Love's Divine

Ava Freeman

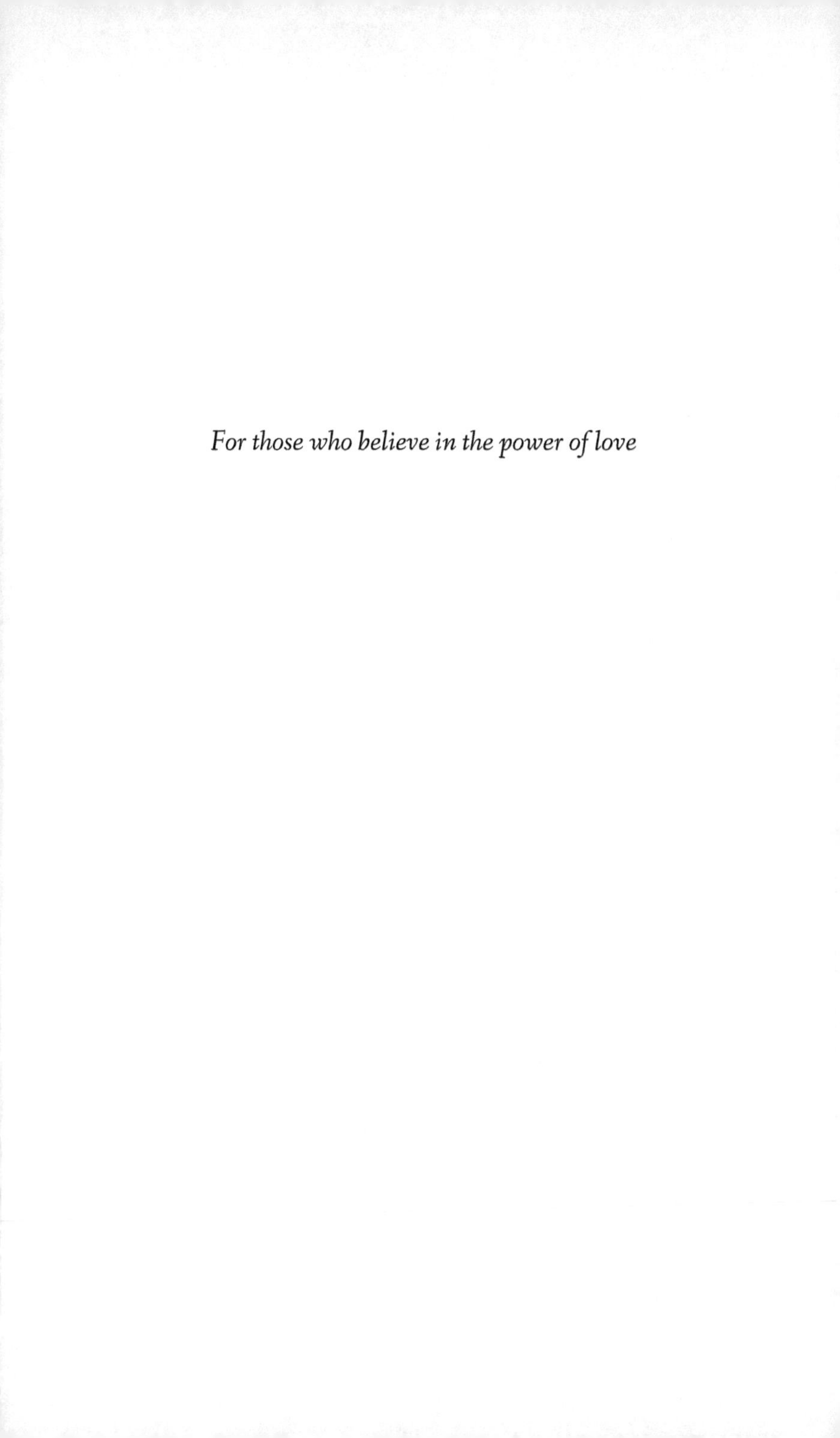

For those who believe in the power of love

Also by Ava Freeman

Four Letter Word

Four Letter Word 2

Fire We Make

Belong to You

Friends & Lovers

Games We Play

Lovers Rock

A Taste of Remy

The Makings of You

Sweetest Taboo

Chapter One

"That can't be right. Can you please check again?"

"Ma'am, I've checked three times already, and there is no reservation listed for you."

Genesis Malone placed her overnight bag down and tried to remain calm. "Okay, is there a manager I can speak with?"

The clerk nodded and excused himself. Genesis prayed to God that there was a glitch, and he was mistaken. She booked the trip to Barbados over a month ago and had no alternate plan. Another room at this hotel, or a different one, were possibilities, but her hopes weren't high. It was the island's busy season.

A man who she assumed was the manager appeared, along with the hotel clerk, several minutes later. He smiled at her and began typing into the computer.

"Hello, Ms.," the manager looked down, "Malone. My name is Henry. I'm the manager here at Sugar Bay. Phillip tells me there is an issue with your reservation."

"Hi, Henry. Yes, I booked this trip two weeks ago and got a confirmation." She dug the paper copy out of her bag and slid it across the desk. "But my reservation is nowhere to be found."

Henry's eyes scanned the paper, and he nodded. "I see what the issue is. You booked through an online company called Travel Bug. We've had issues with them in the past. Their servers don't always connect with ours, so they often have outdated information. We have attempted to rectify this to no avail."

Genesis sighed and rubbed her temple. "Is it possible for me to get another room?"

Henry typed into the computer again. "There are no rooms available for the next several weeks. We are one of the premier hotels here on the island."

"Yes, I know. That's why I was so excited about the deal," Genesis said, frustrated. "Do you know of any other available hotels?"

"The odds are slim, but I can't say for sure. I can call around and see what I can find."

Genesis thanked him and took a seat in the lobby. With no plan B, she would have to turn right back around and go home if he couldn't find her a room. The thought made her nauseous.

She placed her overnight bag beside her. It was all she brought, along with another small bag of toiletries. The plan was to spend all of her time on the beach and at the swim-up bar. Her vacation "wardrobe" consisted of bathing suits and several maxi dresses to wear in the evenings. This time was for her, and she had been happy not having to worry about being put together like she always did when she was home.

Home. She wasn't even sure she could call it that anymore. Her ex-wife Shannon had filed for divorce two years ago, leaving her solely responsible for a house she hadn't even wanted. The only thing that kept her there was laziness and her dog, Kuma. A wildly beautiful husky, Kuma adored the ample space. Regardless, she knew soon she would need to get on top of things and speak to a real estate agent about selling.

"Ms. Malone, I found something," Henry said as he took the seat beside her. "None of the hotels have availability until next week, but there is a place that might be suitable. It costs more, but the price is negotiable."

"This isn't a dump that no one wants to stay at, is it?"

Henry chuckled. "Not at all. It's the guest house of Ms. Zuri Baker. We know her well on the island, and she's an American too. Her family has owned the property for many years and rents out the guest house. I spoke to the property manager, and she said the space is available."

Henry held out a small card that contained the address of the house. Genesis took it from his hand. "Is it at least near the beach?"

He laughed again as he stood. "How about you visit and decide for yourself? I have the hotel van waiting for you out front, and the ride over will be of no cost to you. We are sorry for the inconvenience."

Genesis thanked him and picked up her bags. He directed her towards a van sitting in front of the hotel entrance. The driver was leaning against the front, a cigarette dangling from his mouth. As she walked towards him, he put out the cigarette and opened the door for her. They greeted each other, and she handed him her bags, which he took and placed in the back of the van.

"How are you today, Ms.?"

"I've been better," Genesis said. She buckled her seatbelt and prayed that the driver wasn't chatty. A headache was looming, and she just wanted to check out this guest house and rest.

"Well, I hope your day gets better. You're going to Ms. Baker's place, so it can't be that bad. My name is Dennis."

Genesis perked up at the mention of the mysterious homeowner. "Dennis, who is this, Ms. Baker? The hotel manager mentioned that most people on the island know her."

Dennis checked his mirrors and pulled out before responding. "Well, Ms. Baker has been coming here since she was young, but her home originally belonged to her grandmother. Their family is from the island. Since she took over ownership of the place, she's used some of her family money to build things like schools and housing. People know and respect her. She is a delightful woman, but a bit of a recluse, at least when she's here."

Genesis had to admit, hearing more intrigued her. At the very least, she figured the home would be lovely, and she wouldn't end up in a shack. She didn't want to be a snob, but she hadn't traveled all that way to rough it on foreign soil.

"Her home is far out, so you can close your eyes if you like," Dennis said, turning towards her. "Any music preferences?"

"Something mellow would be nice."

"Okay, I got you." He fiddled with his phone while they waited in traffic. The strains of a guitar filled the van. Pleased, Genesis put her head back and relaxed against the cushion.

* * *

"Ms. Malone? Ms. Malone, we are here."

Genesis sat up, startled. It embarrassed her to find drool in the corners of her mouth as she wiped her face. She wanted to sleep, not pass out.

"I am so sorry. I didn't mean to fall asleep that deeply. How long was I out for?"

"It took about 30 minutes to get here," Dennis said as he pulled out her bags. "You travel light."

"I don't normally, but this is me being spontaneous. Are you sure we are in the right place?"

As she woke up out of her sleep-induced fog, she surveyed

the home. The palatial property in front of her was not what she had been expecting. The nonchalant way the hotel manager and Dennis spoke of the mysterious Ms. Baker, she just assumed she was a rich lady with a fancy home. What stood in front of her was a compound on some Jay Z and Beyonce level of rich. She looked behind the car and noticed that they had driven through a gate and across an expansive driveway.

"This is it. There is Ms. Taylor now; she's the property manager. She takes care of the place for Ms. Baker. Anything you need, you go through her."

Ms. Taylor looked like a woman who meant business. She had a short stature but carried herself like someone much taller. Her hair was in a tight bun, and she wore a gray pinstriped suit jacket and skirt with a white blouse. Her heels clicked on the stone path as she headed in their direction. With flawless dark brown skin, Genesis couldn't place her age, but she figured her to be at least in her early 50s.

"You must be Ms. Malone, a pleasure to meet you."

"You can call me Genesis, and the pleasure is all mine. Thank you for taking me on such short notice."

"No worries, Ms. Baker likes to help in any way she can," Ms. Taylor said with a smile. "Dennis, so good to see you. How is your mom?"

"She's good; told me to thank you for that pie you sent over. I need to say thank you as well since I ate most of it."

They both laughed and continued to chat. Genesis left them to catch up and walked over to the bushes near the front door. Their style was impeccable, each cut into a perfect square. She brushed her hand against one and was in awe of how soft the branches were despite the blunt tips.

"Our gardener, Michael, is brilliant. Very precise with his work," Ms. Taylor said, as she appeared beside Genesis.

"Gather your things, and I will show you where you'll be staying."

Genesis waved goodbye to Dennis and followed Ms. Taylor inside. The entrance to the house was tall and had a large wooden door. It looked like they built it for a giant.

The foyer was not impressive, but it opened up into the living area, which boasted an oversized television set and a bar. A table for 12 was near the windows, and there was even a pool and a cabana behind them. The glass glittered in the sunlight like shimmering water under the trees. Genesis wondered if she could see the ocean from there.

"Zuri renovated the home in 2012, but she tried to maintain the integrity of the space. This is the primary entertainment area, but there are more intimate rooms throughout the house. The eat-in kitchen, movie viewing room, office, etc."

"I'm speechless; this is a beautiful home. Not at all what I was expecting."

Ms. Taylor chuckled. "That's what everyone says. Even those who know Zuri's status in the industry expect the space to be more quaint."

"What industry is she in?" Genesis asked as they walked through the house.

"Movies mostly. She runs one of the largest production companies in Hollywood. I'm sure you've heard of it, Ellis Films."

"Oh my goodness, yes. I love their movies."

Genesis remained quiet as Ms. Taylor continued to show her the spaces available to her during her stay. She had access to the guest house and most other areas in the home other than Zuri's private wing. After twenty minutes, they finally exited on the opposite side of the house and walked along a path toward the guest house. She expected a small cottage; what she got was a whole other house.

"Everything you need is here. There's a kitchen, living room, bathroom, two bedrooms, and a study complete with a library if you like to read. Also, access to the beach is right behind the house here," Ms. Taylor said, opening a back door that led to a patio. "Should you get bored or run out of anything, you are free to visit the main house. As I mentioned, anything in there is available to you."

Genesis dropped her bags on the couch and plopped down beside them. "This is amazing, and I am beyond grateful, but I don't think I can afford this. I'm supposed to stay here for two weeks; there's no way this house rents for what I would pay at a hotel."

Ms. Taylor smiled as she closed the patio door. "Don't worry about that. Zuri often allows the hotels to use the space as a courtesy when she isn't renting it out. At the end of your stay, whatever you would pay for the hotel will be more than enough. Now, if you'll excuse me, I have some things to check on. There's a phone in the kitchen which connects to our intercom. Use it if you have a question or need help."

Genesis thanked her and waited until she was alone before she started jumping up and down. She ran all over the house to take everything in, and when she got to the bedroom, she flung herself on the California king bed. Her body sunk into the cozy blanket that lay on top of it, and she let out a deep sigh. She did not understand how she had gotten so lucky, but it felt like things were going her way for the first time in months.

She pulled her phone from her pocket and searched for the owner of the house. Judging by the luxury surrounding her and owning a movie studio, Genesis assumed the woman had to be much older. After a few searches, she found an article on the creation of Ellis Films ten years ago. Zuri started it with her twin cousins, Reggie and Elijah. They named it after their grandmother, Hazel Ellis. Ellis was a famous Black actress that began her career in the 1940s. Genesis remembered watching some of her films with her parents growing up. Her mom was an actress as well named Veronique Milian. She was huge in the '80s and early '90s.

At the bottom of the article, she found a link to photos taken for the magazine. As the first picture came up, Genesis was shocked to find that all three were far younger than she thought. Elijah and Reggie were handsome and tall, with light brown eyes that stood out against their dark brown skin. Zuri's complexion was golden brown, but she had the same piercing eyes although much darker. She stood between her cousins, her hands on their shoulders. Although she didn't have their height, she was tall for a woman and wearing the hell out of the suit she had on. It was black, fitted, and noticeably missing a shirt.

Genesis tried not to stare too hard, but it was impossible not to notice Zuri's curves. Her hair was gorgeous as well. Thick black dreadlocks that cascaded down to the middle of her back. The confidence she exuded in front of the camera was sexy.

"Who is this woman?" she mumbled to herself.

After going back to her original search, she looked over the articles about Zuri alone. One Cosmopolitan magazine article detailed Zuri's dating stats as one of their most eligible bachelorettes. She was 39, a pescatarian, and owned a stake in her favorite sushi restaurant. At the time of the article, she was single, but what caught Genesis' eye was her sexual orientation; lesbian.

Although it shouldn't have, it still surprised Genesis whenever she came across someone famous who was out. After growing up in a strict religious household, it took years to get over the hangups she had about her sexuality. It was nice that the world was slowly but surely progressing.

After reading more about Zuri, she finally closed her phone.

As intriguing as this other woman was, the odds of their meeting were slim. Curiosity satisfied, she planned to enjoy her time in Barbados and leave everything, and everyone, on the back burner.

Chapter Two

Zuri Baker tapped a digital pen against her tablet. She was in the second hour of a long day involving newbie screenwriters pitching scripts, and she was already over it. The young man standing in front of her was unprepared and attempting to salvage what little he could of the meeting. Although she wanted to end his pain, her cousin Reggie was trying to coach him through it. He clearly liked the guy.

"So, Stewart, you're going with the horror angle?" Reggie asked.

"Yeah, yeah. Picture Get Out meets Rosemary's Baby type thing, you know?"

Zuri let out an exasperated breath. "No, we don't know. That's why you're here trying to convince us to sink money into this idea." She put down her pen and folded her hands on top of the table. "How old are you, Mr. Macintosh?"

Stewart shifted in place and looked down. "Um, 25, ma'am."

Zuri cringed at being called ma'am, but let it go. "You're young, and I commend you for having the guts to come out today and pitch us your idea. But here's a piece of advice;

always be prepared. Even if you think you don't have a chance in hell of getting somewhere, act as if you do. We have dozens of people out front ready to come in here and sell us on their project. Trust me, some of it will be shitty, but the presentation is what will get you called back. Understand?"

"Yes, I do," he said.

"Good. So we will end this right here, and I suggest you come back to us when you have something more concrete." Zuri took a business card from the stack she had on the table. "This has my email on it. Contact me once you've crystallized that jumble you've got going on in your head."

Stewart smiled and grabbed the card. "Thank you so much, Ms. Baker and Mr. Cole. You'll be hearing from me."

Zuri and Reggie shook his hand and watched him tumble out of the room with his folders.

"That was nice of you to give him a lifeline," Reggie said, walking over to the coffee machine.

"His idea is interesting, but it needs more polish. If he takes my advice, I think it will be worth buying his script, but he needs to put in the work."

"Pitch Week," as they called it at the studio, was a yearly endeavor that Zuri implemented the second year after Ellis Films was born. It was a chance for up-and-coming screenwriters to pitch to the studio instead of through an agent or third party. She loved it because it gave them access to raw talent, and every year, at least one film they produced was from an amateur writer.

Reggie handed her a mug of her favorite espresso and took a seat next to her. "I thought you didn't like it. You looked annoyed the entire time he was speaking."

"That may be, but you have a nose for talented writers. I could tell you were digging him, so I figured he was worth giving a shot."

Zuri owned the studio, along with her twin cousins Reginald and Elijah. The three of them had a significant trust fund courtesy of their grandmother, the world-renowned actress Hazel Ellis, and they used it to open the studio. Films and their creation ran through their blood. Aside from their grandmother, Zuri's mother, Veronique Milan, was an award-winning actress in her own right, and her father, Frederick Baker, was an Oscar-winning director. Her aunt Lynn, Reggie and Elijah's mom, was a screenwriter and film producer. As the third generation of the Ellis family, they felt it was their duty to continue the legacy their grandmother fought hard to create.

"Thank you for that vote of confidence. Now tell that to my brother," Reggie said.

"Are you two fighting again?" Zuri asked. She adored her cousins, but they were always either fighting or the best of friends; there was no in-between.

"There's a film I'm passionate about making, but he thinks I'm only humoring it because of Delilah."

Zuri raised an eyebrow. "Well, are you?"

Delilah was Reggie's long-time girlfriend who had left a career as a journalist to become a screenwriter. She was a talented writer, having published several fiction books, but was looking to branch out.

"Of course, I'm going to give her more support as my woman, but that doesn't mean it's bad. She's a brilliant writer who's trying a new format. Other than needing some guidance in that area, the bones are good."

"Okay, so what you're saying is you need me to be the tie-breaker here?" Zuri asked.

Reggie clapped his hands together. "Please. You can see whether I'm biased or my brother is being a pompous ass."

"Will do," Zuri said. She heard her phone buzz and checked

to see who it was. Her face lit up when she saw Sheree Taylor's name appear.

Ms. Taylor, as everyone called her, had been working for their family since she was young. Her mother was the property manager of the house when Zuri's grandmother was still alive. After Hazel Ellis's passing and Sheree's mother retired, she offered to take on the manager's job. Zuri was more than happy to have her there because she was like a second mother and one of the wisest people she knew. With her monitoring the house, Zuri's mind was at ease when she was back home in the States.

"Auntie, how's everything going?" Zuri said, putting her on speaker.

"Everything is well, my darling. I hope you aren't working yourself into the ground like you tend to," Sheree said, hints of her Bajan accent underlying the words.

"Not at all. You can ask Reggie. He's here with me."

Reggie leaned towards the phone. "Hey, Auntie, she's lying through her teeth. I have to force her to go home most nights."

Zuri smiled and put up her middle finger.

"Reggie, sweetness, how are you and your brother? You two need to come down here for a visit. I haven't seen you all in two years."

Zuri left them to catch up while she poured herself some more espresso. Reggie wasn't lying about her inability to pull herself away from work. It seemed there was always something essential that needed to be done, and if she didn't do it, her mind would run wild with all that could go wrong. She gulped espresso as if it were a fast-disappearing commodity, since it was the only thing that could keep her awake. Her friends and family kept telling her a crash was coming soon, but she felt like she had more stamina than when she started.

"Zuri, I was calling to let you know about a possible new houseguest," Sheree said. She paused, then read off the information sent to her by the hotel. "Her name is Genesis Malone, and she bought a two-week stay at Sugar Bay, but the booking didn't go through. Now she's stuck out here with nowhere else to stay."

Zuri sat back down and sipped her drink. "As long as no one else is renting at Ellis Manor, I'm fine with that."

"Great, I just like to ask first. On that note, kids, I'll speak to you later. Zuri, let me know when you're coming down."

They all said their goodbyes.

"I still chuckle to myself when I think of Grams naming that old house Ellis Manor," he said with a smile.

"Grams was bougie as hell, but that's why we loved her. She was fabulous in every way." Zuri picked up her tablet and eyed the long list of names. "We've got about twenty more people to see today. What do you say we get back to it?"

"I'm ready, cuz. The next is a collective of screenwriters. They say they've got the next big dark romantic series this side of 50 Shades of Grey," Reggie said, reading from his notes.

Zuri rolled her eyes and pressed the intercom system to reach their admin. "Stacy, please send in the next group. Thanks."

* * *

Zuri made it to her home in Laurel Canyon around 8 pm that night, earlier than usual. Her on-again-off-again girlfriend, Tracy Scott, was in town. Seeing her was one of the few things that could get her to leave early, and even that wasn't always true. But Pitch Week could be rough. Even workaholics like her had limitations.

As she unlocked the front door, she wished she had a dog to greet her when she got home. Growing up, she owned several, but over time they passed away, and once her career took off, there was no time. She was always traveling and didn't think it was fair to get a pet when she knew that someone else would need to take care of it. Still, the thought of having someone excited to see her every night was nice.

After putting her bags down, she entered the kitchen and had a glass of orange juice. She leaned against the counter as she drank it and looked across the room toward the outside. Her house had a magnificent view of the mountains and trees that surrounded Laurel Canyon. It was what drew her to the area. The home itself had walls of glass that provided stunning canyon views in all directions. Along with being airy and sun-drenched most days, it was an open concept with bamboo floors and high ceilings.

Although Zuri came from money, she was never foolish about it. She took after her grandmother in the strategic way she spent and earned what she had. Her home was the only thing she had splurged on in the entirety of her adult life. Now that 40 was around the corner, she was wondering if maybe she had spent too much time being cautious and not enough time living.

As she cleaned her glass, she eyed a bag of food on the counter and smiled. It was from her favorite Japanese restaurant, Kiraku Inn, and that meant Tracy was already there. Although they didn't see each other as often as she would have liked, Zuri was always happy when they did.

She and Tracy had been in a relationship for more than five years, and many of her close friends didn't understand why she wouldn't find someone who wanted to commit. But the situation suited her; they were both busy people who enjoyed each other's company when their schedules aligned. Still, Zuri desired something deeper, yet after two broken hearts from long-term relationships, she was content with what she had.

She bound up the stairs and caught Tracy as she exited the master bath wrapped in a towel.

"Jesus, Zuri, you scared me," Tracy said, her hand over her heart.

"I'm sorry, babe, just happy you're here," Zuri said, opening her arms.

Tracy stepped into her embrace and nuzzled into her neck. "God, you smell good."

" It's nice to come home to you." Zuri kissed the top of her head and sat on the bed. "How was your flight?"

Tracy sighed. "Don't get me started. I had this gross man sitting near me who was picking at his toenails for half the flight. Who does that in first class?" Tracy shuddered at the memory.

When she dropped her towel and began applying lotion, Zuri couldn't help but admire her body. Tracy was in phenomenal shape, necessary as an actress, but she went beyond just working out to please casting directors. She had been a track star in her former life and likely would have gone on to Olympic status had an unfortunate injury not sidelined her.

After getting her fill, Zuri got up and took the lotion out of Tracy's hand. She squirted some onto her skin and massaged it in. Tracy looked down at her as she sat at her feet and rubbed the lotion onto her legs. Her hands played in her locs.

"You know I can do this myself, right?" Tracy said.

Zuri continued to apply more lotion. She loved Tracy's skin. The rich cocoa brown color was so smooth and blemish-free that it reminded her of silk. It was hard for her to keep her hands to herself when they were around each other.

Zuri looked up at her. "When are you returning to Miami?"

"I'm cleared through the weekend. They expect me back by Tuesday."

"I'm surprised they let you leave. Normally you're required to shoot straight through, no?" Zuri said as she stood up and began applying lotion to her back.

"Well, it's one perk of being a star. Plus, I already negotiated to have this weekend off when I signed my contract."

Zuri smiled as she finished and turned Tracy around to face her. "You took my birthday off in advance?"

Tracy nodded and wrapped her arms around Zuri. "I sure did. There was no way I was going to miss your 40th."

Zuri felt her face get hot from the kind sentiment. She placed the bottle of lotion on the nightstand and pulled Tracy into a tender kiss. Tracy squealed when she lifted her off the floor and and gently laid her down on the bed. She let her hands roam in a far less innocent way and pressed herself into her lover. A sigh of pleasure was her reward.

Zuri's lips trailed kisses along her chin and neck as her breathing became sporadic. She knew it wouldn't be long before Tracy came; it was always like that the first time when they hadn't seen each other for months. She liked to think it meant she missed her.

"Happy birthday to me," she mumbled as she kissed her way down.

Chapter Three

Genesis spent her first few days lounging on the beach and meditating. She was more relaxed than she had been in years. Reading, listening to music, and generally zoning out were a part of her daily routine; it was paradise. So much of her adult life had been taking care of her sister and ex-wife. Now she was making herself a priority.

After a deep stretch, she got out of bed from her afternoon nap and went to get a snack from the fridge. She chose a bowl of pineapple and walked out to the patio to eat. The cool evening breeze and the smell of the ocean made her smile. Every day began with a visit to the beach, and she couldn't wait to go back the following morning. As she sipped on a glass of water and ate the fruit, she pulled out her phone to check her email.

She swiped through her messages and clicked on one from her sister Kenzie. Her younger sibling worried about her and was not happy when she discovered she was traveling out of the country alone. Accustomed to her sister's behavior ever since their parents died when they were young, Genesis understood why she was so clingy. They only had each other, so Kenzie liked to keep tabs on her. When they discussed the trip, she had to make her understand that this was something she needed for herself. It was a concept that went out the window when she became a pseudo-parent at 22.

Her fingers flew over the phone keyboard as she typed out a response to Kenzie, assuring her she was okay. After she sent it off, she saw another message from her ex-wife, Shannon. Her finger hovered over it. She wasn't sure she wanted to see what it said. Their divorce had been finalized over a year ago, although the heartache from it was still very much present.

At one point, Shannon had been their person. The three amigas, as her friend Andrea, liked to call them. Shannon made them feel like a real family, and for a time, their loss didn't hurt as much. Now, she was still close to Kenzie, but Genesis refused to allow her back into her life. The way she left was disrespectful to what they had built, and forgiveness was not something she was ready to give.

"Not today," Genesis mumbled as she erased the email without reading it. This trip was about her finding herself again, and she would no longer give access to people who only used it to hurt her.

She answered a few more messages from close friends, then turned off her phone. Emails and web surfing were activities best left at home. Barbados was a chance to live in the moment. So she jumped up and changed into one of her bathing suits. The heated pool Ms. Taylor showed her during the tour was calling her name.

* * *

Genesis laid back poolside on a lounge chair and looked out towards the ocean. The night was beautiful, but there was a slight chill in the air, which balanced out the heat emanating from the pool. It was her first time using one with that feature, and she had to admit it was a genius invention. She raised her glass to drink more of the rum and cranberry juice she had been enjoying, but realized it was empty.

"Another wouldn't hurt," she said as she got up and headed inside.

She hummed to herself as she poured more rum. The sound of the ocean's waves crashing into the beach was comforting. The quiet bothered her less than she thought it would. As she continued to hum, she recalled Ms. Taylor mentioning that the sound system would come on if she spoke to it.

"Google assistant, play Rihanna?" Genesis hesitated and was going to repeat the request when she heard the instrumental from the song Rude Boy. "Louder, please?" The music soon filled the entire house with the sounds of one of her favorite singers.

Genesis finished making her drink, then twirled around the living room, her feet barely touching the floor as she moved. The music from the stereo filled the space and lifted her spirits, the notes and lyrics acting like a balm for her weary heart.

Her body stayed in motion as the next song played. The music drowned out everything, so much so that she didn't realize someone else was in the room until she opened her eyes for a second. She cried out, startled to find a woman standing by the entrance.

After a few moments of confusion, she recognized who it was. Zuri Baker stood in front of her, looking more beautiful than she did in her photos online. A duffle bag was at her feet.

"Don't stop on account of me," Zuri yelled over the music.

"Lower music, please," Genesis called out. The sound lowered to a reasonable level, allowing them to talk without screaming.

"Polite even to artificial intelligence? You'll do well when the robots take over," Zuri said, removing her jacket.

"I'm sorry I was getting carried away. Might have put a bit too much rum in this drink," she said, lifting her glass. "I can get out of your way if..."

Zuri smirked at her and continued to get undressed. Genesis looked away to be polite, but not before checking her out. When she snuck another peek, Zuri had on a fire engine red bikini that made Genesis's one-piece bathing suit look childish.

"I'll be right back." Zuri took off, running towards the pool.

She dived into the deep end but came up a minute later and performed laps from one end to the other. Not sure what to do, Genesis walked back out and sat on the abandoned lounge chair. After several minutes, Zuri appeared next to her and climbed out of the pool.

"Sorry about that. I was dreaming of a swim for most of the day. It's the first thing I do when I come here."

Genesis just nodded as Zuri laid back on the lounge chair beside hers. Unable to resist, she let her eyes roam over the other woman's body. Voluptuous women rarely caught her eye, she had a thing for slim athletic types, but she couldn't stop looking at Zuri. Her figure was coke bottle status, and everything matched, so she was likely not surgically altered. Her plump bottom and thick thighs made the small bathing suit look damn near indecent, but Genesis had no complaints.

"You know if you keep staring, I might have to charge you," Zuri said with a smirk. Her eyes remained shut.

"I'm sorry," Genesis stuttered out. She quickly looked away, scolding herself for showing her interest so blatantly. It had been a while since she met another woman who stirred something inside her.

Zuri chuckled. "I'm just messing with you. This suit isn't leaving much to the imagination."

Genesis watched her get up and head back into the house.

Her body was even better in motion. Zuri turned and gave her a bright smile.

"I make superb waffles; perhaps you'd like to join me in the kitchen around 10 am?"

She didn't wait for a response and strolled inside. Genesis remained seated and tried to pick her jaw off the floor.

* * *

The next morning, after spending more than an hour getting ready, Genesis made her way to the main house. It was quieter than the day before, and she remembered that Ms. Taylor mentioned how most of the staff got weekends off.

Music was playing low throughout as she tried to remember the path to the kitchen. The sheer size of the house's layout was a bit confusing. She listened and ended up following the sounds of pots and pans. When she entered, Zuri greeted her as she stirred what she assumed was waffle mix and manned an omelet on the stovetop. She had on fitted jogger pants and an off the shoulder white t-shirt that had the word LOVE written in script across the front. Her locs were up in a messy bun. Even dressed down, she looked good, really good.

Genesis strolled over to the stove and picked up the spatula beside it. "How about I handle these and leave you to your superb waffles?"

"Ah, you remembered. Superb waffles are coming right up," she answered with a wink.

Genesis's stomach flip-flopped. *Control yourself.*

She cleared her throat. "This kitchen is beautiful and so big. The one I have at home is a good size too. It makes cooking so much easier."

"Where do you live?" Zuri asked as she poured the batter into the waffle maker.

"Glenwood, California. Been living there for going on ten years. I'm an accountant."

Zuri stood there, waiting for the waffles to cook as her eyes lingered on Genesis. She licked some excess batter from her fingers. Genesis swallowed and turned to flip her omelet.

"So I'm dealing with someone who has an analytical mind. My favorite," Zuri said, returning to her task. "And I live in Laurel Canyon, so we're neighbors."

Genesis chuckled. "Yes, we are. And I didn't realize it was possible to have favorite minds."

"Sure, or maybe it's more personality types. I'm attracted to pragmatic people since I'm more emotional. It can be fun getting someone in touch with their feelings."

"Is that what you're doing now? By being coy about who you are and flirtatious?"

Genesis surprised herself. That wasn't what she meant to say, but for once, she didn't hold back her thoughts to be polite. Despite not answering, she could tell by her smile that the other woman liked her directness. They continued cooking for several more minutes. When they finished, each walked over to the table with their food. Fresh fruit and other accouterments for the meal were already on the table.

"Before we eat, I should introduce myself. My name is Zuri Baker, but you can call me Z."

Genesis smiled as she cut into her waffle. "I know who you are, Ms. Baker."

Zuri raised an eyebrow as she scooped fruit onto her plate. "Been doing your homework, have you?"

"Well, I couldn't stay in a home no matter how beautiful and not learn a bit about the owner. Plus, I don't know if you're aware of this, but you're famous."

Zuri nodded and chuckled. "So I've heard."

"Thank you for letting me stay here," Genesis said.

"Oh, it's nothing, but you're welcome. I must apologize for my intrusion last night. Next weekend is when I scheduled time to be here, but I needed to get away sooner."

"Please don't apologize, this is your home, and I am grateful for your kindness. I would have been back in Cali by this point the way things were going."

"Well, I am glad that didn't happen," Zuri said with a smile. "I enjoyed your dancing."

Genesis blushed and almost choked on the strawberry she was eating. "I'm so embarrassed... I don't do that."

"Do what? Have fun?"

"No, I mean, just letting it all hang out. I'm on the conservative side."

"I hadn't noticed." Zuri's eyes danced with mischief.

Genesis continued eating and tried to think of what to discuss next. She was enjoying their conversation, but the knot of nervousness in her stomach was killing her. It had been years since anyone made her feel that way. Despite that, the quiet between them was nice too. She could be self-conscious when she wasn't filling up space by talking or trying to keep the other person engaged. Zuri seemed just as happy to sit there in silence.

After several minutes of just the sounds from utensils scraping their plates, Zuri paused and observed her.

"You're exquisite; you know that? The way the sun is hitting your skin right now is everything."

Genesis blushed. "Thank you."

"You're welcome," Zuri said, as she popped a grape into her mouth. "So, you must have someone back home?"

"Not anymore. I've been divorced for over a year now."

"Sorry to hear that. No prospects in sight?"

Zuri's fishing for information amused her but was flattering. "No, my wife is the only woman I've ever been with."

Zuri raised her eyebrows and paused her eating. "You've only been with one person?"

"Yup," Genesis said, looking away.

"Don't do that," Zuri said, reaching out to touch her hand. "Your experience, or lack thereof, doesn't matter."

"Well, we've known each other since we were teenagers but didn't start dating until college. Before her, there was no one."

"I see. Well, I can relate."

"I don't believe you," Genesis said. "You're trying to tell me you had trouble finding people to date?"

"I was a late bloomer too. All of this did not come along until I was older." Zuri said, running her hand along her body. "Before that, I was all gangly limbs, crooked teeth, and hair I didn't know how to style. Plus, I was a bookworm; I was way more interested in the romances I read than in pursuing anyone."

Genesis threw her head back and laughed. The image of Zuri being anything other than put together was amusing. It made her far less intimidating.

"I'm glad the pain of my former awkward self is putting you at ease." Zuri winked at her as she grabbed their empty plates and took them to the sink. " I learned that personality hooked people in when your looks didn't. So I became way more outspoken, perhaps to a fault."

Genesis began clearing the table. "I wish I could do that."

"Do what? Dance like no one's watching?" Zuri said. "I believe we already witnessed that last night."

Genesis chuckled. "Yes, but do that even when people are. Isn't that the sentiment behind the saying? To be unapologetic and live free of caring what others think."

Zuri placed the items she brought over on the counter. "Yes, you just need to find out how to do that in a way authentic to you. Now, back to your ex. What's her name?"

"Shannon," Genesis said, leaning against the kitchen island. "Did you realize you referred to her as your wife earlier?"

"Oh my God, I did." Genesis wanted to kick herself. Nothing like mentioning a wife when trying to be flirtatious. "What do they call that, a Freudian slip?"

"Yes, revealing your subconscious feelings with words or behavior by mistake." Zuri filled up the dishwasher. When she finished, she let her eyes wander over Genesis. "You know what I think?"

Genesis licked her lips to calm the nervous tick that began as soon as she felt Zuri's eyes on her. "No, tell me."

"That Freud was full of shit. I was always a Carl Jung fan myself."

Once again, Zuri caught her unawares, which caused her to burst into a fit of giggles. This woman was definitely a charmer.

"You've got syrup on your chin." Zuri reached out to clean her face. Her fingers lingered near her lips, then dropped. She started back putting items away, appearing unphased by their moment.

Genesis stood frozen in place and unsure of what to do next. The sound of a woman calling for Zuri from the front of the house saved her.

"Z, are you here?" The voice yelled out again.

"Shit," Zuri mumbled under her breath.

"You've got a visitor."

"Yes, an uninvited one," Zuri said, her mouth turned down into a frown. She dried her hands with a dish towel and walked to the kitchen entrance. Before leaving, she stopped and said, "I had a delightful time with you this morning. If you're free tomorrow night, I'd like to have you for dinner. One of the best restaurants on the island, The Sea Breeze, is not too far from here."

Genesis chuckled and nodded, yes. "You said to have me for dinner, not have dinner with me."

Zuri bit her lip and grinned. "Did I? Another Freudian slip, I guess."

Genesis watched her walk away and couldn't stop smiling. Despite some missteps, breakfast had been everything she hoped it would be and more.

Chapter Four

"What are you doing here, Rain?"

Zuri stood in front of the bratty starlet with her arms crossed and wearing a scowl. The young woman knew better than to show up at her place unannounced. Usually, she would have taken such a disruption in stride, but she had been enjoying the company of her new houseguest.

"Z. OMG, I know you like your privacy, but this is an emergency, and I couldn't get you on your phone. I came down on the spur of the moment."

"If you can't reach me by phone, that's by my design."

Rain rolled her eyes. "Okay, but I'm here. Can we talk, please?"

Her whiny voice was like nails on a chalkboard. Zuri flinched at the sound. Rather than listen to more, she dropped her arms and decided to hear her out. "Let's go to my office."

Rain Phillips could be annoying, but she was a star and one that Zuri's studio had created. She became famous because of a trilogy of films known as the Star Crossed Saga. Based on a set of young adult novels, it was on Twilight's level in its heyday.

The movies grossed an ungodly amount of money due in large part to the rabid fan base. Although she felt like anyone who starred in the movies would have become just as popular, Zuri had to admit that Rain was talented. She used her time in the spotlight to show her range and starred in several blockbusters and indie films that garnered her awards and even more attention. Now she was working on a new series of films for Zuri and making her regret it every second.

"I told my agent that he should just reach out to you, but he swore I was ridiculous."

"Oh, I can't wait to hear this," Zuri said sarcastically.

They rounded the corner to her office and ran into Genesis. Zuri couldn't help but smile at seeing her again. She had a slightly startled expression on her face, and she wondered why she found her so adorable.

"Hey Genesis, this is Rain. We're working on a movie together." She emphasized the work part so that the other woman wouldn't make any assumptions about their relationship.

"Oh wow, I would know that face anywhere. Nice to meet you, Rain."

Rain barely acknowledged her with a curt smile as she scanned her phone messages. Zuri laid her hand over the screen and made her lookup.

"Don't be rude," she said, nodding towards Genesis.

"Oh, sorry, it's a pleasure to meet you," Rain said, looking Genesis in the eyes.

"That's better. Go on in and have a seat," she said, holding the office door open. Rain slid by with a sheepish look on her face.

Zuri motioned for Genesis to walk with her. "Sorry about that; she acts like a spoiled brat. I'm used to it, but it can be a lot sometimes."

"No worries. Maybe if I were a fifteen-year-old, I'd be crushed, but she's just a kid."

"Twenty three now, not so much a kid as a diva in training. Anyway, I have to talk her off a proverbial ledge. I have some other things to take care of, but I will see you tomorrow night?"

"I'm looking forward to it."

Zuri watched Genesis as she walked towards the back of the house. She was wearing denim shorts and a peasant top, nothing special, but she elevated the clothes. When she complimented her earlier, it wasn't just for flattery. She genuinely glowed. Whatever was going on with her marriage might have dimmed her light, but it was shining through, regardless.

When she walked into the house the night before, she didn't mean to startle her, but the way Genesis moved entranced her, and she didn't want her to stop. Genesis danced deliberately, not like someone just having fun but someone who knew how to move to the music. Her toned body and gracefulness made her wonder if she used to be a dancer. How such a dynamic woman could be so subdued was beyond her, but it intrigued her enough to want to learn more.

Zuri entered her office and sat across from Rain. The young woman was typing away on her phone and finally looked up after a few minutes.

"Sorry, I needed to respond to an email from Lyle."

Lyle was Rain's agent and the one Zuri usually did business with if she could help it. Somehow he could tame the young woman's sometimes manic behavior, but it seemed this time around she'd gone rogue.

"I was hoping I could ask you for a huge favor," Rain said, leaning forward.

"What type of favor?"

"Can you fire Jackson?"

"You want me to fire Jackson Montgomery? Are you kidding me?"

Jackson was the male equivalent of Rain. He became a star in his late teens because of his starring role in a television series, which he parlayed into a successful movie career. The two of them together in the studio's upcoming film was highly anticipated.

"You don't understand. I can't work with him. If I had known he would be my co-star, I would have never signed on."

"First, you signed your contract, understanding that you would work with whoever we decided was best for the role. Second, you did the screen test with Jackson, and your chemistry was off the charts, so please tell me why you suddenly...." Zuri stopped mid-sentence and leaned back into her chair. "You two slept together, didn't you?"

Rain looked down and nodded. "I didn't mean for it to happen, but like you said, we had so much chemistry. Then we exchanged numbers and started talking all the time, went out to places where we could avoid the paparazzi. It was like we had our own world. Then after four months, he ghosted me, and next thing I know, I see his face plastered all over the tabloids with some other chick."

"Rain, I don't want it to seem like I'm unsympathetic to your plight, but Jackson is a known player."

"Yeah, but I thought I was special," Rain said, sniffling.

"Yeah, that's what players do. Guys like him know how to make you feel as if you're the only one in the world until they get bored. I can guarantee you that whoever this unknown girl is, she'll be gone in a few weeks too."

Rain nodded but didn't look convinced. "I was hoping you all wouldn't choose him for the role. There's nothing you can do?"

"I know this will sound outrageous but hear me out." Zuri

indicated for Rain to get closer by sitting forward in her seat. "Do what you're being paid that ridiculous salary for, act. I don't care how, but you need to convince the world that you two are absolutely in love on screen. Do we understand each other?"

Rain threw herself back in the chair and frowned. She nibbled on her lip and agreed. "Okay," she mumbled. "Can I at least stay here for a few days, get my thoughts together."

"Fine, you can leave when I do. Just don't get in my way."

Rain sat up and gave her a bright smile. The blonde highlights in her brown hair glistened as the sun hit them, and her green eyes sparkled. Her tan made her usually pale skin look sun-kissed, even though she rarely visited the beach. Objectively she was a beautiful woman and looked to be getting even better with age, but her personality could be tiresome. She expected to be catered to, and nine times out of ten, she was. Zuri had a feeling that despite Jackson's reputation, he had likely found her off-putting, which is why he disappeared. It wasn't possible to fake the chemistry they had, and she had seen many actors succumb to it. But sometimes, it only worked artistically and was disastrous in real life.

"Did you ever do something like this?" Rain asked, her eyes suddenly downcast.

"Fall for a player?" Zuri contemplated how personal she wanted to get with the young woman. "Sure, it's happened a time or two."

Rain's hand fell across her mouth. "Omg, so I was right. Tracy Scott is playing you."

Zuri rolled her eyes. "Don't put words in my mouth."

"Whatever, Zuri, Tracy is the only person you're involved with at the moment. Meanwhile, she's always out with, well, lots of women."

Zuri took a deep breath and let it out slowly. "Tracy and I

are not in a committed relationship. We enjoy each other's company, and that's it. She is free to see whoever she likes."

"Okay, but then why aren't you seeing anyone?"

"Because I don't want to," Zuri said, gritting her teeth. "I have lots of other shit to deal with, like spoiled actresses who work for me."

Rain lifted an eyebrow but said nothing else. "I'm going to go get my overnight bag."

"It sure sounds like you had no idea you would stay," Zuri replied, referencing her spur-of-the-moment comment earlier.

"Well, I couldn't just hop over to another country and not bring my things."

Zuri waved her off. "You know where the guest rooms are."

Rain got up and answered her phone on the way out. "Yes, I'm staying for a few days. Lyle, I can reschedule that interview. I need time to myself to think."

Zuri shook her head as she powered on her computer. Although she was taking several days off, she still needed to stay up to date on what was happening back home. Ellis Films was her baby.

It surprised everyone when she began working behind the scenes instead of in front of or even behind a camera. The shadow of her parents loomed large. As their only child, everyone assumed she would take up their mantles, and while their influence led to her love of film, she had no desire to direct or star in them. She was more interested in the force behind the movies, the movie studios. To be the one that got to decide what films would get made seemed like a better use of her time, and her cousins agreed.

Almost as if reading her mind, her office phone rang, and she saw her cousin Reginald's name pop up. "Reggie, what's up?"

"Hey cuz, just wanted to give you a heads up that Rain might pop up at the house."

Zuri chuckled. "Too late, her annoying ass is already here."

"Damn, sorry about that. I only listened to her message a little while ago. She's been driving Elijah and me crazy with her demands. This latest one takes the cake, though. Does she seriously think we're going to search for a whole new co-star when production starts next week?"

"Apparently, but I got her to settle down. A few days here, and she'll get over it. I need a favor, though. Talk to Jackson and have him apologize to her so they can be civil to each other."

"I will do that," Reginald asked her to hold on while he told his assistant to get Jackson on the phone. "Done. Are you planning on staying over there or coming back on Wednesday?"

"I think I'm going to stay until the end of the week. Possibly longer depending on how things unfold," Zuri said as her mind shifted back to the image of her finger swiping syrup from Genesis' mouth. Her lips curled into a smile at the memory.

"Really? I can't think of the last time you left us to handle things by ourselves."

"I'll be available if you need me. Don't be scared, little cousin; I have faith in you."

Reginald laughed. "All right, all right. We'll hold it down, and you know that. I hope whatever has you staying is worth your time."

"Oh, believe me, it is."

Zuri hung up and fingered the ring she wore on her right hand. Tracy surprised her with it a couple of years ago for their "anniversary." They didn't have an official one, but they liked to celebrate during the month they met. It surprised her that Tracy would give such a gift knowing the ring's implication, but she said she thought it suited Zuri when pressed about it.

And that was what irritated Zuri the most. She knew Tracy

had feelings for her; it was evident in their interactions, yet somehow she always slithered out of any commitment. They said I love you in passing, extravagant gifts tended to be given at random, and their lovemaking felt like it was less about love and more about climaxing.

Zuri didn't want to play the victim; she had known all along what their relationship was. Tracy told her explicitly that her priority was her career, and she had no interest in an all-consuming romance. So why, after five years, was it starting to bother her so much?

After meeting Genesis, the answer was becoming abundantly clear. She missed the intimacy of a proper relationship desperately. The short conversation the two had earlier held more promise than five years worth of time spent with Tracy. It hurt her to think that she had wasted so many years wishing and hoping for change, only to realize it would never happen.

Of course, she knew nothing about Genesis, something she hoped to remedy at dinner the following night. She could feel the potential, and it had her giddy. Still, she needed to protect her heart as best she could, and she was going to, but that didn't mean she couldn't enjoy herself along the way.

Chapter Five

The following evening, Genesis ran around the guest house like a madwoman trying to make herself presentable. She called her best friend Andrea and had her on speakerphone while she made up her face.

"Say that again. You are staying in Zuri Baker's home, and you didn't tell me?" Andrea screamed. "You are aware of how much I love her mom, right?"

Genesis laughed out loud. "Am I? I remember how when you broke up with Tina, you had me come over, and we watched Heart Sick on repeat."

Although Genesis tended to be coy when meeting anyone, she was excited to tell Andrea. From the first day they met in college, they had been the best of friends. Even after they left school, they never lost touch, no matter how far apart they lived. She was ecstatic when Drea moved to Denver from Pennsylvania because it meant they could see each other more than once a year.

"So, what's she like in person?"

Genesis pictured Zuri in her bikini. "Down to earth and charming. She's stunning; pictures don't do her justice."

"Wow! She's a hot bohemian version of her mom." Andrea paused, then said, "Are you aware she's a lesbian?"

Genesis nodded, then remembered Andrea was unable to see her. "Yes, I read about her online. I'm calling because she and I are going out to dinner."

"What?" Andrea screamed again. "Sorry, I could have sworn you just said you were going on a date with Veronique Milian's daughter."

"It is not a date," Genesis said.

Is it a date? Although Genesis had been flirting with her, she wasn't sure it would go beyond that. She had seen the pictures of her girlfriend, Tracy Scott, and there was no comparison. Someone dating a woman of that caliber would not want someone like Genesis. Not that she didn't believe she was attractive in her own right, but there were levels, and she was not on Hollywood actress level.

"Hmmm, if you say so. Of course, it doesn't mean you can't have fun," Andrea said.

"What are you going on about?"

"When I told you to get laid during your trip, you said that not only weren't you going to find any gay women but that you aren't, and I quote, as friendly as I am."

Genesis cracked a smile at the memory of their conversation. "I am not sleeping with Zuri. I'm just excited to meet someone interesting. Besides, she has a girlfriend."

"Okay, but if it's offered, don't pass it up." They both laughed. "Anyway, everyone knows that she and Tracy aren't serious."

Genevieve shook her head. "And may I ask how you're aware of her business?"

"Because unlike you, I live and breathe celebrity gossip."

Genesis ended the call after their chat and looked at herself in the mirror. She looked good; she just needed something to wear. Her first attempt at minimalistic travel couldn't have come at a worse time. Clothing options were limited, but she would have to make it work.

After finding her favorite dress, the one "dressy" item she had with her, she placed it on the bed and went in the shower. She put her hair up and stepped inside, allowing the steady stream of water to massage her shoulders. After hearing the gossip about Zuri's superficial relationship with Tracy, she now wondered if there might be a possibility of them hooking up. It was not something she did, but she had to admit she wanted it. Ever since her divorce, she had been so lonely and needed a fun, passionate affair. Perhaps Zuri would be the one to give it to her.

* * *

ZURI

Zuri stood in front of the full-length mirror in her bedroom and looked at her outfit. She was trying to decide what she wanted to say with her clothes. When she was into someone, what she wore tended to be more provocative, but Genesis had already seen her in a skimpy bikini, which left little to the imagination. While she wasn't shy by any means, she didn't want to go overboard and come off as too aggressive. Their flirtation was fun, but mental foreplay was more her style. Despite the short time they had, she saw no reason to change up her tactics.

"That jumpsuit is beautiful on you."

Zuri sighed as she turned to see Rain standing in her doorway. Wearing a bathing suit and munching on a bag of popcorn, she had a pair of headphones dangling from her neck with the sounds of Ariana Grande pouring out.

"Thanks, but this is my private suite. Note the word private."

"Always acting as if you don't want me around makes me want to be near you even more," she said with a wink. Rain entered the bedroom and sat atop the bed with her legs crossed. "Are you going to dinner with that pretty lady staying here?"

"Your face was so deep into your phone I'm surprised you even saw her," Zuri said, spraying on perfume. "Anyway, maybe I'm going out with someone else."

"I looked after you made me," Rain said with a smirk. "Besides, I can tell you like her by how annoyed you were with my behavior. Any other time, you just ignore my insubordination."

Zuri chuckled. Rain was annoying but witty and observant. "Remind me to never underestimate you, despite your tendency to irritate me."

"You're the big sister I never had; it's my job to irritate you," Rain said, as she threw some popcorn into her mouth. "So, first time meeting?"

Zuri stared daggers at her as she scooped up the popcorn she was spilling onto the floor every time she dug into the bag. "We just met yesterday. She's staying here for a couple of weeks. Which reminds me, try to stay in your part of the house."

"Why, are you afraid I'll scare her away? I can be charming too; thank you very much."

Rain gave her one of her photo-ready smiles. Zuri ignored her and leaned into the mirror as she applied her lipstick.

"So, guess who texted me?" Rain asked.

"Please, don't keep me in suspense."

Rain ignored her sarcasm. "Jackson. He apologized for being a jerk and asked me out to talk everything over. He said he didn't want animosity between us before we shot the movie."

Zuri feigned surprise. "Is that so? I'm glad to hear it. You two will be dynamite on screen."

Rain didn't respond and instead squinted at her and continued chewing. Zuri turned back towards her mirror. She smoothed the front of her jumpsuit. It was sexy without being over the top. As she walked over to her dresser and began putting on jewelry, she felt Rain watching her.

"If you're going to be a weirdo, can you at least come over here and help me put this on?" Zuri said, her hand outstretched with the necklace she wanted to wear.

Rain placed the bag of popcorn down and jumped off the bed. She grabbed the necklace from Zuri's hand and placed it around her neck. "It's obvious you guys told him to do it, but I wanted Jackson to apologize on his own. It's not the same. Now he'll think I can't fight my own battles."

Zuri thanked her and grabbed a pair of earrings. "You can't; that's why you came to us. Both of you are kids playing at being adults, and I don't have time for you to figure your shit out and jeopardize my film."

"Whatever." Rain walked back over to the bed and grabbed her popcorn. "I'm going to go chill by the pool. Have fun on your date and wear your nose ring. It's sexy and highlights your face."

Zuri took out the diamond stud she wore in her nose from her jewelry box. She put it on and checked her face in the mirror. Rain was right; it worked with her outfit for the evening. When she located her purse, she grabbed it and headed out to pick up Genesis.

* * *

Zuri knocked on the door of the guest house several times. Music was blasting from the inside, which was why Genesis couldn't hear her. A slight push opened the door, and she knocked again as she poked her head inside.

"Genesis?" she called out. The longer it took her to answer, the more concerned Zuri became. As she walked inside and shut the door, Genesis entered the living room in her towel.

"Oh my God," she cried out, jerking back.

"Shit, I'm so sorry. I was knocking and calling your name; I got worried," Zuri said, backing up. As hard as she tried not to stare, she lingered on the exposed parts of Genesis's skin. Her arms, chest, and legs glistened from the steam of her shower, small droplets of water still clinging to her.

"Second time you caught me off guard.. I get in a zone when I'm listening to music. In case you haven't figured that out." Genesis let out a nervous giggle. Her hands gripped onto the towel as if she feared it would fall at any moment. "I should be ready in fifteen minutes. Is that okay?."

"It's cool; I'm early. Take your time. I'll wait for you in the car." Pushing down her lustful thoughts, Zuri turned and walked back outside.

Twenty minutes later, Genesis knocked on the passenger door of Zuri's Audi. She unlocked the door and breathed in deep as Genesis sat down. The perfume she wore was a lovely and light floral scent that was strong but not overpowering— fitting for the person wearing it.

"I expected a driver," Genesis said as she put on her seat belt.

"Sometimes I use one, but I don't make anyone other than security work on the weekends. I can take care of myself for a few days."

"I would never have guessed," Genesis said, smiling.

Zuri smiled back. Genesis appeared more relaxed than earlier, and that set her at ease. She wasn't nervous, but she was more aware of her behavior. It had been a long time since anyone made her want to impress them.

"So I have to ask. What's up with the name?" Zuri asked as she drove toward the gates of the estate.

Genesis chuckled. "My mom was a born again Christian. She chose it over naming me after someone in the bible. When I was a kid, I hated it because I got made fun of by other kids. Eventually, I grew into it."

"It's a lovely name. Different can be difficult sometimes, but adversity builds character, no?"

Genesis agreed but didn't respond further. Zuri worried she might have offended her.

"I'm sorry, I'm not dismissing your experience..."

"No, it's okay. You said nothing wrong," Genesis replied, placing her hand on Zuri's knee for reassurance. "I have hang-ups when it comes to my childhood and my parents."

She removed her hand, and Zuri hoped she would place it there again. "I have issues with mine, so I get it. Anything you want to discuss?"

"How much time do you have?" Genesis said with a chuckle.

"An entire dinner. I want to learn more about you."

Although her eyes were on the road, Zuri felt Genesis's eyes on her.

"Sounds good," Genesis replied after a pause. "I want to learn more about you too."

Chapter Six

"This place is gorgeous," Genesis said as they entered the restaurant.

With a warm decor that evoked the Caribbean, she felt calm as soon as they entered. The server, who introduced himself as Paul, led them upstairs while Zuri chatted with him. It appeared they were familiar with each other, but according to her driver earlier, there weren't many people Zuri didn't know on the island.

They had the whole top of the restaurant to themselves per Zuri's request. It was outside and had a fantastic view of the town of St. Lawrence Gap as well as the Atlantic Ocean. Zuri pulled out Genesis's chair, and she could feel her eyes admiring her. Although her outfit wasn't anything special, just a teal wrap dress, it did highlight one of her favorite features, her legs.

"You come here often?" Genesis asked as Zuri went to take her seat.

"I do; this is my go-to spot if I'm not eating at home."

Genesis lifted the menu and began going over the options. "Food must be good then."

"I should hope so. I own the place and expect nothing less,"

Zuri said, scanning the menu. Genesis stared at her until she looked up. "What?"

Genesis chuckled and went back to the menu. "I'm just fascinated by your nonchalance about your wealth."

Zuri placed her menu on the table. "I'm very fortunate, and I made sure I put myself in a position to maintain the lifestyle I'm accustomed to having. Does that bother you?"

Genesis placed her menu down too. "Not at all. I find your confidence, among other things, very sexy."

Zuri looked flustered for a moment, and that pleased her. She didn't want to be the only one constantly caught off guard.

"Good," Zuri said as she picked up both their menus. She called the server over and ordered several items off the menu for them to share.

"What if I don't like what you ordered?" Genesis said, with a playful glint in her eye.

Zuri licked her lips and said, "I'm certain there will be something in there that will satisfy you."

Genesis looked away but smiled. She pointed out towards the ocean. "That is what I was looking forward to being around. I'm enjoying it so much. I just wanted to be a beach bum for two weeks."

"I hope I didn't derail that for you?" Zuri said as she poured them both wine.

"Not at all. I had a lovely afternoon at the beach, and a private one at that," Genesis said, turning back to her. "It's silly to keep thanking you, but I'm grateful that I got the chance to stay. I didn't want to go back home."

"The divorce you mentioned, was it mutual?"

Genesis sipped from her wineglass and shook her head no. "We were having problems, but I didn't think they warranted a divorce. Shannon thought otherwise."

"I'm sorry to hear that. The end of a relationship is always heartbreaking."

"Yeah," Genesis said, looking away. "I just assumed we would be together forever, but I guess that was stupid."

"No, it's never stupid to love someone with all of your heart. If you don't do that, then what's the point? I'd say we all go into a relationship with the hope it will never end. At least I do, but it has yet to work out that way."

Genesis raised her eyebrow. "How is that no one has snatched you up?"

"If I knew the answer, then I suppose we wouldn't be sitting here." Zuri sat back and looked thoughtful. "I've had relationships but a hard time finding someone I can truly be intimate with."

"I'm assuming when you say intimacy; you mean more than sex?"

Zuri nodded. "Yes. I am also not a fan of casual sex, but I won't pretend I haven't had it. Someone with whom I can share my innermost thoughts and who gets to see all of who I am is more elusive. It's tough when I'm in such a superficial industry."

"Have you dated any actresses?"

"I have," Zuri said without elaborating.

"Are you dating one now?" Genesis said, looking into her eyes.

Zuri wagged her finger. "Don't play coy Genesis, if you want to ask me about Tracy, you can. You had to have come across something online."

Genesis hesitated. "Are you in a relationship with her?"

"We have a mutual understanding and spend time together. It isn't a traditional relationship, but it works for us."

Genesis nodded and looked out towards the water. Although they were just getting to know each other, she couldn't hide her disappointment. It wasn't like Andrea hadn't already told her, but hearing it from Zuri silenced any uncertainty. Now the question was, would she let that stop her from pursuing things further.

"Hey, listen," Zuri said, leaning towards her. "What I have with Tracy in no way means I can't spend time with anyone else. If it did, I wouldn't be here with you. I like you, and you already have me acting out of character."

Genesis turned to her, her brow knitted. "How so?"

Zuri waited to respond as Paul came over with their first course. He laid several small plates on the table and left them to eat. She took Genesis's plate and asked her which items she wanted to try. Once she filled it up, she placed it in front of her and refilled her wine glass.

"Are you always so accommodating?" Genesis asked as she started eating.

Zuri began to fill her plate. "I like people I'm with to feel taken care of at all times. Some like it more than others."

"I like it," Genesis said as she looked into her eyes. "You didn't answer my other question, though. How are you acting out of character?"

"I don't give up my time here to anyone," Zuri said.

"You own an estate on a Caribbean island, and you're telling me you've brought no one here?"

"Not a romantic partner, only friends and family. I decided a long time ago that I needed something that was just mine. A place where I could go..."

"And just be," Genesis said, finishing her sentence. "Yeah, I understand that desire."

"I figured that if I ever got serious with anyone or married, then that would be the time to share it. No one has made it to that level. Tracy has been here once but not anytime since."

"That explains why they say you're a recluse."

Zuri laughed out loud. "This is my sanctuary, so yeah, I

spend most of my time here holed up at home. Life back in LA is hectic. When I'm here, I just want solitude."

Genesis nodded, and her eyes lit up as she bit into an appetizer. "Oh my God, this fish cake is perfect. The crispness on the outside and the flavor inside is so good."

"Yeah, that's one of my favorites, but everything chef Huey makes is phenomenal."

Genesis made her way through the food, loving it all. Zuri watched her with amusement as she devoured everything in front of her.

Only once she was full did she take a break. Genesis wiped her mouth and patted her stomach. "That was so good. Anyway, we were supposed to talk about our parents. Although God only knows why we would want to put a damper on things by doing that."

"Well, if it makes you feel more comfortable, I can tell you about my upbringing first," Zuri said. She thanked Paul as he came by to remove their empty plates. "My parents were self-absorbed and not into having a kid. I think my mother had me because she reached an age where she felt it's what she had to do, and my father obliged. They were good to me, but I didn't grow up in the most loving home. I got that from my grandparents, and my mother's sister Lynn, God rest her soul. Reggie and Elijah, my cousins, are more like brothers because my aunt always had me at her house. She knew how my mom was."

"It's a blessing she was in your life. Sometimes the universe gets it right. How is your relationship with your parents now?"

Zuri thought about her mom and dad, who had been living in Paris for the past ten years. They were semi-retired from the film industry and popped up at industry award shows or events now and then. She saw them at least twice a year.

"Things are good now. I'd say they are better parents to me as an adult than they were to me as a child. I'm still getting used to the change in them, and I can't lie and say I don't harbor some resentment. But they took care of me and loved me as best they could."

"Well, that's something. I try to remind myself that parents are human beings and have all the faults that come with that." Genesis sipped on her wine, her fingers stroking a strand of her hair. "My parents were the opposite of yours. They always maintained a level of control over me and my sister's lives. Both were super religious, and it was crucial to them we be good, Christian girls that never strayed from the fold. They controlled every aspect of our lives, from our clothes, to how we spoke; it was all very structured. Our life revolved around our church. We weren't close to family because my parents felt they weren't true servants of the Lord. I think we spent time with our grandparents and other extended family members only a handful of times. They looked at the church members as our genuine family."

Zuri scrunched up her face in distaste. "This sounds like a cult, was it?"

"No, it was just a small Pentecostal church in Virginia, but the control the pastor had over his congregation was absolute. He was the voice of God. It colored every interaction we had with our parents, but there were good times; they loved us very much. They wanted to give us a better life than what they had growing up. One filled with faith and devotion to God. A purpose that was greater than us I guess."

They put their conversation on pause as Paul returned with their entrees. He placed the food on the table, and Zuri pointed at the various selections. "I asked them to cook some staple Bajan food. So we've got some fly fish, macaroni pie, rice and peas, a pepper pot and some chicken curry. I'm sure you're going to love it all."

Genesis filled up her plate with a bit of everything. She gave

Zuri a thumbs up after several bites. "This is wonderful, thank you."

Zuri dug into some of her food. "You talk about your parents in the past tense. Are they still with us?"

Sadness washed over her face as Genesis sat back and sighed. "No, they passed away a few months after I graduated from college. My sister Mackenzie was 16. Thank God I was old enough to take her into my custody. It was a freak accident; they died in a head-on collision on their way home from church. My sister stayed behind for Bible study, which is why she wasn't with them."

"I am so sorry, Genesis. That must have been hard for you both?"

"It was tough, and I became a parent overnight. My sister took it even harder than me, and there was no one to help me deal with that. I thought the church would be there, but once they knew about my relationship, they distanced themselves from us."

"How did they find out?"

"Shannon and I had just started dating then. The town was small, so it was hard to hide anything. We moved around a bit until we settled in California. My sister had a long rebellious phase. She settled down at some point, and now she is a very responsible adult that thinks she's in charge of me," Genesis said with a chuckle.

Zuri steered the conversation into lighter territory, talking about her cousins and some aspects of running a studio. Genesis was in awe as she described the day to day inner workings of what they did. The more she talked, the more Genesis was drawn in. Not only was she a pleasure to look at, but she was funny and endearing. Every once in a while, she would say something arrogant, but when Genesis called her out on it, she just said something else self-deprecating.

"Well, we have laid quite a lot on each other at this dinner," Zuri said. "How about we take what's left to go?"

"Yes, please, I would love some of this for lunch tomorrow." Genesis looked at the food and bit her lip. "Who am I kidding? I want all of this for lunch tomorrow."

Zuri laughed at her enthusiasm. She waved Paul over and requested to wrap everything up, and added a few dessert items. As they sat waiting for his return, Genesis swayed her head to the music playing in the background. She didn't want the night to end.

"Hey, I thought it would be nice to grab another bottle of wine and walk on the beach when we get back to the house. You'll never see a fuller moon than the one here at night," Zuri said.

Pleased by the eagerness in her voice, Genesis smiled and said, "I could go for that. Let's do it."

Chapter Seven

After grabbing a bottle of wine from her cellar, a beach towel, and a basket, Zuri dropped off the leftovers and led Genesis to her favorite spot on her private beach. Having that space to herself was something she loved about the house. It wasn't just the solitude she was into, but the memories. She spent many summers there with her grandmother playing as a child and then having long discussions about life and her dreams as she got older.

Hazel Ellis had been an actress from a young age and became best known for her work on the stage. Although she grew up during segregated times, she built a stellar career through grit and unmatched talent. She bought and built the massive home in Barbados because that was where her family originated. Her parents were a part of a significant immigration wave from the country to the United States in the early part of the 20th century. Still connected to her roots, Hazel wanted to make sure she left her family a piece of their history.

Zuri shared all of this with Genesis. She was inquisitive but allowed Zuri the room to tell her story, and it was a story she loved because of how much her grandmother meant to her.

"Did you ever feel like your parents were pushing you off onto your grandmother?" Genesis asked.

"No, I looked forward to it. My parents weren't home often, so I was at my aunt's house or with my nanny. When I came here, I got one-on-one attention."

"A nanny? I keep forgetting you all are rich, rich," Genesis said with a wink.

Zuri laughed as she pointed to an area for them to sit. Walking the beach at night with the stars sparkling above and no one else around was a unique kind of peace. Zuri didn't share it with anyone, yet she was more than happy to be there with Genesis. Her energy was refreshing. She wanted nothing more from her than conversation. It had been a long time since she met someone without an ulterior motive.

Once they reached their destination, Zuri placed down the towel she brought for them to sit on. She placed the basket on the sand beside them and pulled out the wine and glasses. There were a few other treats inside in case they wanted to snack. As she sat down, Zuri noticed Genesis shiver, but she wasn't complaining. Although it was warm out, the breeze off of the ocean could be brisk at night. She pulled off her sweater and placed it over Genesis' shoulders.

"Oh, you don't have to do that. I've been out here at night; I should have brought my own," Genesis said, about to remove it.

Zuri waved her off. "No worries, I'm used to the weather here. I'll be fine."

Genesis pulled the sweater closed. "Okay, thank you."

After she poured them some wine, Zuri waited for Genesis's response after she took a sip. It was one of her favorites, and she hoped she liked it.

"Mmm, this is good. I don't like red wine, but this isn't dry like most." Genesis lifted the bottle to look at the label.

Zuri took a sip herself and let it sit before swallowing.

"They use overly ripe grapes to give it a more fruity flavor. Not as sweet as some white wines, but also not as dry like you said."

Genesis drank a little more and side-eyed Zuri. "Your family doesn't own a vineyard, too, do they?"

Zuri let out a throaty laugh. "No, although I have been thinking about it. Wine is a good business, so is liquor. I'm a connoisseur of both, and it would be pretty awesome to invest in it and not just consume."

Genesis nodded and looked out over the ocean. "Can I ask you something?"

Zuri sat back as she let her hair down. "Of course."

She could sense Genesis's gaze on her as she fluffed out her locs. When she turned to face her, there was blatant lust in her eyes. Zuri laughed out loud, and it seemed to snap Genesis out of her haze.

"Sorry. I love your hair," Genesis said as she cleared her throat.

"Thank you; these are my babies. I have been growing them for fifteen years. My mother hated the style at first, but she's coming around. So what did you want to ask me?" Zuri said, taking out some cheese.

"Oh, I was just curious about what it's like to never want for anything, as far as money."

"That's a loaded question," Zuri said. She handed her a piece of cheese and popped a bit in her mouth. "It feels good. I've never known insecurity about food, having a home, or any of the basics that money can provide. I'm not bragging; that's just a fact. My life was easier by being born into a wealthy family."

Genesis regarded her, and a small smile appeared. "Thank you for being honest. Had you said anything other than what just came out of your mouth, I would have had to call you out."

"That's not my style. I will give it to you straight no chaser all day every day, but not everyone can handle that." Zuri stared out over the horizon. "My grandmother was one of the bluntest people I've ever known, and I loved that about her. My mother found it distasteful, but she didn't care. She used to tell me she regretted sending my mom to those bougie boarding schools because it made her soft. God, I miss that woman."

"Didn't you attend those same schools?" Genesis asked.

There was no malice in her voice, so Zuri didn't take offense. "I did, but my mom and I have such opposite personalities. I've always been comfortable existing outside of the mainstream. My mom, not so much." Zuri averted her eyes. "It's always been hard between us because of that."

After a few minutes of silence, Genesis leaned forward and touched Zuri's arm. "Hey, where did you go?"

Zuri shook her head and looked over at Genesis with a grin. "Sorry, just got hit by a random memory. Pay me no mind—anyway, enough about me. I have a question for you. Were you ever a dancer?"

Genesis tilted her head and said, "What made you ask me that?"

"Last night, when I saw you dancing, something about the way you moved made me think maybe you were a professional or at least studied it," Zuri said, trying not to smile too hard at the memory.

"You're very observant," Genesis said, gathering the sweater closed again. "I studied modern dance in college. Ever since I saw an Alvin Ailey performance on a video in school, I knew that's what I wanted to do. I used to practice all the time, so I would be perfect when I got my audition. My parents never knew. I figured I would live in New York performing with the Alvin Ailey Dance Theater before they were any wiser. Then life happened."

"I'm surprised your parents let you leave Virginia for college."

Genesis shrugged. "It was a Christian school so they figured I wouldn't be led astray."

Zuri noted the sadness that passed over her face, and it made her heart constrict. "So I take it that once they passed away, you didn't pursue dancing?"

"I had my sister to think about all the time. So when we moved to Cali, I studied accounting because I've always been good with numbers, and by the time she graduated, I had a career. The pay was good, and I could find work easily," Genesis said. Her jaw clenched as she continued. "Shannon was always practical, so she preferred it."

Zuri waited for her to finish, then asked, "And what did you prefer?"

"I preferred the steady pay and stability," Genesis said, her voice missing conviction.

Unable to stop herself, Zuri pushed. "Was that your true preference?"

Zuri watched Genesis and saw a subtle shift in her demeanor. The corners of her mouth turned down. When she spoke, her voice was firm but low.

"It was devastating when I realized I could never make up for the lost time. Once Kenzie graduated high school, I was 25, then I had to help pay for college, and when she finished, I was going on 30. There was a point where I thought maybe I could return to it, but that time never presented itself." Genesis looked up, her eyes burning with defiance. "My dreams are unfulfilled, but that's the price one pays when you aren't born with a silver spoon in your mouth. You don't get all the choices, you only get some, and often, they may not be the ones you want."

Zuri fought the urge to sit forward and kiss Genesis, even though the desire was strong. She loved that she pushed back at her line of questioning but also gave an honest answer. It showed she had a backbone and didn't mind being transparent. It was rare for Zuri to come across people that exhibited either quality, let alone both.

"I'm sorry if that was out of line," Zuri said, breaking their eye contact.

Genesis pursed her lips, then finished her wine. "It's fine, I wasn't frank with you, and you called me out. I've spent a long time convincing myself that I made the right decision."

"Thank you for your honesty," Zuri said. "But you did what was best for your family. There's nothing wrong with that."

Genesis nodded. "Okay, now that we have gotten into each other's business," she said with a big smile, "how about we talk about something fun. What does a movie mogul do in her spare time?"

Zuri sat back and leaned on her elbows. "I mentor young women of color. I started a foundation, Beacon Academy, where we focus on providing resources for them to develop skills in their areas of interest. Everything from coding to the creative arts. We get them internships and help them connect with people they wouldn't otherwise meet. I have a young woman now, Avery, whose dream is to direct movies, and she just got into one of the top film schools in the country. I've been mentoring her since she was in junior high school."

Genesis gave her a small clap. "Bravo, using your resources to uplift young people is wonderful. What drew you to that?"

"I can do it, so why not? It's good; it keeps me grounded. My grandmother was all about that. She used to have me volunteering all the time, taking me to places where those less fortunate lived, especially here in Barbados. Not to pity them, but to understand that I was well off, and I needed to do what I could to lift up my brothers and sisters."

"She sounds so amazing; I wish I could have met her."

"Me too; I know she would have liked you." Zuri poured them some more wine. "Your turn. What does a brainy accountant do during her downtime?"

"Well, this will sound cheesy, but I hug babies," Genesis said.

Zuri raised an eyebrow. "Like you just go up and hug random babies in the street?"

"No, silly," Genesis said, slapping her leg. "I volunteer at Brookdale Hospital as a cuddler. Babies in the NICU need extra TLC, and since their parents and staff can't be there all the time to give it to them, we fill in the gaps."

She didn't think Genesis could get any more attractive, but somehow she had. Who hugs babies in their spare time? Someone with a kind heart and she had it in spades.

"That's not cheesy at all; it's wonderful. And I bet those babies love every minute," Zuri said.

Genesis's eyes crinkled as she nodded in agreement. "They do. It makes me happy that I can give them the comfort they need, but I also get some back. After the last couple of years, I think I needed it more than they did."

Zuri hesitated, then asked what had been at the back of her mind. "Do you miss your ex-wife?"

Genesis sighed. "I'd be lying if I said I don't. She's family; we've known each other for so long and grew into adulthood together. But I don't know if I miss her as my wife. The romance was out of the picture for quite some time."

Zuri did an internal fist pump after hearing that. It meant she had less to worry about than she thought.

"Now that we have interrogated each other, I think it might be time to go inside. It's getting pretty cold out here," Zuri said.

She began packing away the wine and glasses. When she turned, Genesis moved in to hug her, but they ended up with their faces close enough to kiss. Zuri wanted to close the distance, and she could see a myriad of emotions playing all over Genesis's face. But she wrapped her arms around her instead and hugged her tight. Genesis reciprocated and stepped back.

"Thank you for everything today," Genesis said.

Zuri handed her the basket and picked up the towel from the sand. "It was my pleasure. I enjoyed your company."

They walked back, chatting about some topics they hadn't discussed earlier. Zuri was pleased to find they had quite a few things in common. Once they got back, she was reluctant to end the night, but the extra time getting to know each other was a bonus. Whatever was going on between them, she could tell it had the potential to be special.

Chapter Eight

The following morning Genesis woke up feeling refreshed and unable to stop smiling. The last couple of days had been so delightful that she didn't think they could be topped, but she was willing to find out.

Zuri was nothing like she thought she would be. There was a slight arrogance about her, which Genesis found intriguing. No doubt it came with the territory of being the heir to a cinematic dynasty. Despite that, she was down to earth and seemed interested in Genesis, plus she enjoyed their conversations.

With her lack of experience in the dating world, Genesis was sure that she would either become a hermit or have the misfortune of endless bad dates after things ended with Shannon. Paralyzed by either prospect, she had opted out of it entirely.

Kenzie, hoping that Genesis and Shannon would reconcile, was okay with that. She kept telling her big sister that they were soul mates. Genesis knew her sister's attachment had more to do with losing their parents and seeing her and Shay as surrogates, but she felt guilty just the same. Still, she had no idea what would come of things with Zuri, but the prospect of being with someone else didn't seem so impossible anymore.

Eager to see if Zuri was around, Genesis showered and got dressed. As she stepped outside, she almost tripped over a basket of beautiful flowers that included a note.

Sorry, I'm not around to see you this morning; I have some errands to run. But I thought waking to something beautiful would make up for it. I left breakfast for you in the kitchen. Perhaps I could persuade you to have dinner with me again this evening. Think about it, Z.

"Oh, I do not have to think about that at all," Genesis mumbled to herself.

After placing the beautiful flowers on the breakfast nook counter, she made her way to the main house. The breakfast Zuri made the other day had been delicious, so she was excited to see what else she had for her. As she entered the kitchen, a figure behind the refrigerator door startled her.

"Oh, shit, my bad," Rain said with a sheepish look on her face. "Didn't mean to scare you."

"It's fine; I just forgot that you were here. Good morning," Genesis said, walking over to the large island.

"Good morning," Rain said, popping a grape into her mouth.

Zuri looked over everything that was on display. More waffles, sunny side up, scrambled eggs, bacon, French toast, fruit, and a tasty-looking smoothie with a note attached: *For Genesis, don't touch Rain.*

"Seems Zuri was expecting you," Genesis said with a smile as she filled her plate.

"Yeah, I love it when she cooks. Breakfast is the only thing she's mastered, but she owns it. I can't boil water," Rain said as she shoved some bacon in her mouth. After she finished chewing, she pointed another piece in Genesis's direction. "How did your date go last night?"

Genesis walked over to the table with her food and smoothie. After placing it down, she settled into her seat.

"Why do you assume it was a date?" she asked.

"Well, you dressed up and had dinner at a nice restaurant. I'm pretty sure that's how dates go," Rain said with a shrug. "But it's cool if you don't want to talk about it."

Genesis ate some food and watched the young woman. She was nosy but could fill in the blanks on Zuri's situation, so she shared.

"Zuri and I are getting to know each other as friends, but we had an enjoyable time, thank you for asking." Genesis poured some syrup on her waffles. "I'm curious. Do you know anything about her friend Tracy?"

Rain sniggered and covered her mouth. "Oh yeah, Zuri's been messing with Tracy for a minute. Their relationship, if you can call it that, makes no sense to me. Honestly, Zuri just puts up with it because she's whipped."

Genesis laughed at Rain's candor. "Please, tell me more," she said.

"They met at this charity event Zuri was hosting. Tracy was there with this other woman named Fiona, a big-time producer. The rumor is that Tracy only attended with Fiona to meet Zuri, and the rest is history. The weird thing is, as soon as things got hot and heavy, Tracy pressed pause, and it's been this weird back and forth ever since. Zuri wants something serious, but Tracy seems to like things the way they are." Rain drank some orange juice. "Anyway, I know all of this because I'm good friends with Stacy, Zuri's assistant. She would never tell me this herself. We have a love/hate relationship."

Genesis found Rain's delivery amusing, but now she was curious about Zuri's relationship even more. When they talked the night before, she made it sound like what she had with Tracy was mutual, but it was clear from what Rain said it wasn't. Did she lie so Genesis wouldn't be scared off, or did she believe that she was okay with Tracy not committing to her?

"So why do you say you have a love-hate relationship?" Genesis asked.

"I'm exaggerating. I irritate her because, well, I can be a brat, but I respect her. She got me out of an unpleasant situation at home when she took a chance on me for that Star Crossed trilogy, and I'll always be grateful for that," Rain said. "So yeah, I'd much rather she be with someone nice and normal. Zuri's not like most of the assholes I've met in the industry; she cares about people."

Genesis raised an eyebrow. "So Tracy isn't nice then?"

Rain rolled her eyes. "No way, she's a total social climber. Let's just say that ever since she started dating the hottest lesbian bachelorette around, her career went into overdrive. I'm not sure why Zuri can't see that she's a user, but I guess love is blind."

Genesis cringed at the use of the word love. "You think they're in love?"

"Zuri maybe, Tracy no, but she's damn good at pretending."

Rain gave Genesis a lot to digest, so she steered the conversation in a different direction. The young woman was more than happy to talk about herself and her career, so that's what they did for the rest of the meal. Afterward, Genesis excused herself and walked back to the guest house to prepare for another day on the beach.

Whatever was going on between Zuri and Tracy was unclear, but she appreciated the honesty. Nothing had changed in her mind. She wanted to wait and talk to Zuri. However, it did give her pause. While she wasn't sure if she was ready for anything serious, she was open to the idea of something with the other woman. She just needed to be sure that it was what they both wanted.

* * *

ZURI

Zuri sped down the highway to her destination with the top down on her convertible. She blasted a song by one of her favorite music artists, Steflon Don.

"Look how you make me feel, Look how you make me get aggressive, Look how you make me feel, Look how you make me get senseless," she sang at the top of her lungs.

To say she was in a good mood was an understatement. While she loved it, she also didn't trust it. She hoped that the next week would give her time to learn more about Genesis and space to figure out what she truly wanted.

Zuri parked down the block from the construction site she was visiting. It was a sports facility she funded. The island needed a new one after a storm destroyed the biggest one three years ago. It took a while, but Zuri cut through the government's red tape to get the work started.

Whenever she had any type of construction project, she went to her cousin Christopher. He owned one of the smaller construction companies on the island, but his work was impeccable. They were close since he was often at her grandmother's home when she would visit back in the day. Most of the Ellis family had moved abroad and made the United States and Canada their new home. One of grandma Hazel's sisters, Patricia, stayed on the island and had a large family that still lived there.

"Hey cuz, what's up?" Zuri said with a wave.

"Nothing much, but I'm happy to see you," Christopher said as he pulled her into a hug. "You haven't been down in a few months; that's not like you."

"Trust me; I hate it. Things have picked up so much at the studio that sometimes it gets overwhelming, but I guess it's what I wanted. Thank God Elijah and Reggie are on top of things because I couldn't do it without them," Zuri said.

"Those two still arguing all the damn time?" Christopher said with a chuckle.

"Yeah, pretty much. I'm just glad that they're both in happy relationships; it makes things a hell of a lot easier." Zuri picked up the plans Christopher had laid out on a cinder block. "I can't wait to see the building when you're finished; it's going to be beautiful."

"Thanks to you, Z. Aunt Hazel would be proud." Christopher walked over and tapped on the paper. "But you didn't come here to talk about this project. What's up?"

Zuri folded her arms. "How's Keith?"

Christopher's eyes crinkled as he wagged his finger at her. "Deflection doesn't look good on you, but I'll bite. He's doing well and moving up the ranks in the police department. He's always been an overachiever that one."

Keith and Christopher had been together for well over ten years but lived in separate homes. Homosexuality was still a crime in Barbados and some other Caribbean countries. Convictions were harsh and carried a life sentence for those caught. While rarely enforced, it still placed a stigma on members of the LGBTQ community. For some, the ostracization they would experience if found out could be just as bad as jail time. It sullied the beauty and love Zuri had for the island since she couldn't be herself. Activists were trying to make changes, but it was slow to take hold.

"Does him going into law enforcement still bother you?" Zuri asked.

"It does, but I understand why. His end goal is to reach a high enough position that he can help change the laws. Doesn't make it easy, though, knowing what it would cost him if others found out," Christopher said.

Zuri nodded. "I have so much respect for what he's trying to do. It's so easy to take things for granted living somewhere that doesn't have this level of restriction."

"Sometimes, we talk about moving to the States, but then what does that mean for the people here who can't just leave? We want to be a part of the change for those who come up after us," said Christopher.

They sat down on some tree stumps close to the construction zone. Zuri leaned into the sunshine as she looked out at the beach at the bottom of the cliff they sat near.

"I met someone," Zuri blurted out.

"I knew it." Christopher clapped his hands. "Who is she?"

"Her name is Genesis; she's staying at the guest house. We've been hanging out, and she is wonderful."

Christopher made a face. "And what does Tracy think about this?"

Zuri tilted her head and gave him a dirty look. " That's a low blow."

Christopher shrugged. "What? You want me to act like you don't have a girlfriend?"

"She's not my girlfriend, something she has made painfully obvious," Zuri said. "We are at most friends with benefits, and that's all she ever wanted. I can't keep putting my love life on hold, waiting for her to love me."

"Do you love her?"

"Doesn't matter."

"It does if you want to get involved with someone else.

Genesis doesn't deserve a half-assed relationship because you're still pining for your ex."

"I don't know anymore what I feel." Zuri sighed and looked at the ground. "At one point, I did."

Christopher placed his hands on her legs and forced her to look him in the eye. "It sounds to me like you met someone with possibility, but you have to be careful that you aren't projecting your needs onto this other person. You just met her. Get your house in order; then you can let someone else inside."

Zuri sucked her teeth. "Do you always have to be so damn right about everything?"

"Isn't that why you come to me for advice?"

What Chris said was on point, as usual. There was an instant attraction between herself and Genesis, but they didn't know each other. And while she had assumed that if anyone were a rebound, it would be her, her feelings for Tracy were still in limbo. It wouldn't be as simple as she assumed to end that situation, no matter how "casual."

Chris clapped his hands. "Hey, why don't you ladies come over for dinner Thursday night? Keith will be on vacay, and he can whip up a meal. Then we can interrogate your little lover girl."

"I'd love that, I'll check with Genesis, but I'm sure she'll be down." Zuri stood up and wiped off her pants. "And she is not my lover girl...yet," she said with a wink.

Chapter Nine

At 9:30 am, Genesis was startled awake by her alarm. She placed it across the room, so she had no choice but to get out of bed; it was the only way she ever woke up on time. After a thorough stretch, she padded into the bathroom and gazed in the mirror. Zuri and Rain kept her up until around 3 am playing board games and watching clips of Rain's guffaws on the red carpet and in interviews. No matter what Zuri expressed, she held some affection for the starlet. There was a camaraderie between them that was clear underneath all the sarcasm and irritation.

She sighed as she washed her face. It would be necessary to hide the dark circles that always appeared if she didn't get enough sleep to be presentable. Zuri told her the night before about an open-air market they were going to visit around 11. Unable to turn down a fun shopping trip, Genesis said yes. Of course, she knew deep down; it was just another excuse to hang out with Zuri.

Her mind kept settling on the question of what would happen once they got back to California. They didn't live far from each other, but Genesis understood that Zuri was busy when she was in L.A., and the type of time she was giving now likely wouldn't be the norm. It didn't stop her from imagining a myriad of possibilities.

The house phone by her bed rang, and Genesis jogged over to answer. As soon as she picked up, Zuri's deep melodic voice came through.

"Good morning. I figured I should call you since we were up late. Do you still want to go down to the market?" she asked.

I'd go anywhere with you. She shook her head and chuckled at the juvenile sentiment. Zuri had her acting like a love-struck schoolgirl.

"What's so funny?" Zuri said.

"Nothing, just a pleasant thought that made me smile."

"Mmm, was it about me?"

Genesis froze at the slight breathlessness of Zuri's voice. Her mind brought up all of the dirty things she could do to entice those same sounds.

"Don't do that," she said.

"Don't do what?" Zuri asked.

"Make those sounds; it's distracting."

Zuri burst into laughter on the other end of the phone, and even though she was embarrassed, Genesis couldn't help but laugh too.

"Okay, fair enough. I'll behave," Zuri said.

Genesis bit her lower lip as she pictured the naughty smile that was no doubt on Zuri's face.

"Thank you for being so accommodating. Anyway, I'm about to get dressed."

"Oh, well then, it shouldn't take too long. You don't have to work that hard to look good."

Flattery tended to irritate Genesis because it always sounded disingenuous, but she found it flattering when Zuri did it. There was a sincerity in the way she spoke to her that was a breath of fresh air. It made her feel seen and appreciated.

"Thank you, that's sweet of you to say," Genesis said.

"I'll meet you out front in a red convertible," Zuri said, then hung up before she could respond.

"Red convertible? Okay then." Genesis headed back into the bathroom and continued getting ready.

* * *

Zuri was waiting for her in a car very different from the one she drove the other night. The color was a deep red that shined in the Bajan sun. It turned out to be a classic car that belonged to Zuri's grandmother. A few years ago, she restored it but didn't use it often because of its sentimental value.

"It's a British sports car called an MGB. My Grams nick-named it speedy," Zuri yelled over the wind whipping past their faces.

Genesis laughed and said, "Did she get it when she was young?"

"Nope, she bought it when I was about ten years old, so she was 65."

"Your Grams was a badass."

"Yeah, she was. I could only hope to be half as cool as she was at every age."

Their conversation slowed down as they listened to music, which was fine by Genesis. She had so much on her mind that she was grateful for the peacefulness of the drive. The last few days she felt like she had truly reached a place of peace. Now it was time for her to think about what was next when she got back home.

Genesis spent years prioritizing her wife and sister. She was neglected, and that was never more apparent than when

Shannon left. It thrust her into a state of confusion not only because it came out of nowhere, but it also forced the realization that her life was fully integrated into her wife's. Any interests that were important to her, including dance, were long forgotten. They shared friends, extracurricular activities, finances, and anything else of importance.

Why did she let Shannon become her world? That question had been plaguing her for months. It wasn't as if the other woman demanded that sort of allegiance. But it was so easy to allow herself to become subsumed by Shannon's more assertive personality. Even now, Zuri's confidence and swagger attracted her like a moth to a flame. Perhaps that's who she was, a weak follower.

Her thoughts made her sick to her stomach. Is this who her parents created from years of demanding respect but not always offering it in return?

"Hey, you okay over there?" Zuri asked, placing her hand on Genesis's arm.

"I'm sorry I got lost in my thoughts. What were you saying?" Genesis said, forcing herself to smile.

"I asked if you would be interested in going to dinner at my cousin Christopher's house on Thursday? His boyfriend is a phenomenal cook, and he invited us."

"Us? You told him about me?" Genesis asked, trying not to smile too hard.

"I did; I hope that's okay," Zuri said.

"It's fine, as long as it was all good things."

Zuri chuckled. "All good. I told him you are a delightful woman that he just had to meet."

"Well, in that case, it would be rude if I didn't go. It would be my pleasure."

Zuri glanced over at her and said, "Good, that's what I was hoping you would say."

"What would you have done if I said no?"

"Then I would have had to find some way to make you say yes," Zuri said, her voice dripping with innuendo.

Genesis shifted in her seat and tried not to appear flustered. Hearing Zuri's words had her clenching her thighs. *It is too early in the morning to be getting this turned on.* Chastising herself didn't stop the feelings, and if she was honest with herself, she didn't want to.

* * *

Once they arrived in Bridgetown, Zuri found parking several blocks away from the fair. According to Zuri, that would allow them to leave and not have to worry about traffic.

Genesis took a deep breath as they strolled towards the town square. The weather was perfect, the same as every day since she arrived. The salt air that wafted over them from the ocean was refreshing. Sunlight beamed down from the bright blue sky and warmed their skin. Although it wasn't quite noon, the sun was already high in the sky.

Delicious smells flowed towards them from the many vendors lined up and preparing food. The crowd was small since it was still early, but it was filled with residents and tourists alike. The fair ran up and down a long stretch of highway, cut off from traffic. On either side were vendors as far as the eye could see. In the distance, steel drums played, their sound traveling through the air.

"What's with all the colorful costumes I'm seeing?" Genesis said as she gestured towards a stall selling masks and other clothing.

"This market is a part of the Crop Over Festival. It's a three-month celebration, and at the very end, there is a big parade full of dancers and music." Zuri pointed towards some people purchasing clothing. "Plenty of tourists like to take part; that's who they sell to here."

"So it's similar to the carnival celebrations I've seen in other countries?"

"Yes, but we all have our reasons, of course. The tradition here started around 1687 to celebrate the end of the sugarcane crop. Now it's way more elaborate, and the finale is the Grand Kadooment Parade. Your fave Rihanna has taken part in the past."

Genesis' eyes lit up. "Rihanna? That's my girl. My timing was off this year, but next time it's on."

"So there'll be a next time?" Zuri said with a smile.

Genesis looked down, then back up again. "Of course."

Zuri's gaze swept over her as she brushed a loose hair from her face. They stared into each other's eyes, and Genesis could feel herself moving closer. A kiss felt inevitable, and she wanted it, but she took a step back and pointed at a vendor selling fruit.

"Maybe we can start over there? That fresh fruit is calling my name," Genesis said.

Zuri looked disappointed but followed behind her. Her mood changed when she saw some of what was for sale.She chose a container with chunks of mango and handed it to Genesis. "You haven't had mango until you've had it straight from the tree."

Genesis opened up and started eating as Zuri paid for hers and another container. Of course, the fruit was divine. Succulent and sweet, the burst of flavor was how she imagined sunshine would taste.

They strolled for a bit, dodging the growing crowd. Some jewelry caught Genesis's eye, and she dragged Zuri over. After purchasing a few items, they moved on to some vendors selling clothes. Now that she knew they were going out to dinner, she wanted to get something pretty to wear.

"This is nice," Zuri said, fingering a skirt.

"Not quite what I'm looking for." Genesis surveyed the items on a rack. A flowing red dress jumped out at her. "This is the one."

Genesis admired the material and pulled it down. She gave it to the vendor to ring up before Zuri caught a glimpse.

"So I can't even see what you picked?" Zuri asked as Genesis clutched the bag.

"Nope. You'll see it when I wear it to dinner."

Zuri rolled her eyes. "Really?"

Genesis stuck her tongue out and giggled at Zuri's mad face. "Anyway, have you ever considered living here full time?" Genesis asked.

Zuri nodded. "Oh yeah, one day. It's not workable now, but I can see myself retiring here. The people, the weather, and my family's history make it perfect. All I need is the right person to come with me."

The intensity in her eyes as she said those words and looked into Genesis's face had her feeling some type of way. *Five days, you've known her for five days.* The reminder was necessary because the jumble of emotions inside had her ready to consider what their last names would look like together.

"So, what does Tracy think about your plans?"

Zuri flinched at the mention of the other woman. Genesis knew it was throwing off their flirtation, but it was something she had to keep in mind.

"She loves the islands, but as I told you, I like to keep this place as my sanctuary. She's only been that one time, but I'm sure she would love to live on a Caribbean island, who wouldn't. Whether that would be with me, I can't say." Zuri stopped walking and pulled Genesis over to a building, away from the streams of people. "I don't want to be presumptuous, but it's obvious that I'm into you, right?"

Genesis shoved her hands in her pockets. "Yes."

"And it's mutual?" Zuri asked, searching her face.

"It is," Genesis said, trying to keep her tone neutral despite the somersaults happening in the pit of her stomach.

"Then don't worry about Tracy. You and I are getting to know each other and enjoying each other's company. It doesn't have to get deeper than that," Zuri said. She lowered her voice and leaned in, then said, "Unless you want it to."

Genesis's eyes dropped again to Zuri's plump lips. Even if Zuri just wanted to have a good time and let it end there, what was wrong with that? They were two consenting adults, and Zuri had let her know more than once that her relationship with Tracy was not exclusive. Even so, Genesis knew herself, and a fling was not in her wheelhouse. If the sex were at all like what she had been imagining, one time would not be enough.

The sound of a horn jarred both of them out of their staring contest. Genesis shook her head. Now wasn't the time. She would know when it was right to move forward.

"How about we get some lunch? The food smells delicious," Genesis said, walking back amongst the crowd.

Zuri's lip poked out a bit, and it was the cutest pout she had ever seen. Genesis decided to have mercy on her, so she grabbed Zuri's hand and squeezed it. Zuri gave her the sweetest smile and squeezed her hand back.

Chapter Ten

"So, this is Coco Hill. What do you think?" Zuri waited for Genesis's response as she surveyed the trail they would be hiking.

"I think I am about to regret this." Genesis saw her disappointment and laughed. "I'm kidding, Zuri, this place is great, but I'm not a hiker."

"Doesn't matter; this place is so beautiful you won't even care. Follow me."

Located in Barbados' Scotland Hills district, Coco Hill Forest covered 53 acres and contained various birds, vegetation, trees, fruits, herbs, and spices. Zuri had visited many times over the years and wanted to share it with Genesis. It had been a couple of days since their visit to the market and she knew the other woman would appreciate the tranquil vibe.

"These trees are amazing," Genesis said, walking up to a Royal Palm.

The trees were tall and thin, with leaves sprouting from the top. They swayed from the breeze blowing off the water.

"I know, this place always leaves me in awe no matter how

often I visit." Zuri dropped to the balls of her feet by a patch of plants. "This looks like basil."

Genesis bent down beside her and sniffed the air. "Smells like it too. It's so fresh; this whole place is a dream to my sinuses right now."

Zuri looked over at her. "You have allergies?"

"I do, but ever since I got here, I've been fine. The best I've breathed in years."

"That's good to hear." Zuri brushed a random leaf from her shoulder. Their eyes locked, but then Genesis turned back to inspect the plant.

After their excursion the day before at the market, Zuri knew Genesis was feeling the same way she did. Everything about her behavior told her so, but she was reluctant to make the first move. Genesis seemed to want things to go at a slower pace, and she had to respect that.

"Can we eat this?" Genesis asked, massaging the leaves.

Zuri laughed. "I suppose we could. Richard, who helps run the farm here, says it's fine as long as you know what you're picking."

Genesis's eyes twinkled as she removed a leaf and popped it into her mouth. Zuri watched her chew and swallow, then pick another leaf.

"Your turn," she said.

Zuri made a face but took the leaf. Genesis shook her head and motioned for her to open her mouth so she could feed it to her. Surprised, Zuri opened and tried not to react as Genesis's fingers brushed against her lips as she laid the leaf on her tongue.

"Now, close your eyes," Genesis said.

Zuri did as she was told and chewed. The flavor of the basil flooded her mouth. It was spicy with a hint of bitterness. While not the best thing she had ever eaten, it wasn't unpleasant.

"What did you think?" Genesis asked.

She opened her eyes to find Genesis watching her. "It had an interesting taste. I didn't love it, but my mouth feels clean."

"I use basil all the time as a palate cleanser when I'm cooking. If you're tasting multiple food items, something heavy, that or some mint is the way to go." Genesis jumped up and held out her hand to Zuri. "I know breakfast is your domain, but maybe I can teach you some other items to cook."

Zuri grabbed her hand and stumbled into Genesis, catching herself as she held onto her waist. *Kiss me.* Their lips were mere inches apart, and Genesis's eyes kept dropping to her mouth. She bit her lip, and Zuri was sure that this time it was going to happen.

"Z, is that you?"

Zuri recognized Richard's voice and cursed under her breath. She let Genesis go and noticed the disappointment on her face too.

"Hey Rich," Zuri said, waving him over. "I brought my friend here to take in all of this beauty."

Richard hugged her, and she introduced him to Genesis. "Well, since you're here, would you like to join the tour I'm giving?" Richard said, pointing to the group of tourists waiting for him.

"Sure, why not, if you want to?" Zuri said, turning to Genesis.

"I'd love to learn more about the forest. Let's do it," Genesis said.

They followed behind Richard and said hello to the tour group. As they started the hike, Genesis's hand bumped hers, then their fingers intertwined. If she could have, she would have done a victory dance in the middle of the forest. Instead, she just smiled and held on tight.

* * *

Two hours later, Richard took the group and headed back to have lunch at the restaurant run by the nearby farm owners. Zuri thought Genesis would be interested in the food, but she seemed content to stay out longer.

Experiencing Barbados through her eyes was something that Zuri enjoyed. It was like she was seeing everything for the first time. Even now, they had discovered a private oasis with the cool green light from the surrounding tropical flora bathing them. She was certain it was never like this during previous visits.

The branch on a nearby tree shook, and a green monkey with a baby clinging to her stomach appeared. She sat and watched them with large, curious eyes.

"Awww, how precious. What is that monkey called?" Genesis said, pointing towards the tree.

"That would be a green monkey. They've been on the island for a long time. They're originally from West Africa. Very adorable, but aggressive if you disturb them." Zuri started walking, and Genesis caught up. "They are all over the island, but mainly in wooded areas like this."

As they walked further, a gap in the trees gave Zuri a view of the sky. She cursed as she noticed rain clouds forming.

"Damn it, I think we're about to get caught in a downpour," Zuri said.

Genesis followed her gaze. "What should we do?"

"We don't have enough time to get to the farm. Let's just hunker down over here; the trees are pretty dense in this area."

Zuri led Genesis over to a tree stump beneath a group of trees that looked like they would provide ample cover. On cue, the wind picked up, and the bit of sky they could see became overcast. The sound of thunder was loud enough to cause Genesis to jump into Zuri's arms.

"Did you set this up?" she asked with a smile.

"Oh yeah, I'm good friends with the god of thunder. Thor and I go way back."

Zuri placed her arm around Genesis's shoulders, and she snuggled into her body. The rain lashed against the tree leaves, and the moist air intensified the smells of the surrounding forest.

"Thank you for bringing me here," Genesis said, lifting her head from Zuri's chest. "I would have never seen the island this way if you weren't here."

"It's been my pleasure. I didn't realize how much I would enjoy exploring with someone else." Zuri hesitated, then said, "I'd love to show you more once we're back in LA."

Genesis sighed. "Oh, there is so much I want you to show me."

Zuri looked into her golden-brown eyes, and she saw what she had been waiting for; permission. That was all it took for her to press forward and kiss the lips she had been fantasizing about for days.

It was gentle and sweet as their mouths pressed together. Zuri closed her eyes, and everything around them disappeared. In the distance, she could hear the drum of the rain, birds cawing, the rustling of the trees as monkeys swung from their branches. None of that compared to the sound of her heart pounding in her chest.

Genesis brought her closer by placing her hand on the back of her head, gripping her locs. Zuri responded by kissing her harder. A deep moan escaped from the back of Genesis's throat. Zuri could feel herself getting wet, and it wasn't from the rain.

The storm halted, a common occurrence during the wet season in Barbados. Rain one minute and sun the next.

Although Zuri didn't want their kiss to end, she knew it was best to head back just in case another bout of rain came down.

Zuri licked her lips when they parted. "Let's walk back to the entrance," she said, leaning her forehead against Genesis.

Genesis gave her a playful pout. "Just when things were getting good."

"Mmm, that was good, but trust me, it can get even better."

"I don't doubt that," Genesis said, biting her lip. She got up and pulled Zuri with her.

Shortly after they began their stroll, Genesis screamed out in pain at the same moment her grip left Zuri's hand. She turned to find her writhing on the ground and holding on to her ankle.

"Oh my God, what happened?" Zuri said, dropping beside her. She looked around and saw that the heavy rain had loosened some rocks and other things from the ground. One ended up in Genesis's path.

"I'm okay, but I twisted my ankle, and it hurts like hell," Genesis said, sitting up.

Zuri helped her stand and had her place her arm over her shoulder. "Put your weight on me. It's going to take us a while; we walked pretty far."

They began the slow walk back, and Zuri prayed they made it back before dark. Richard said they walked the trail to ensure there were no visitors left behind, but there was no guarantee this would happen. While the place wasn't dangerous at night as far as she knew, she didn't want to find out otherwise.

Chapter Eleven

Genesis blew bubbles away from her as she sunk further down. Zuri insisted she use the Japanese soaking tub in her suite to take a relaxing bubble bath. Having never used one before, she didn't expect it to be so deep.

She wiggled her foot under the water and winced. It had taken them over two hours to get back. Zuri knew a doctor on the island who made house calls, and he looked her over. It was a sprained ankle but a mild one, so he said she would only need a day or two off of it with elevation and some ice.

When she first fell, the pain had been so excruciating she was sure that the injury was more serious. She sent up a silent prayer of thanks that it wasn't because she hated the thought of spending her last days in Barbados laid up.

"How are you, beautiful?" Zuri said, appearing in the doorway.

Her hair was up, and she had changed into leggings and a tank top. It didn't seem to matter what she had on; she looked good. Genesis turned away so she could stop drooling over her.

"I'm okay. This tub is everything. I wish I had one like it at home because baths are so much better than showers."

Zuri leaned against the door frame and sipped on the drink in her hand. "I agree, but there's so little time for them."

Genesis shook her head. "There's always time for pampering. I try to do something nice for myself every weekend."

"How long have you been doing that?"

"Since my divorce," Genesis said, her voice losing some of its perkiness. "That's why I'm here. I spent too long neglecting myself."

Zuri walked further into the bathroom, and Genesis tried to cover up. Then she remembered what happened between them earlier and decided there was no need. It seemed silly to act overly modest.

"Here, it's time we put some ice on that foot of yours," Zuri said, holding up a large towel.

"Do I have to? It's so nice in here." Genesis sank further. "Five more minutes."

Zuri rolled her eyes. "You've been in there for over an hour, and your dinner's getting cold."

"You cooked for me?"

"I wish, but I had food brought over from The Sea Breeze. Since I own it, that's just as good as cooking it, right?" Zuri said, wiggling her eyebrows.

Genesis laughed. "Not quite, but I'll take it."

Zuri held the towel up again. "I have some dessert that's just for you if you want it."

The huskiness in her voice made Genesis's insides feel like molten lava. Their kiss earlier had been chaste, but still ignited her in a way she hadn't expected. Now she couldn't look at Zuri without wondering what she would be like in bed.

"I think I can get myself out of the tub," Genesis said, holding out her hand.

"Don't be silly. Once you stand up and have to put pressure

on your foot, you're liable to fall. Let me help you." Zuri continued to hold up the towel, but this time averted her eyes.

Genesis appreciated the effort, and as she stood up, she thought maybe her foot was okay after all. Then she put more weight on it. Her arms flung out to the sides, and she fell back. She held her breath, preparing to go under the water, but then a body pressed against hers.

Zuri stood in the tub halfway, holding her just above the water. Genesis was hyper-aware of her nakedness as Zuri's clothing soaked through. They were both breathing hard as Zuri positioned them upright. Her hands remained on her back but could have slid down to her bottom. She kind of wished they had.

"Can't stay on your feet around me, it seems," Zuri said with a smirk.

As Zuri backed away from her, Genesis didn't cover up her body. Instead, she stood there staring into Zuri's eyes. She could see that her behavior surprised her, but rather than ogle her, Zuri gave her an appreciative once over, then grabbed another towel.

"I'm sure you don't need me to tell you this, but your body is beautiful." Zuri handed her the towel and extended her arm. "Let me help you out; then I'll give you privacy to change."

Genesis reached out and held onto her arm as she gingerly climbed out. She allowed herself to sneak a peek of her own as she wrapped the towel around her body. Zuri wasn't wearing a bra, and her erect nipples looked tempting underneath the soaked tank top.

Despite her attempt at being discreet, Zuri caught her stare. She just smiled and gave her a wink.

"Meet me on the patio, in ten."

Genesis waited for the door to close before she let herself fall back against the vanity. It was large and black, with double sinks and one continuous mirror. It stood out in the otherwise white bathroom.

Mindful not to make the same mistake again, Genesis hobbled around as she got dressed in shorts and a T-shirt. She fixed her hair as best she could, but the humidity from her bath made it hopeless, so she wrapped it in a scarf. Not very sexy, but the throbbing in her foot wasn't leaving room for more primping.

The sheer size of Zuri's room took her breath away as she entered it again. It was the size of two master-bedrooms in one. At the center was a huge four-post bed. Floor to ceiling windows lined the opposite wall, along with two doors that led out to the patio on the other side.

The walls were painted black, which would have made it too dark in any other space. Instead, with all the light from the outside during the day and the bright light fixtures, the contrast worked. Colorful artwork adorned the walls with canvases of various sizes. A large white bureau stretched along the wall opposite the bed underneath an enormous television.

The ocean breeze greeted her as she stepped outside. Zuri appeared minutes later, carrying their food.

"Sit here, and you can use this chair to prop your foot up." Zuri situated her foot on a cushion and placed a large ice pack on top of it.

Genesis sighed. "Oh, that's nice."

Zuri placed a pill in her hand. "Tylenol for the pain."

"Thank you." Genesis gulped a glass of water and downed the medicine. "What is Rain doing?"

Zuri waved her hand dismissively. "Holed up in her room. I think she's practicing her lines and obsessing about Jackson."

Genesis laughed as she cut into her chicken. "Leave the girl alone; she's young. I think we all obsess about the people we date at that age. Unrequited love can be the worst."

They were quiet as they ate, breaking the silence now and then, but enjoying the meal more than anything else. Genesis caught Zuri watching her a few times. When they finished, Zuri disappeared and returned with a couple of beer bottles.

"This is from a local brewery, a pale lager. One of my favorites." She opened the bottles and placed them on the table.

Genesis picked one up and took one sip, then another. "This is good, refreshing. I'm not a big beer drinker, but I like it."

"Stick with me kid, you'll get all the good stuff," Zuri said, snickering.

After taking another long swig of beer, Genesis worked up the nerve to say what had been on her mind ever since they got back. "So, are we going to talk about that kiss earlier or..."

"We can talk about it, reenact it, whatever you want." Zuri turned to face her. "It was the best first kiss I've ever had."

Genesis blushed at how sincere she sounded. "The best? That's saying a lot."

"Well, I've kissed plenty of people, but this afternoon was something else. The atmosphere and the vibe between us."

"It was special," Genesis said, twisting the bottle in her lap. "What is it you want from a relationship?"

Zuri leaned onto the table. "The basics; loyalty, love, passion. Someone that makes me a priority, and we can depend on each other. Someone who makes me laugh and holds me when I cry but puts me in my place when necessary."

"I want those same things, but I also need a woman who doesn't need to control everything and respects what is important to me."

"Sounds like you've experienced that yourself?" Zuri asked.

Genesis stared at the table. She wanted to open up, and if they were going to move forward, Zuri needed to know about her past. "Shannon was controlling. Never abusive or anything like that, just very particular about the way things needed to be and what she wanted from me. I never questioned it because it felt familiar. My parents were the same way, and I think there was a level of comfort in that with them gone."

Zuri moved her chair closer and repositioned the ice pack on her foot. "Was the sacrifice worth it?"

"In retrospect, she never seemed to place much value on the things that mattered most to me, and she would undermine me when I would discipline my sister. She thought dance was a frivolous pursuit, despite knowing how much I loved it. I accepted all of it and just buried my feelings because that's what I'd always done." Genesis nibbled on her lip, then took a sip of beer. "We were happy for a while until we weren't."

"Are you relieved that you're free?"

Genesis looked at Zuri's face and smiled. "I am. The world is such a big place, and I'd be doing myself a disservice if I didn't open myself up to other possibilities."

Zuri raised her bottle of beer and motioned for Genesis to do the same. "Here's to other possibilities," she said, clinking the bottles.

* * *

After another drink, Zuri convinced Genesis to visit the home theater to watch a movie. Even though she was tired, she didn't want the night to end, so she agreed.

The theater had seating for at least eight people, with white leather recliners near the front and a large cream sectional couch in the back. Along the side was a popcorn maker and a small bar. Genesis walked over to one of the six framed movie posters on the wall and recognized Zuri's grandmother. They had similar features.

"I know this lady," she said with a smile. "Was this her first film?"

Zuri nodded and gazed at the poster with pride. "It was her first and her favorite, according to her. This poster was one she had here in the house when she was living here. Come and sit." Zuri patted one recliner, and Genesis sat down.

She pressed a button on the side of the chair and elevated her legs. "I can't guarantee I won't fall asleep. This chair feels like a bed," Genesis said, shifting herself until she felt comfortable.

Zuri laughed and opened a hidden cabinet in a panel on the wall. "You better not. I'm about to pull out a black movie classic right here."

Zuri showed her the DVD box, and Genesis clapped. "Love Jones, that's such a great movie." She took the box as Zuri set up the projector. "I used to have such a crush on Nia Long. Who am I kidding? I still do. The woman is flawless."

"Same here, although I liked Larenz Tate too. I always found him sexy."

"Hush, they might take your lesbian membership away," Genesis said with a chuckle as Zuri turned down the lights.

Zuri giggled and settled in next to her. "Well, I never said I was a lesbian. The magazines and papers decided I must be because the last couple of people I dated were women. I like people, so I would describe myself as pansexual. I dated a couple of guys; one was a trans man. So yeah, I'm open to whoever makes me happy." She turned to Genesis. "Is that an issue for you?"

Genesis gripped Zuri's hand and laid back as the movie started. "Nope, not an issue at all."

"Good," Zuri said, raising her hand and kissing it. "Now, let's watch these two beautiful people fall in love."

Chapter Twelve

The following day, Zuri felt like she was on cloud nine. Other than Genesis's minor injury, their time together had been fantastic. She felt like they were getting to know each other, and the more she learned about Genesis, the more she could see a potential future with her.

The question was, now what? They both were leaving on Sunday, and she had high hopes for what was to come. Her life was hectic, but she wanted to make room for the right person. There was just her relationship with Tracy. Genesis was not comfortable with their arrangement, no matter how casual, and that was understandable. It was on Zuri to do something about it.

Zuri parked in the garage and headed into the house to check on Rain. She wanted to leave a bit earlier, and she promised to drive her to the airport. On a whim, she ran out to pick up some of the fresh fruit she knew Genesis liked first and was now late. It didn't matter; she was more than worth it.

As she walked inside, she noticed two suitcases by the door. They didn't belong to Rain because she usually brought a duffle bag when she came to visit. Zuri strolled into the foyer and heard glasses clinking by the bar. An all-too-familiar figure stood with their back towards her, mixing up a concoction of some sort.

"Tracy?" Zuri said. "What are you doing here?"

Tracy turned and smiled. "Well, hello to you, too. One second, I've been working on preparing a Bahama mama," she said, turning back around. After shaking up her concoction in a tumbler and pouring filling up her glass, she took a giant sip. "Perfection."

She put the drink down, skipped to Zuri, kissed her on the lips, and then wrapped her arms around her. "I knew you were here for a couple more days, and they postponed production. I'll tell you more later. Anyway, I wanted to surprise you. Are you happy to see me?"

Zuri hugged her back, then stepped out of her embrace. "Of course, babe. I'm always happy to see you. It's just..."

Tracy held up her hand. "I know what you're going to say about this being your private getaway, but it's been years since I stayed here with you. I need to talk to you about something important."

Before she could respond, Rain came strolling out from the back of the house. She took one look at Tracy and rolled her eyes as she dropped her duffle bag onto the floor.

"Rain, I didn't know you were here," Tracy said, barely hiding the irritation in her voice.

"Funny, I was about to say the same thing," Rain said. She turned to Zuri. "Z, I spoke with Lyle, and he said it's cool if I just leave when you do."

Zuri furrowed her brow and walked over to Rain. "What are you talking about?"

Rain brought their heads together and spoke low. "I can leave, but then that means you'll be here with your current lover and your new potential lover. Not sure how you like those odds."

Zuri glanced over at Tracy, then turned back to Rain. "That sounds good, Rain. It's only a couple of more days."

Rain winked at her and strolled over to the bar where Tracy had returned to finish her drink.

"So Tracy, how's that movie you're shooting? Word is they're over budget already," Rain said, grabbing a cola out of the mini-fridge.

Tracy frowned. "Well, whoever your source is, they don't know what they're talking about. We are not over-budget; shooting is barely underway."

Rain sipped from the can and squinted her eyes. "Exactly, so why are you here?"

"Not that it's any of your business, but a good portion of the crew got food poisoning, including the director, from some bad salmon. As soon as everyone is okay, we'll be back in Miami." Tracy put down her glass and tilted her head. "What about your film? Jackson is quite the charmer. He's bedded several of his co-stars. Better watch out there, Rain."

Zuri saw Rain's body stiffen, and she was sure the young woman was about to let loose a tirade on Tracy, so she jumped in.

"Honey, why don't we take your bags into my suite and get you settled. I'm sure you want to get on that beach," Zuri said as she got the suitcases.

"Sure, baby," Tracy said, giving Rain a sickly sweet smile.

They began walking to her suite when Zuri spotted Genesis coming inside from the guest house. She had hoped she would have time to speak with her before introducing Tracy, but it seemed the universe was not on her side.

"Hey Z, I was wondering..." Genesis stopped speaking

when she noticed Tracy behind Zuri on her phone. "Oh hi, I'm Genesis," she said, offering her hand.

Tracy glanced between the two of them, then shook her hand. "Hello, Tracy. Pleased to meet you."

Zuri could see a look of suspicion on Tracy's face. "Genesis is staying in the guest house because of a mixup at the hotel. She had nowhere to go, so Ms. Taylor asked if she could stay here," she said.

Recognition lit up in Tracy's eyes, and she relaxed. "Oh, that's right, you've mentioned that before. I forget how much of a sweetheart Zuri can sometimes be," Tracy said, wrapping her arm around her waist. "So, how do you like Barbados, Genesis?"

"It's beautiful, my first time here. Not sure why it took me so long to visit," Genesis said, looking down for a moment. "My ex preferred visiting less tropical countries."

"You never mentioned that," Zuri said.

Genesis looked into her eyes, and for a moment, it was like they were alone again. Tracy cleared her throat beside her, breaking the moment.

"Well, you got lucky staying here. Babe," Tracy said, gripping onto her. "I'm tired; you think we can get to the room?"

"Yes, of course," Zuri said. She tried to read the expression on Genesis's face, but it had gone blank.

"Nice meeting you," Genesis said.

Zuri stopped her as she passed by. "You wanted to ask me something."

"It wasn't important. Take care of your lady."

Zuri pulled back at the tone in her voice. Although her face was neutral, there was enough bite behind Genesis's words to betray her genuine feelings. She had no choice but to let her go, but she hated not having the space to explain to her what was going on.

* * *

"Ugh, how can you stand that little brat," Tracy said as she sat on the bed and removed her heels. "Seriously, Zuri, she is so rude. And for the life of me, I cannot understand why she dislikes me so much. I've done nothing to her."

Zuri sighed as she rolled Tracy's luggage into her walk-in closet. "Rain is annoying, but she is a phenomenal actress and loyal. She has worked with us over some major studios several times."

"Well, she needs to learn to respect her elders. I haven't spent 20 years in the business, so some twit from a Twilight rip off could talk to me like a fucking extra on set."

"I will speak to her about it," Zuri said. She sat beside Tracy and cupped her face, pulling her into a firm kiss.

For the first time that she could ever remember, her actions felt forced. Usually, she was so excited to even be in Tracy's presence that she couldn't keep her hands to herself.

"Mmm, I need more of that as soon as I take a shower," Tracy said, breaking the kiss. "Care to join me?"

"I'm going to check in with Christopher. We're having dinner with him tomorrow night."

"Ooh, I love him and Keith. That should be fun. Okay, I'll be out in a few," Tracy said with a wink.

Zuri smiled at her and watched as she made her way into the bathroom. As soon as the door closed and music started playing from her phone, she went to look for Genesis. Tracy always took extended showers, so she had at least thirty minutes before she finished.

Genesis and Rain's laughter spilled into the living room and Zuri followed the sounds out to the pool. Despite their rocky initial meeting, the two seemed to have hit it off.

"What's so funny, ladies?" Zuri said as she stepped outside.

"Gen was just telling me about a time when she knocked a groupie into a pool who was pushing up on her wife," Rain said with a chuckle.

Zuri sat on a pool chair. "Groupie?"

Genesis scratched the back of her head. "Um yeah, my ex Shannon played for the WNBA on the San Francisco Sparrows."

Zuri's eyes opened wide. "Your wife was Shannon Colbert?"

Genesis nodded and looked away, embarrassed. "I don't mention it much because people get weird about it."

Shannon Colbert had been one of the top players in the WNBA for her entire career. Straight out of college, she went to play for San Francisco and led them to three championships. A career ending knee injury forced her into retirement, and she was now the coach of a women's team at a university in California. Occasionally she popped up as a talking head on the sports analysis shows on ESPN.

"I understand. People have lots of expectations once they sniff a hint of fame," Zuri said.

Rain jumped up from her chair and clapped her hands together. "I am going to go get ready. Gen and I are going out tonight."

"Where?" Zuri asked as Rain passed by her.

Rain pretended to zip her mouth shut and strolled inside.

"She realizes that I can get you to tell me anyway, right?" Zuri said with a smile.

Genesis didn't smile back and instead laid on the chair and looked out over the horizon.

"There's a party at a club in Bridgetown that Paul mentioned to her. They have some events as part of the festival."

"Paul is always partying, but he's a decent guy. You'll have fun. Make sure you stay with him and his friends; they'll look out for you."

Genesis glanced at her and raised an eyebrow. "I'm not dumb. I did my research on the club and the events. It's going to be full of tourists, mostly."

"I never said you were," Zuri replied. "I'm sorry."

"Why are you sorry? The woman you're dating surprised you by visiting. Objectively you've done nothing wrong."

"Objectively..but you feel differently?"

"Not about you," Genesis said, her voice low.

Zuri leaned on her knees towards Genesis. "This changes nothing. Everything I've said still holds true."

"Listen, Z, I came here to relax and finally do something nice for myself. You were a surprise."

"A delightful surprise, I hope," Zuri said.

"Yes, a wonderful surprise," Genesis said, nibbling on the corner of her lip. "It's just, I'm not interested in anything complicated, and this whole situation with Tracy is exactly that."

"But it's not. Tracy and I have been little more than friends with benefits for years."

"So you're not in love with her?"

Zuri wished she could unequivocally answer no, but that would be a lie.

"I'm not sure," she finally said.

"That's what I thought." Genesis stood up and placed her hand on Zuri's shoulder. "Until you can answer that question, I think we should leave things as they are."

* * *

After getting off the phone with Christopher and making him aware of the extra guests, Zuri went back to her room. Tracy was still in the shower, so she grabbed her laptop and checked her email. Fifteen minutes later, a burst of hot air billowed from the bathroom, followed by a nude Tracy. Any other time this would have made her hungry with desire, but now, nothing.

"Thank God I braided my hair. Between the humidity in Miami and here, there is no way I'd be able to tame my bush," Tracy said, strolling over to her luggage.

"I love your afro," Zuri said. It was true; she loved Tracy's natural hair. It was full and glorious, but she rarely wore it out. Either she rocked a weave or had it flat ironed bone straight.

"That's why I wear it out for you," Tracy said, wrapping herself in a silk robe.

Zuri barely registered the statement. She was too busy reading an email from her cousins. They were deciding on the finalists from pitch week. The bed moved, and she watched Tracy crawl towards her.

"Did you hear what I said?" Tracy asked.

"Sorry, sweetie, I was responding to an email from Elijah and Reggie. What's up?"

Tracy pushed the laptop off of her lap and straddled Zuri. "So Genesis, huh? She's a pretty lady."

Zuri sighed. She hoped the conversation wasn't going in the direction she thought. The biggest downside to dating an actress was dealing with their insecurities. There was never enough praise or attention that could wipe that away.

"Yes, she is," Zuri said. She wrapped her arms around Tracy's waist. "But why are we talking about her?"

Tracy picked at the neck of Zuri's shirt and shrugged. "I'm just surprised you didn't mention her when we talked."

"I never mention the houseguests who stay here; she's no different."

The words sounded fake, at least to her ears, but Tracy

seemed satisfied with her answer. She ran her hands over Zuri's locs and brought her closer.

"Doesn't matter anyway," Tracy said, loosening the belt of her robe and shrugging it off. "I've missed you."

She worked her way under Zuri's shirt, unfastened her bra, and then brought her hands around to caress her breasts. Despite herself, Zuri sighed and leaned into her.

"You missed me, or you missed having sex with me?" Zuri said.

A sly smile crossed Tracy's face as she said, "Both, but let me show you just how much."

Zuri allowed Tracy to kiss her, then pulled away gently. "Babe, I can't."

"What do you mean, you can't?"

"I'm not in the mood. I'd much rather just chill and hang out with you. Is that okay?"

Tracy stared at her for a moment in disbelief, then reluctantly nodded as she pulled her robe back on. "Is everything okay?"

Zuri said nodded and kissed her forehead. "Why don't you go put on one of your pretty bathing suits, and we'll go down to the beach. I'll bring some food, and we can have dinner there."

Tracy's eyes lit up as she went to change. Zuri closed her laptop and tried to ignore the ache in her chest. She got up to change and decided not to think about who she would rather go to the beach with for a night time picnic. Tracy was visiting, and she would give her the attention she deserved, even if she wasn't the one on her mind.

Chapter Thirteen

Genesis scowled into her glass of whiskey sour. As much as she wanted to go out initially, she realized her mistake once they arrived. Nothing about her mood was conducive to a good time, and she found the festive spirit around her grating. Rain sat beside her on the edge of her stool, bopping to the music blasting.

"You should finish that drink and down a few more. It will help lighten your mood," Rain said, leaning towards her.

"I've already had three, so I don't think that's the solution," Genesis said, turning around to face the room. "I noticed you aren't drinking."

Rain raised her glass, filled with cola. "Sugar is my drug of choice. Alcohol reminds me too much of the unfortunate environment I grew up in."

Genesis turned to her. "I'm sorry."

"It's cool. That's the past, and I have moved way beyond it. I'm a motherfucking superstar now, baby," Rain yelled out.

Those in the crowd who heard her yelled their approval and raised glasses towards her. While most had been polite, there were more than a few people who recognized the young actress and came over to chat or fawn over her. Rain took it in stride and even took selfies with anyone who asked. The bar was a tourist spot and catered to them with the music and general atmosphere. She was disappointed because instead of feeling like Barbados, they might as well have been in any of the bars she frequented in California.

"What is that like?" Genesis asked, gesturing towards the crowd.

"What, having fans? It's weird, but it comes with the territory. Lots of people love who they think I am."

"And who are you?"

Rain shrugged. "Sometimes I don't know, but I'll tell you who I'm not. I'm not some chick with magic powers who can't choose between a demon and an angel," she replied with a chuckle. "Star Crossed gave me so much, but it also took a lot away from me. I had to work my ass off so that others would take me seriously as an actress. But it's a struggle to maintain who I am in the face of constantly being told who I should be."

"It was weird when Shannon and I went out to events or just hung out together, and people would come up to her gushing, wanting to take pictures."

"Did you ever get jealous?"

"No, but I found it invasive. And we always had to be conscious of how we behaved outside, just in case people were watching. She wasn't on your level of fame, so I can only imagine what it's like once you're a bigger star."

"I've gotten used to it, but there is never a time when I don't believe it could go away. I try my damndest to maintain my image, or at least what people think my image is." Rain looked off into the distance for a moment, then turned to Genesis. "My birth name is Sarah, by the way."

Genesis smirked and put out her hand. "Pleased to meet

you, the artist formerly known as Sarah. I have to say; I thought your parents had named you Rain."

Rain shook her head. "I wish, but they weren't cool enough for that. No, they gave me a generic name because I was one of many. Your name is unusual, but it meant something to your parents. Me and my siblings look like they opened a list of most common names and just picked from the top 20."

Genesis burst into laughter. "I'm sorry, I know you're serious. But perhaps they just liked simplicity."

Rain scoffed. "I am one of ten. They just needed something to put on the birth certificate. If there was something to be smoked, sniffed, or shot into their veins, my parents were into it. We were just a result of them being negligent when it came to birth control. Anyone can have a child, but it takes someone special to be a parent."

Genesis reached over and rubbed her arm. "I'm sorry, honey. That sounds awful."

"It was, and that's why I changed my name. As soon as I turned 18, I moved out and visited the county courthouse, and put in the paperwork. Rain was born, and I never looked back. The following year I got the part in Star Crossed, and the rest is history."

"You are out here proving every day just how much of a badass you are. You should be proud. I am, and I barely know you," Genesis said, smiling.

"To know me is to love me," Rain said. "So what happens when you go back home?"

Genesis shrugged. "I go back to a house I can't afford and a job I haven't liked in years."

"Well damn, don't sugarcoat it," Rain said.

"I will tell you one thing, being an adult is bullshit," Genesis said, finishing her drink.

Rain furrowed her brow. "You realize I'm a grown-up, right?"

Genesis waved her off. "I know, but you're still in the infancy stage. Get back to me when you're pushing 40 and can't stop thinking of all the things you didn't do."

"You're almost 40, not 80. What's stopping you from doing what you want?" Rain rested her hand on Genesis' knee. "I had no choice but to follow my dream. The only other path in front of me led to destruction, and I wanted to live. You have the luxury now of the wisdom you've gained to get yourself where you need to be."

Rain's observation took Genesis aback. "Okay, I guess you're not an infant after all," Genesis said, rubbing her hand. "Don't mind me, anyway. I'm just in a mood."

"Tracy got you feeling some kind of way, huh?"

"There's nothing for me to feel. Zuri isn't mine."

"Yet, Zuri isn't yours yet. I'm rooting for you, Gen," Rain said, slapping her on the arm. "Now, I think we should have fun. You wanna dance?"

Genesis threw her head back and mouthed yes. Rain let out a joyous yelp as she jumped down from her seat and grabbed Genesis' hand to pull her onto the dance floor.

* * *

The next morning, Genesis woke up with a massive hangover. The sunlight that she had been soaking up without reservation for the past week now had her scrambling to close the shades. She sighed as she slipped down to the floor beside the bedroom window. The sounds of the ocean called out to her.

After a few minutes, she forced herself up to take a shower. There were only a couple of days left in Barbados, so she had to make the most of it.

They didn't return to the house until almost 4 am, the latest she had been out in years. Once they started dancing and hanging out with some other tourists, the time flew by. Rain was a lot of fun, and Genesis realized that she would miss spending time with her. She resembled a less uptight version of her sister.

Thinking of Kenzie made her pull out her phone. She needed to let her know what time she was due at the airport on Monday. A message from Shannon popped up, one of those annoying open-ended greetings. *Hey, how's it going?* No doubt Kenzie had told her she was out of the country, so either this was her weird way of checking up on her, or she wanted something.

When they first got together, Shannon appeared to be everything Genesis wanted in a mate. She was kind and nurturing. If there was such a thing as an ideal first girlfriend, it was her. When they were teens, they both knew the other was into girls, but it was a fun secret they shared between them. They would often talk about how it would be once they left their small town and could embrace who they were. It was Shannon's idea to attend the same college.

Best friends, their relationship remained platonic for years. Then when they were seniors, something changed. It was around that time when Genesis bloomed and stopped being so awkward. She paid more attention to her appearance, and her shyness took a back seat. Dance had brought this about. When she was moving, she felt like the most beautiful being in the world, and after a couple of years, it translated into her everyday life.

Shannon noticed, and even though basketball took up much of her attention, they started spending more time together one-on-one. Soon their "hangouts" became dates, and Genesis could see the desire in Shannon's eyes.

Once she knew Shannon wanted to be with her, it became

inevitable. They were inseparable, so the added intimacy was natural. When her parents died, Shannon made it known that she wanted them to be a family, along with Kenzie. So not too long after, they had a commitment ceremony, and then when California legalized gay marriage, they made it official.

The first several years of their marriage were bliss. They moved to San Francisco when Shannon made the Sparrows team, and she was a phenom right out of the gate. Instead of going abroad like the majority of athletes during their hiatus, Shannon made extra money with sponsorships and was selected to be an ESPN commentator. She didn't want to leave her and Kenzie, something Genesis appreciated. Her sister was still going through a rebellious phase, and they often had to drive out to her college to check up on her. Sometimes Shannon was the only one who she would listen to, and Genesis welcomed the support.

It was hard to pinpoint when things went wrong. There wasn't a particular incident or event that incited what would be the end of their romance. Instead, it was a gradual change that Genesis took notice of too late. Shannon stopped paying her attention. Affection between them became forced, and the passion that had once burned so bright disappeared.

Andrea used to refer to what they were going through as "lesbian bed death," which is a theory that suggests the longer two women are together, the less sexual attraction there is between them. Genesis thought it was nonsense and didn't buy it. She did still want Shannon, but it was obvious the feeling wasn't mutual.

Genesis tried everything to get them back to where they were, and it was then that she saw herself disappear. She catered to Shannon to make her happy. Instead, she got lost in the process and lost the woman she loved, anyway.

Now here she was on vacation, supposed to be jump-starting a new life for herself, and once again, she was pining for someone. She didn't believe that Zuri meant her any harm, but her current entanglement was not conducive to them getting together. When she saw Tracy standing there with Zuri, that gut-punch was so familiar.

Zuri was a fantasy, and although it pained her to do it, she would have to let go. It was better for them both.

* * *

After her shower, Genesis walked into the main house to look for Rain. She could have gone to the beach by herself, but she wanted company. It was easier not to think about what was wrong in her life when she had someone else around to distract her.

As she passed the living room and headed towards the set of bedrooms on the other side, she spotted Tracy out of the corner of her eye. She was at the bar mixing a drink, and when she turned towards the pool, she saw Zuri sitting on a pool chair lounging back in all of her glorious splendor.

"Oh, hello, Genesis. Care for a drink?" Tracy said, her smile obscenely bright.

"No, thanks. I indulged a bit too much last night," Genesis said as she turned to continue to Rain's bedroom.

Tracy cleared her throat and said, "Nothing like a little fun before returning to regular life, huh?"

Genesis turned back around and gave her a polite smile. It was clear Tracy wanted to talk.

"I've been taking advantage of it," she said, walking to the bar.

Tracy pulled a soda out of the fridge and slid it across the bar top to her. "I've been all over the world, and this is one of my favorite destinations."

"How often do you come here?"

"Oh, all the time. It's Zuri's second home, so it's mine as well."

Genesis tilted her head. Zuri said Tracy had only been there once, but never returned. It was a curious thing to lie about.

Genesis popped open the soda. "Must be nice."

Tracy took a swig from her glass. "It is! Do you have a special lady or man in your life?"

"Not anymore. I'm recently divorced, so I'm learning to be okay by myself."

"Sorry to hear that. Relationships are hard." Tracy leaned into the bar. "Zuri and I have had our difficulties, but we love each other. My goal is to make sure that nothing changes that, you know?"

Genesis nodded and realized what their conversation was about; Tracy was marking her territory. "I hear you, and I get where you're coming from."

Tracy flashed a smile. "Good, I'm glad we're on the same page," she said as she walked from behind the bar. "Care to join us by the pool?"

"No, Rain and I are heading to the beach for a bit."

"Okay, well, I guess we'll see you two at dinner."

"I'm looking forward to it."

Genesis watched as Tracy strolled outside and handed one of her drinks to Zuri. As she bent down for a kiss, Genesis got up and walked away.

Chapter Fourteen

"Here's your drink, baby."

Zuri opened her eyes to find Tracy standing beside her, holding out a glass. While she went inside to make them something to drink, Zuri drifted off to sleep. Her mind had been in overdrive ever since Tracy's arrival, and she had yet to land on whether she was sure about continuing their relationship. Meeting Genesis upended what she thought they had and what she believed she wanted for the future.

"Thanks, babe," Zuri said.

Tracy bent down for a kiss and she obliged. Ever since she arrived, Zuri had noticed a difference in her behavior. The woman she was used to dealing with was way more selfish about affection and always straddling the line between attentive and distracted. This new Tracy wouldn't leave her side and kept finding excuses to kiss or touch her. She liked it, but was unsure of its sincerity. Had she changed for the better, or was she simply reacting to the perceived competition?

"So, I wanted to talk to you about something," Tracy said as she sat in the chair beside Zuri.

"Right, you mentioned that yesterday. What's going on?" Zuri asked as she sipped her drink.

"Sure Fire studios contacted my agent about a television role that they think I would be perfect for."

"I didn't realize you were interested in television."

"I wasn't, but when they laid out what I'd be making and the fact that I would be the star of the show, I had to rethink my stance. I read the script, and it's brilliant. It's been years since I came across such a meaty role."

Zuri smiled and took her free hand. "That's great, honey. It sounds like you should put yourself out there. As an actress, especially a Black actress, you need to make your mark when you get the chance."

Tracy agreed and said, "That's why I said yes."

The solemnity in her voice surprised Zuri. "You don't sound happy about it."

"I am happy, but I realized something. I will film in London for six months out of the year. Which means we will barely see each other."

"Yeah, but we've had to do that before. I can always visit you," Zuri said.

"It's not that." Tracy put her drink down and moved her chair closer to Zuri. She twisted the ring on her finger and let out a deep breath. "I don't want to be away from you that long. At least not without some sort of formal commitment."

Zuri narrowed her eyes and sucked her bottom lip. She gave herself a moment to fully digest what Tracy was saying to her.

"What makes now different from before?" Tracy looked away, and Zuri gently squeezed her hand. "Say what's on your mind."

Tracy turned back to face her. "I'm in love with you and have been for some time. I know we both agreed to keep it casual, but.."

"You told me that's what you wanted," Zuri said, interrupting her.

"It was," Tracy lifted her hand and cupped Zuri's face, "but it isn't anymore."

This was the moment she had been waiting for since she first fell in love with Tracy. Now, as if she was aware of the conflict happening inside of Zuri, she was giving her the one thing that she always thought would be elusive.

Five years ago, Zuri held a fundraiser for her non-profit and wasn't fond of having to deal with the snobbish attendees who fussed more over their looks than the cause at hand. But, it was a necessary step to raise enough money to help sustain Beacon Academy, and in addition to that, she donated generously herself. In the middle of the night, she had stepped up to the bar and was laughing with both bartenders when someone tapped her shoulder.

"Is this seat taken?" a woman asked her with her hand on the barstool beside Zuri.

"That depends on who's asking," Zuri said as she allowed her gaze to take her in.

Tracy had been in the industry for a while by the time they met, so Zuri recognized her. The times she had seen her on-screen didn't do her justice. She could still remember the deep red dress with a leg split and her radiant smile.

"Tracy Scott," she said, putting her hand out.

Zuri took it into hers and gave her a firm shake. "Zuri Baker, nice to meet you, Ms. Scott. Please have a seat," she said, pulling out the stool for her.

A beautiful face wasn't enough to capture Zuri's attention because beautiful people surrounded her. Integrity, kindness, and intelligence were the characteristics she preferred in the women she dated. Years of experience in the shallow world of entertainment had dampened her enthusiasm for actresses, so while she appreciated Tracy's beauty, she had already dismissed her. But as they talked, she saw that there was more to her than she assumed. They read the same books, had similar extracurricular activities, and Tracy had the most sensual laugh she had ever heard.

"So what's the deal? There's no way you came here alone," Zuri said.

"I came with Fiona," Tracy said, pointing across the room.

Zuri looked over and recognized Fiona Cooper, a well-known producer. "Well, if I remember correctly, Fiona doesn't take kindly to any sort of competition."

"Is that what you are? I thought we were just talking," Tracy said, leaning towards Zuri.

"We are," Zuri said with a smile. "I'm trying to figure out if that's all we'll be doing."

Tracy smiled and licked her lips. "Are you hitting on me, Ms. Baker?"

Zuri shrugged. "Only if you like it."

"Well, Fiona and I aren't together. We're friends, and she needed someone on her arm tonight."

The band began playing a song that Zuri loved. She stepped down from her seat and smoothed the black cocktail dress she was wearing. Tracy grinned as she held out her hand.

"Dance with me," she said.

Tracy took her hand, and they danced into the wee hours of the morning. It was the beginning of something special, and despite how she was feeling, Tracy still made her heart skip a beat. Was she willing to give that up for the unknown?

"Say something, Z," Tracy said, her voice cracking.

Zuri snapped back into the present, and her heart clenched at the emotion in Tracy's voice. She looked at the woman she had loved for the past five years and said the only thing she could say. "I love you too, baby, and I'm yours, just like I've always been."

* * *

"Hello everyone," Christopher said as he threw open his front door.

They arrived at Chris's home at 7 pm, right on time. Zuri squeezed her cousin close and introduced him to Genesis and Rain. He and Tracy were already familiar with each other and exchanged kisses as she handed him a couple of bottles of wine.

"I picked some delicious ones from the cellar," Tracy said with a wink.

"See, I knew I liked you for a reason, girl." Christopher gave her a high five. He led them into the living room. "Come in, make yourselves at home. Keith is making some delectable food for us, but he'll be out to say hello."

Zuri admired the renovation work her cousin had done on the house. Passed down to him from his grandmother, they also owned the surrounding land. He had done a build-out, added extra rooms, and extended some existing ones.

"The place looks great, Chris. I'm impressed with how large this space is now. Remember when we were little, and everyone would come over how cramped we would be?" Zuri said, taking a seat beside Tracy.

Chris laughed out loud. "Do I? Grandma Pat would grumble the whole time even though she was the one always trying to have an extended family dinner."

"Is your family large?" Genesis asked, posing the question to them both.

"I'd say so, yeah," Zuri answered, looking to Chris for confirmation.

Christopher nodded. "Great aunt Hazel, Zuri's grandmother, was busy with her career, so she just had two children. But my grandmother, her sister, was a homemaker, and she did what they expected back in the day and had several kids. Then their siblings also had many children."

"Let's just say we have more cousins than we can count on two hands," Zuri said with a chuckle.

"It must be nice having a large family that is close," Rain said, a wistful expression on her face.

Zuri smiled at Chris. "It has its pros and cons for sure, but it is nice."

Chris excused himself and headed into the kitchen, leaving the four women to sit in awkward silence. Between the dislike Rain and Tracy had for each other and the awkwardness Zuri was experiencing with Genesis, they had remained in their separate corners of the house. Their current forced proximity was nothing less than torture. Luckily, Keith came in to greet them. His bright smile stood out against his chocolate skin.

"Hey ladies," he said, carrying a tray with wine glasses.

"Keith, I've missed you," Zuri said, jumping up to hug him. "The food smells so good."

After introducing himself to the other women and hugging Tracy, he handed them each a glass. "Thank you; I've been prepping all morning. It seems I don't deserve a day where I'm not working," Keith said, directing his comment to Chris as he entered the room.

"I popped open the wine," Chris said, shaking one bottle. He looked over at Keith as he began pouring into the glasses. "And you love every minute."

Keith agreed with a smile and raised his glass for a toast. "Here's to good food and good company."

* * *

After some small talk as they waited for the food, they all sat down at the table in the dining room an hour later. The menu included stew chicken, rice and peas, fried plantain, grilled fish, a side salad, and macaroni pie. Zuri couldn't resist taking a little of everything.

"So Keith, Zuri told me you're a police officer," Tracy said.

"I am, and I love it. It's a bit of a family tradition. My father and grandfather were officers as well," Keith said.

"You don't find it a conflict of interest?" Genesis asked.

"Because of Chris and I? Yeah, it is, and we look forward to it changing, but it's hard. We live on an island, and both have long family histories here. Activism has been going on, and our prime minister is more LGBTQ friendly, but change is slow. I hate the thought of having to choose between someone I love and the work that I love to do." Keith looked over at Chris. "But I would give it up for him if I had to."

"Awww, you guys are relationship goals," Rain said.

"Well, you could open up a restaurant because this food is delicious," Tracy said, patting her stomach. "I never eat this much."

Keith did a slight bow in his seat. "Well, I am honored that Ms. Tracy Scott is breaking her actress diet for me."

"It's going to be the last time for a while, so I have to savor it. I'm working on a film; then I'll be heading to London to start a new television series."

Zuri saw Rain roll her eyes, and she signaled for her to stop. She appreciated how protective she was of her, but didn't want to hear Tracy's complaints about Rain's behavior again.

Chris lifted his glass and took a drink. "I don't know how you two do it. I can't imagine being away from Keith for such long stretches of time."

"We make it work, don't we, baby," Tracy said, taking Zuri's hand.

"That we do," Zuri said, smiling at her.

Although she could feel Genesis's gaze on them, she refused to look over at her. She knew if she did, the guilt would make her shrivel up inside. No matter what she was thinking, she owed it to Tracy to give their relationship a chance, and it was pretty much what Genesis told her to do. Zuri just wished it didn't feel like she was betraying her.

* * *

After dinner, everyone gathered on the deck behind the house for dessert. Christopher and Keith were wonderful hosts, so the tension that had been percolating for the past couple of days almost felt nonexistent.

Other than a few glances here and there, Genesis kept her distance from Zuri, and while she understood, that didn't make it hurt less. They had gotten close so quickly that it felt weird to act as if they were strangers. Watching her off to the side, laughing up a storm with Rain made her chest ache.

Unable to take it anymore, she let Tracy know she had to use the bathroom and escaped. After she finished, she made a detour to the front porch. She placed her hands on the railing and closed her eyes. *Am I making the right decision?*

The sound of the screen door swinging made her open her eyes, quickly wiping away the wetness around them. Christopher appeared with a drink in hand. He gave it to Zuri and stood beside her, silent. They both stared into the quiet night sky for several minutes before speaking.

"Z, is everything okay?" Chris asked, laying his arm around her shoulders.

Zuri leaned into him. "How many people do you think there are out there for us?"

"You mean like soul mates? Well, I think it varies for each

112

person. For some, there might be one; with others, it could be several. When it comes to love, there are no rules." Chris squeezed her to his body. "So Tracy, huh?"

"Had this been any time before, even a month ago, I would have been so excited for her to be here," Zuri said, stepping out from under his arm. She leaned against the railing and turned to face him. "Now, it's like she's intruding, and I'm stuck, you know? I can't drop a five-year relationship over a woman I just met."

Chris raised an eyebrow. "Didn't you say you were thinking of ending things, anyway?"

Zuri folded her arms. "I thought I would have time to process all of this." She got quiet and put her head down. "Tracy told me she's in love with me."

"Aww, honey, that's wonderful. Isn't that what you wanted all along?"

"It was, but now..." Zuri shook her head and pushed off from the railing. "Genesis makes me feel things I never have before."

Chris sat on the bench behind him. "Okay, so maybe it's time to let Tracy go if that's how you feel."

"But Tracy and I never had a real relationship. She's offering me the love I've been trying to get this whole time."

"So then stay with Tracy," Chris said with a sigh. "Sounds like you're trying to have your cake and eat it too, cuz. You have to make a choice."

Zuri took a sip from her glass and sat beside Chris, laying her head on his shoulder. "Tell me what to do, Christopher."

He chuckled and patted her hand. "Whatever you decide, don't second guess yourself. Sometimes the universe gives us what we need at the point in our lives when we need it. That might mean Tracy now and Genesis later, or it could mean the opposite. Maybe you met Genesis because you needed to know what's possible."

Zuri nodded and snuggled closer to him. Whatever decision she made, someone was going to get hurt. She just prayed she didn't live to regret it.

Chapter Fifteen

"Have you spoken to Shay?"

Genesis threw herself back on the bed as she continued her conversation with her sister. She called her about picking her up from the airport, and somehow the conversation landed on Shannon. While she was aware of how devastating their divorce was for Kenzie, it annoyed her that somehow she blamed it on her, even though Shannon was the one who left.

There were many times over the years that she could tell her sister preferred her wife, and she had come to terms with that. Since Genesis had to perform most of the discipline, of course, Kenzie would side with the person who was fun and less harsh on her. But now that they weren't together, her refusal to accept that they were over was more than bothersome.

"No, I haven't, and I don't plan to. We've been divorced for over a year; I'm not required to speak with her if I don't want to," Genesis said, trying to keep her voice calm.

"Okay, but she said she's been emailing you and tried to text you. I get that what she did wasn't cool, but if she wants to make amends, I don't see why that's a problem."

Genesis pulled the phone from her ear and stared at it for a moment before putting it back. "I'm sorry, but last time I checked, you're my sister. So all of this pushing you're doing for Shannon is ridiculous. We're divorced.What don't you understand about that?"

Kenzie sucked her teeth, and it took everything in Genesis not to hang up on her. She had no idea if her ex was filling her sister's head with nonsense about them getting back together, but she was over it. It had taken her a while to come to terms with the end of their relationship, and she was more than ready to move on. The last thing she needed was her sister invalidating her feelings because she liked Shannon better.

"Whatever. Can you talk to her, please?" Kenzie said in a less aggressive tone.

"When I get back, I'll see. Right now, I'm trying to enjoy my last few days here in Barbados."

"Have you been hanging out with Rain?"

Kenzie was a massive fan of the Star Crossed series when it came out and obsessed with Rain and her co-star, Drake Michaels. It devastated her when their supposed "relationship" ended after the series concluded.

"I have, and I even got her to write you a postcard with her signature and everything. Should come in the mail," Genesis said.

"That is so cool. Wait until I tell my girls. They were all obsessed like I was back in the day."

"Well, if you stop getting on my nerves, maybe I could set up a lunch with the three of us."

Rain had already given Genesis her cell and mentioned them hanging out once they were back in California. It touched her that the young woman had grown to like her so much, and she felt the same.

"Are you kidding? Okay, you are the best sister ever," Kenzie said with a squeal.

Happy for the distraction, Genesis got Kenzie to fill her in on a new job she had just started at a tech company. After deciding on the best time for them to meet at the airport, they ended the call on a much more pleasant note than when they started.

While she had to admit she was curious about what Shannon had to say for herself, it no longer mattered. She had no desire to let her back in after having such a hard time getting over her. Even though things didn't go in the direction she had hoped with Zuri, it was nice to realize that she was ready to move on. Her heart was open, and she looked forward to whoever grabbed it next.

As if on cue, she heard a knock at the door. She jumped off the bed and went to answer. To her surprise, Zuri stood on the other side, looking as beautiful as ever. The sunset lit her up from behind and made her glow. The woman was breathtaking.

Genesis patted her head. She had forgotten that she still had on her scarf from the night before, but it was too late to remove it without looking like she was trying too hard.

"Hey, how are you?" Zuri asked.

Genesis brushed a stray hair out of her face. "I'm fine; I just got off the phone with my sister. She's picking me up from the airport tomorrow."

"Ah, yes, tomorrow. Are you ready to get back home?"

"I could stay here forever, but I'm as ready as I can be. What about you?"

Zuri shrugged and leaned against the door frame. "I'm going to miss the peace I had the first few days I was here. Things are hectic when I'm home."

Genesis didn't miss the reference to their time together as being when she was at peace. She sighed; how was she supposed to respond to that? Zuri made it clear at dinner the night before that she took her advice regarding Tracy. There was no point in reminiscing about a time that would be nothing more than a blip on her radar soon enough.

"Why are you here, Zuri?" Genesis asked.

Zuri cleared her throat and stood up straight. "Chris invited us out to a private party a friend of his is throwing. It might be a fun way to end your time here."

Genesis contemplated the invitation, then said, "Sure, I'm down."

"Great, meet us out front around 10. See you later."

Genesis watched Zuri leave, then shut the door. *Why did I say yes?* She couldn't stand watching Zuri and Tracy together as it was, but now they would all be hanging out at a party, which meant more PDA and more distress for her. Rain would be a good buffer, but that would only distract her but so much.

* * *

The music spilling out from the surrounding speakers had Genesis moving in her seat. They had been at the party for a couple of hours, and the atmosphere had her in a good mood. On the way there, Zuri informed them that the event was a special one for the LGBT community on the island. Since there were no bars to visit openly, people often held private events only known through word of mouth. Understanding how vital even this small thing was for the people who lived there, Genesis appreciated being able to celebrate with them.

As she continued to move, Genesis saw a woman watching her from the other side of the bar. She was leaning against the bar top and sipping on what looked like brown liquor. After a few more glances between them, the mystery woman raised her glass in Genesis' direction and finished it. Genesis looked away.

Since her divorce, she had avoided interacting with other women because of her inexperience, but she longed to be bolder.

When she looked back to where the woman was sitting, she wasn't there. Disappointed, Genesis turned to order another drink when someone tapped her on the shoulder. She spun back around and smiled when she saw it was her mystery woman.

"I saw you finished your drink, so I bought this," she said, setting a glass down beside her. "I guessed you were a rum and coke type of woman."

"You guessed right," Genesis said with a smile. She offered her hand and said, "My name's Genesis."

"Ooh, biblical, I like it. My name's Taylor," she said, shaking Genesis's hand but not letting go. "Can I just say you are the most beautiful woman I've seen here tonight?"

A blush crept over her cheeks. "That's sweet, thank you. You're not so bad yourself," she said.

Taylor was her type; tall and slim, her dark brown hair cut into a shag with bangs. She wore a sleeveless black tee that showcased her muscular arms, with tattoos adorning both. Genesis noticed a slight pinkness to her skin that meant she and the sun were not friends.

"No tan for you, I see," Genesis said, brushing over Taylor's arm as she sipped her drink.

Taylor raised her fist. "Damn my Irish heritage," she said with a grin. "I'm milky white or burned; there's no in-between. I slather on sunblock like nobody's business. We aren't all blessed with sun-kissed skin like yours."

"Ah, but Black people can burn too."

"Of course, but something tells me you don't. You're glowing," Taylor said, reciprocating the arm brush.

Her touch was nice, really nice. *Geez, am I that deprived?* She drank some more and shook off the feeling.

"So, how did you hear about this party? I'm told they keep things pretty low key on the island," Taylor said, moving in closer.

"Oh, my friend's cousin lives here, and he told us about it. How about you?"

"The guy who's giving the party met my friends and me at the resort where he works. He picked up on our lady-loving vibes and figured we'd enjoy ourselves."

Genesis laughed out loud. "I'd say his gaydar was on point."

Taylor shrugged and said, "The Birkenstocks and basketball shorts gave us away."

"Oh, you're funny," Genesis said.

Taylor smiled at her as she sipped from her glass. Genesis looked into her deep blue eyes and noticed just how large they were. The urge to close the distance between them and kiss her was intense. It had been way too long since someone touched her with desire, and she wanted it more than she cared to admit.

"So, how is it possible that someone hasn't snatched you up yet?" Taylor asked.

"Well, I'm divorced, so I'm taking baby steps getting back into the dating scene."

"How's it going?"

Genesis tilted her head. "Well, let's see, I have yet to go on an actual date, so I'd say not that good."

Taylor scrunched up her face in disbelief. "No one has asked out a pretty lady like you? I find that hard to believe."

"Oh, they ask, but I just never say yes." Taylor raised an eyebrow, causing Genesis to laugh. "That sounds like an oxymoron. I want to date, but then never do it. Guess I need to ease into it."

Taylor smiled and moved in closer, speaking into her ear. "Maybe I could help with that transition."

Genesis shuddered as her lips grazed her ear. "Yeah, maybe you could."

* * *

"Be careful; this area is steep," Taylor said, putting out her hand to help Genesis down.

The house had a generous backyard, and the party had spilled outside. Smokers were milling about, and a few groups were having heated drunken discussions. Genesis wasn't sure about their location on the island, but the drive out had been quite a distance. The homeowner had made sure that the party and its participants were safe from prying eyes.

Taylor led her to a dark corner that was just secluded enough to do the same for them. They had been chatting and drinking for over an hour, and when she suggested they head outside, Genesis didn't hesitate to say yes. She was tipsy, verging on drunk, but for once, she didn't care. It was nice not to get so caught up in the what-ifs.

"Listen to that," Taylor said, pointing to the ocean as they sat. "It sounds so soothing."

"I like it too," Genesis said, swaying to the oceanic symphony.

Taylor closed the distance between them and placed her lips against Genesis. The other woman was warm, and the cologne she wore, a mix of citrus and wood, smelled pleasant. She gasped as Taylor's hands gripped her. Her strength and the intensity of the kiss made her body feel electrified.

The rhythm of the reggae music spilled out into the night and added to their interlude. The drinks, the music, and Taylor's persistent tongue were invading her senses and sending her into overdrive. Yet, one person sat in the corner of her mind. *Zuri.* What she wouldn't give to be with her instead. Then, as if she manifested her, she heard Zuri's voice yelling over the music.

"Get your hands off of her before I remove them myself," Zuri said, appearing beside Genesis and Taylor.

"Zuri?" Genesis gasped. She jumped back from Taylor as if her parents had caught them.

"Who the hell are you?" Taylor said.

"Who I am doesn't matter. All you need to know is she's off-limits," Zuri said, getting in her face.

Taylor's lip curled up. "Let me guess, you've been running behind her and couldn't seal the deal," she said, licking her lips. "Well, I can tell you, she tastes as sweet as she looks."

Genesis saw Zuri's eyes fill with anger as she balled up her fist. They looked like they were about to come to blows, so she lurched forward to separate them.

"Z, it's okay," Genesis said. "Nothing happened that I didn't want."

Zuri glared at Taylor, then turned to Genesis, her face softening. "You've been drinking most of the night. You're not in your right mind."

"Listen, are you with her or something? We were having a good time," Taylor asked Genesis.

Genesis turned to her and steadied herself by holding onto her arm. "She's a friend, and she's right. As much as I was enjoying myself, I've had a bit too much to drink."

Taylor nodded and gave Zuri a dirty look. She took Genesis's hand and said, "I'm staying at the South Gap Hotel for the next few days. If you change your mind and want to chill, call me there. Room 214"

Taylor kissed her hand, gave Zuri the middle finger, and walked away. Genesis turned to Zuri, whose face was filled with concern.

"Where's Tracy and Rain?"

"Rain couldn't find you, so I had Chris take them home while I looked for you." Zuri grabbed onto Genesis. "Are you sure you're okay? You don't look so good?"

She wasn't sure if adrenaline had been keeping her steady earlier, but she suddenly felt nauseous. As if she saw it coming, Zuri spun her around so she could throw up on the side of the deck.

"Oh no," Genesis said as she thought about the homeowner finding her mess.

"Don't worry about it, baby. One sec," Zuri said. She returned with a bottle of water and washed away the vomit.

As Zuri took a napkin and poured water on it to wash around her mouth and face, Genesis registered that she had called her baby. Hearing the word come out of Zuri's mouth made her warm inside. She took the bottle to rinse out her mouth and then handed it back.

"Finish drinking it. You need to balance out some of that liquor in your system. Come on; I'll drive us home."

Although she knew she should be indignant about being treated like she was incompetent, she followed Zuri without saying a word.

Chapter Sixteen

Zuri tapped her hand against the steering wheel as she drove back to her estate. Genesis sat with her head against the passenger seat and appeared to be asleep. She wanted to apologize to her for overreacting. While her approach was perhaps too aggressive, she refused to stand there and do nothing while that other woman mauled her. The way her hands gripped Genesis so possessively had triggered her.

When she went looking for her earlier and only found Rain, the young woman had told her Genesis disappeared. She mentioned her chatting up a woman at the bar, and warning bells went off in her head. Genesis was inexperienced with women, and the idea that someone might take advantage of that and hurt her was a concern. Tracy wasn't happy when Zuri asked Chris to take her and Rain back to the house, but she preferred to deal with it after the fact.

Zuri glanced over at Genesis and admired her. She was so pretty without even trying.

As if sensing that Zuri was watching her, Genesis sat up and wiped some drool from her mouth. Zuri chuckled; it was the cutest thing she had seen all day.

"Where are we?" Genesis asked as she stretched.

"We are almost back at the house; it should be another 10 minutes. How are you feeling?" Zuri asked.

"Like shit. I've had more to drink in the last couple weeks than I have in years. But thank you for inviting me out; the party was fun."

Zuri raised an eyebrow. "Well, that much was obvious."

Genesis sucked her teeth and adjusted her seat belt. "Not sure what you expected to happen. I am single, Zuri, and it's not like I was doing anything wrong. Do you have any mints?"

"I never said you were. Check the glove compartment."

Genesis rummaged and found a box. She hastily popped a couple into her mouth.

"Then why did you storm over like I was your child? You acted as if we were having sex."

Zuri frowned at the mention of sex. "You don't know how it is out here, Genesis. You were with Shannon from a young age."

Genesis scoffed and folded her arms. "Okay, then tell me how it is?"

Zuri glanced over at her and noted her defensive stance. "I'm not trying to start an argument."

"Neither am I, but since you seem to know more than I do, please let me know what it's like."

After a moment of hesitation, Zuri said, "Well, did you let her buy you a drink in front of you, or did she bring one over?"

"She brought the first one over," Genesis said. "But the rest she bought in front of me."

"Never take a drink from someone if you didn't see it being made. Too much of a chance for them to slip something in it. Also, don't turn your back on your drink; always keep it in hand."

Genesis shook her head. "That didn't even occur to me. Do women do that sort of thing?"

"Women are people. While they may be less likely to spike a drink than a man, that doesn't mean it's impossible. A friend of mine had it happen a few years ago."

"Was she alright?"

"Yeah, she recognized what was happening and found one of us before the woman took her off somewhere. You just have to assume people are horrible."

"Well, that's excellent advice. Thank you," Genesis said.

Zuri pulled up to the estate and used the remote on her keys to open the gate. "Also, be wary of someone that waits until you're intoxicated to fool around. They know your inhibitions are down. Limit your drinks to an amount you can handle without getting drunk. That way, you know what's happening around you. You need to be in control at all times."

Genesis was quiet for a little while, then said, "I'm so stupid. I didn't even think about any of what you just said."

"You're not stupid, just naïve; there's a big difference." Zuri drove the car into the open garage and pulled to a stop. "Now, you know. You can have fun, just be safe," she said, resting her hands in her lap after she turned off the car.

"That's not why I feel stupid. It's the reason I thought you barged in on us."

"What, you figured I was just a jerk?" Zuri asked with a chuckle.

"Not quite," Genesis said, looking away. She stared at the dash, then said, "I thought you were jealous."

Zuri froze at her admission. Of course, she had been jealous. When she pictured the other woman's hands on Genesis, she felt herself getting worked up again. But the fact remained that she had no right to feel that way about someone who was not hers.

Zuri rubbed the back of her neck. "Well, I can't say that some of my aggression didn't come from a place of jealousy."

"Stop doing that," Genesis said, sounding annoyed.

"Doing what?" Zuri asked.

"Talking in circles. You've been doing some version of that ever since Tracy got here. No one else is in this car, but us, be honest with me."

Genesis unbuckled her seat belt and moved closer to Zuri. Her light brown eyes stared deep into hers, and she felt herself getting pulled in. The fruity smell of her body wash blended in with the musk of her sweat and created an intoxicating scent.

She was right; there was no one else around. Would it be that bad to say what they both knew?

"Genesis, nothing can come of this, at least not right now," Zuri said, trying not to stare at her plump lips.

"Does it matter? I just want to hear you say it," Genesis said.

Her voice low, Zuri said, "Say what?"

Genesis leaned into her ear. "That you want me."

Zuri clenched her fist and tried her best not to do what was running through her mind, but Genesis wouldn't have it. She stroked her hand along Zuri's arm, sending chills all over her body as she unclenched her hand.

Holding hands had never been something she found sexy, but at that moment, they might as well have been naked in bed together. The feel of their flesh pressed against each other made her breath catch in her throat. Their fingers linked, and she closed her eyes. Suddenly she was taken back to their hike in the forest as they walked hand in hand.

"I want you," she murmured into the silence of the car.

It felt so good to say what had been on her mind for the last few days. In response, Genesis closed the distance between them. Their breathing was shallow, as if they didn't want to disturb the spell they were under. Zuri kept her eyes closed, finding honesty easier in the darkness behind her lids.

When Genesis' lips pressed against her own, Zuri's body

relaxed. The tension between them had become unbearable, and this was the release they needed.

Zuri's free hand slipped down the curves of her side to rest on her hip as she drew her in. She tasted a hint of alcohol, but the softness of her lips stood out the most. When Genesis slid her tongue inside to meet her own, it was the sweetest invasion imaginable.

Heat rose from the pit of Zuri's stomach and unfurled in her chest. The hunger behind Genesis's kiss was unexpected, but very welcome. She was so reserved that Zuri figured the liquor had emboldened her, but she wasn't complaining. It was everything she wanted at that moment.

Rendered weak by the kiss, Zuri didn't know how much time had passed when Genesis pulled away. She opened her eyes as she untangled their hands and sat back.

Genesis's voice quivered as she uttered the words, "If you couldn't tell, I want you too." With a lurch of emotion, Genesis ripped open the car door and charged out into the night.

* * *

When she got to her bedroom, Zuri threw her keys down on her dresser and fell back on the bed. She was out of it, physically and mentally. Barbados was her home away from home, her peace. Now she couldn't wait to get back to LA and bury herself in work. Genesis would hopefully want to be friends because she didn't want to lose contact, but it was a bitter pill to swallow when they both wanted more.

Their kiss lingered, and she brushed her fingers across her lips. She had kissed plenty of women, but something about Genesis's kiss set her ablaze. Then she left her sitting there, turned on and confused. How was it possible to be in love with Tracy but desire someone else so much?

"You're home," Tracy said, strolling out of the bathroom. Steam followed her as she walked over to the dresser and pulled out her pajamas. "I take it you found Genesis?"

Zuri rubbed her eyes and nodded yes. Her cheeks flushed with guilt at the mention of Genesis, and she prayed it wasn't visible. "She was hanging out with the woman Rain saw her with."

"I see," Tracy said.

After she finished putting on her pajamas, Tracy walked over to the bed. She climbed on top and sat in a lotus position. Zuri followed her movements and sensed she wanted to talk, so she climbed further onto the bed and faced her.

"You look like you have something on your mind," Zuri said, stifling a yawn.

"I do." Tracy looked down and picked at a loose thread on the comforter beneath them. "It amazes me how you can read me so well."

Zuri shrugged. "We've known each other long enough."

"That's just it. We have known each other for quite some time now, but I don't completely know you. You've always been so hard to read."

"Or you've never taken the time to see me," Zuri said. The statement came out sounding harsher than she meant it to. "I'm sorry, that sounded mean."

Tracy reached out to squeeze her hand. "No, not mean at all, but truthful. I've kept you at bay for a long time because it was easier for me, but it wasn't for you. I'm sorry that it took me so long to open up."

Zuri sat up. "Well, we are trying to move forward, and that's most important."

Tracy stayed quiet, and Zuri didn't badger her to continue. She was curious about what was on her mind, but deep down, she knew. It was evident in the look she gave Zuri when she told her to go home with Rain and Chris while looking for Genesis. There was a mistrust that had never existed between them before, at least not from Tracy's end.

"Something is going on between you and Genesis," Tracy said.

There was nothing accusatory in her tone. She simply stated it as a fact. Zuri remained quiet, choosing not to deny or confirm what she said. They weren't exclusive when she met Genesis, so she had no reason to feel guilty.

"You have been nothing but respectful since I arrived, and I appreciate that, but it's obvious something happened before I got here, which is fair. I set the tone for our relationship. I just want to say that I will not give you up without a fight." Tracy paused. "I just hope I'm not the only one fighting for this."

Although Genesis started the kiss earlier, Zuri had been more than receptive. It had taken a herculean effort on her part not to pull her out of that car and bring her back to the guest house. They had some intense chemistry, but her heart told her she would regret not seeing things through with Tracy. Whether she was still in love, it was possible those feelings could return.

"Do you remember the first night we met?" Zuri asked, taking Tracy's hands.

"Of course. I liked you right away," Tracy said with a smile.

"I knew that I wanted you from the moment you spoke, and that hasn't changed. You're right, Genesis and I had a connection, but once you arrived, I put a stop to it. I'm all in, I promise."

Tracy embraced her and snuggled into her arms. It was a small lie, but necessary if she was going to move on. Nothing good would come from admitting they had kissed, or that she wanted more of it. God, how she wanted more.

Chapter Seventeen

The morning after the party, Genesis woke once again with a headache. That was one aspect of her trip she would not miss. She needed to take a break from alcohol. It wouldn't be that hard; she wasn't a huge drinker in her everyday life. Something about being in Barbados had her acting out of character.

The thought brought back the memory of what happened the night before, causing her to slap her hand against her forehead. Why had she kissed Zuri? The answer was obvious; she wanted to throw caution to the wind. All of her life, she had done the right thing, but good girls didn't always reap the benefits of their goodness. It hadn't stopped her parents from dying, her sister from resenting her, or her wife from leaving her. It felt good to just live in the moment.

What a moment it was. She remembered how Zuri's body tensed up, then relaxed as they touched. It was clear she had tried her best to fight what was happening, but she wanted it as much as Genesis did. Her skin felt so soft as she brushed against it, and when they held hands, it was like finding home.

Genesis was aware of Zuri's desire to be friends since she

had mentioned it on multiple occasions. But the more she thought about it, she wasn't sure it would be possible. And now that they had kissed more than once, she couldn't imagine being in the same room as her and not wanting to do it again and again.

"Knock, knock," Rain said as she entered her bedroom.

Genesis groaned and threw the blanket over her head. "Rain, what are you doing here?"

Rain placed something on the nightstand and jumped into the bed. She dove under the covers and tickled her.

"Oh my God, stop," Genesis said, as she moved between laughter and annoyance. "I have such a headache."

"Told you drinking is the devil." Rain stopped tickling her and laid back on the pillows. "As for what I am doing here, I came to check on you, and since you left the door open, I made you some coffee. You're welcome."

"Thank you, but I don't think I'm ready to get up yet."

"Why not? We only have a few more hours before we have to get to the airport. I thought you would want to go visit the beach one last time."

"Ugh, don't remind me about going home," Genesis yelled as she placed her pillow over her face.

"Please tell me you are at least packed? Zuri is a bitch on wheels when things don't go according to plan, and she expects us ready at-," Rain looked at her phone," - 9 am and it's already 7:30 am."

"I'm not beholden to Zuri. I have my flight, and it leaves later."

"Is that so? Well, she booked you a first-class ticket to Los Angeles with us, so..."

Genesis moved the pillow. "Did you say first class?"

"Yes, I did, and as long as this flight is, that extra space sure would be nice," Rain said, nudging her.

"Ugh, fine, I'll get up, and we can do a beach stroll. I am all packed; I did it yesterday afternoon."

Rain scrambled out of bed. "That's right, you're old, so of course you're prepared; what was I thinking?"

"Ugh, you know I hate you, right?" Genesis said, throwing a pillow at Rain.

"Love you too," Rain yelled from the hallway.

* * *

Large sunglasses and a sun hat were Genesis's armor as she strolled arm in arm with Rain on the beach. The sand felt so good underneath her feet. Although she lived in California and was not a stranger to the beach, her time in Barbados was something else. Now she believed with certainty that it was time to start the next phase in her life. If her interactions with Zuri and even Taylor had taught her anything, it was that she needed to take charge of her love life.

"You're quiet," Rain said.

"Sorry, lost in my thoughts. I have some changes I want to make in my life once I get back home. I'm tired of being on the sidelines of my own life."

"You need to be out there running things."

"Speaking of running things, how are you planning on handling that Jackson situation?"

Rain's body stiffened at the mention of his name. For such a confident woman, it was interesting how he made her turn insecure.

"I guess I'm going to keep it professional, like Zuri said. Do the job I'm damn good at. I can't let his petty ass throw me off my game."

Genesis nodded and leaned into her. "You like him a lot, don't you?"

Rain sighed and threw her head back. "I do, and I hate it. Most guys are for entertainment, but with him, it was real. We used to sit for hours and talk. He didn't even try to sleep with me. I was the one who initiated. I wish I knew what I did wrong."

"You may have done nothing wrong. One minute someone is into you, and the next they aren't; that's how it is sometimes. I'm still not sure what happened in my marriage, and I was with my ex for years," Genesis said, the memory of Shannon leaving their home flickering through her mind.

The day she left had devastated her. All Genesis remembered was an argument, and she woke to find Shannon shoving clothes into her suitcases. They had been having petty fights off and on for months before that, but she thought it was some sort of relationship fatigue. They had been together so long at that point. When she suggested therapy, Shannon dismissed it right away and said it was a rough patch they would get through. It was sobering to find that what had been a "patch" seemed to have turned into the Grand Canyon in no time at all.

"What are you doing?" Genesis had asked.

Shannon was already stacking her suitcases in the living room by that point and was filling one more. Her wardrobe was huge, so it was no minor feat that she had gotten so much done while Genesis slept, which meant she had started early.

"Were you planning on leaving without saying anything?" Genesis followed behind her, the silence angering her. "Answer me, damn it."

Shannon turned to her and threw up her hands. "What do you want me to say, Genesis? This right here," she said, pointing between them, "has been over for a while now. We're room-mates at this point."

"Over? I love you, Shay. That has never changed. If you want this to work, we have to do it together," Genesis said, stopping her hand as she placed more clothes away. "Please, look at me."

Shannon lifted her head but wouldn't look her in the eyes.

"Gen, I love you, but I'm not happy, and I don't have time to waste on something that's already over," Shannon said, pulling away.

"You don't have time? What are you even talking about?" Genesis asked, standing outside of the closet.

It was a massive walk-in that Shannon insisted on having built out. Genesis was never one for spending unnecessary money, but Shannon had expensive tastes and could afford it, so she let her do as she liked. Now she looked around their home, and all she saw were items that she never wanted. The thing she wanted most, love, was about to walk out of the door.

"Never mind, this is what's best for both of us," Shannon said. She finally stopped and looked into her eyes. "I'm sorry that... I'm just sorry."

"Shay," Genesis yelled

Her pride wouldn't let her physically stop her, and what would have been the point? Shannon made it clear that there was no possibility of reconciliation, and the way she dismissed her didn't sit well with Genesis. They had known each other too long for her to treat her in such a cruel way. That was why, when Kenzie kept coming at her about forgiveness; she wasn't having it. The time to talk had been years before she left. Now any bit of reconciliation was going to be on Genesis's terms.

"You're right; I have better things to do than worry about Jackson. But I may text you for moral support while I'm on set because that man looks so good," Rain said, biting her lip.

"You're a trip, but do you boo. If you want him, have fun, but don't get caught up. It's obvious he can't handle that."

"Got ya," Rain said, giving her a side hug. "Are you ready to head back?"

Genesis nodded as she gazed at the endless blue ocean for the last time.

* * *

At the airport, Genesis sat flipping through a magazine. Rain was busy taking selfies to post to her social media accounts, and out of the corner of her eye, she saw Zuri and Tracy chatting. She thought maybe Zuri would behave funny after the kiss, but she acted as if nothing happened. While she was happy not to have to go through an awkward exchange, she was a bit hurt that she seemed so indifferent. *I know she felt something.* The way she held onto Genesis' hips, how she clenched her hand as their tongues moved against each other.

"Genesis, they're calling for our flight," Rain said, tapping her arm.

Startled out of her memory, Genesis shook her head to clear her mind. "Sorry, I was somewhere else for a minute." She picked up her suitcase and pulled it along as they began walking.

"Everything okay?" Rain asked.

Genesis thought about sharing what happened. Rain would be more than ecstatic to hear that things had progressed between them, but it didn't feel right. The moment was so intimate that she wanted to keep it to herself.

"I'm good. By the way, don't forget about that lunch with my sister. She's been messaging me about it ever since I mentioned it," Genesis said with an eye roll.

"I won't, in fact, how about you guys come and visit me on set? I can give a brief tour, and you two can watch me in action."

"Wow, she would love that. I'm going to win all the cool points."

Rain laughed as she handed her boarding pass to the airport

staff . Genesis waited to be next, but a tug on her shirt caused her to turn around. She found Zuri standing behind her, and suddenly she felt breathless.

"Can I talk to you for a minute?" Zuri said.

Unable to speak, Genesis nodded in response. Zuri led her off to the side so the other passengers could board.

"I was hoping to catch you before we got on the plane, but..." Zuri didn't finish her sentence.

"Tracy would not be a fan of us chatting too much," Genesis finished for her.

"Yes," Zuri said. She shoved her hands into her jeans and looked at the ground. "I'm not sure what to say. I just didn't want us to head back and not talk about that kiss."

Genesis pressed her lips together to keep from smiling too big. Knowing she wasn't the only one caught up in the memory made her feel better.

"I should apologize for being so forward. That liquor got to me I guess," Genesis said, a blush spreading across her cheeks. "I hope it didn't make you uncomfortable."

Zuri looked up at her and stared into her eyes. "Not at all. It was good. Almost too good," she said, her voice falling off. "It's just, I have this thing with Tracy, and I promised her I would give it a chance."

Genesis's heart sank, even though what she was saying wasn't a surprise. That didn't stop her from hoping that maybe the kiss would make Zuri drop it all for her.

"I understand; she is Tracy Scott after all," Genesis said, looking away.

Zuri placed her hand underneath Genesis's chin so she would look at her. "You are a dynamic woman. Beautiful, sensual, kind, and all the other good adjectives I can't think of right now." Genesis laughed. "Trust me when I say that you can more than give Tracy a run for her money. She simply has the advantage of time with me."

Genesis nodded and took a step back. "I understand about investing so much in a relationship that you'll do anything to make it work. Trust me, I don't fault you for it, but that doesn't mean I'm not disappointed."

"Friends?" Zuri said, putting out her hand.

"Yeah, friends," Genesis said, gripping it tight.

Once they entered the plane, they walked over to their respective seats next to Rain and Tracy, but she caught Zuri watching her every so often. *Friends? Who were they kidding?*

Chapter Eighteen

S**ix Months Later**

"Zuri, you have got to give me the name of your interior designer. This place is impeccable."

Zuri looked up at the woman speaking, Sylvie Mack, and nodded. Sylvie was a director known for her provocative black and white indie films. She was one of those people who seemed to know everyone, and even though she wasn't rolling in money from her work, it helped that her husband was a successful investment banker. According to her, he financed most of her work and allowed her to maintain her integrity as an artist.

"I will give you his contact info, Sylvie. Galileo is brilliant, and he's a good friend," Zuri said.

"Ooh, Galileo, I'm intrigued already. If he can do half of what he did here for our place, I would die a happy woman. Our last designer made our home about as interesting as an Ikea showroom but with pricier furniture," Sylvie said, making a face.

"Now Sylvie, it's not possible to duplicate Z's style," Tracy said, making her appearance. She kissed Zuri and grabbed an already filled glass of champagne. "Most of what you see in here is one of a kind."

"Is that so? Well, money's not an object if our space can look this nice. Don't forget to send me the info."

"Already sent," Zuri said as she swiped and forwarded Galileo's number to Sylvie.

"Wonderful. Let me go find Richard and tell him we're getting an upgrade." Sylvie did a little dance.

"God, that woman is a twit," Tracy said, dropping her smile as soon as Sylvie walked away. "Does she ever have an original idea? Now her home is going to be a lame version of your house, just like her films are bad Kurosawa impersonations."

Zuri snickered at Tracy's comment. "She's harmless and entertaining, and that is why she always gets invited to parties. Besides, it will thrill Galileo to get her business."

The party was Tracy's idea. Now that she was staying with Zuri, she kept pressuring her to throw one. She wasn't that into having parties in her personal space, but she wanted to be accommodating. So she invited a small guest list of industry people who she didn't find completely insufferable.

"Thank you," Tracy said, wrapping her arms around Zuri's neck. "I know that this isn't your scene."

"Anything for you, baby," Zuri said, lowering her head to kiss her. "By the way, I wanted to ask you..."

Tracy squealed, cutting Zuri off. "Jessica, oh my God."

Tracy dropped her arms and ran over to the woman who had just entered the party. Jessica was a fellow actress and one of her closest friends. Zuri liked her fine, but ever since Jessica didn't get called back for a role at Ellis Films, she'd held a grudge against Zuri. That was one big reason she limited the number of people she considered friends in her industry. Too many were looking to leverage relationships instead of cultivating a meaningful connection.

Not interested in the inevitably strained exchange with Jessica, Zuri wandered out onto the balcony. She breathed in the fresh air and sighed. The party would be enough to appease Tracy before she left. In another month, she would head out to London to film her new show. Although she would miss her, Zuri was also eager to have her space back.

When Tracy finished her film in Miami, two months after they returned from Barbados, she asked Zuri about staying with her for a while. She was in-between homes and didn't see a point in renting an apartment when Zuri had such a large house. Happy to have Tracy to herself, Zuri said yes.

At first, it was great to have someone to come home to every night, and Tracy played the part of the perfect girlfriend. She made dinner, always looked flawless, attended events, listened while Zuri complained about work issues, was ready, willing, and able to make love whenever and wherever she wanted.

At some point, though, the facade dropped. Zuri wasn't sure if it was that the newness of it all wore off, but she questioned the sincerity behind Tracy's newfound domesticity. It felt like an audition meant to convince her that Tracy could be a suitable wife. There was such a difference in their relationship than in the past that she figured her feelings were because of Tracy's 180-degree change, but she wasn't sure.

"Beautiful night, huh?" a raspy female voice said beside her.

Zuri moved over to see who was speaking and found Fiona Cooper. She stood there puffing on a cigar and blew the smoke in the opposite direction.

"Fiona, it's been a minute. How are you?"

"I've been well. Working hard, same as you. I have a few projects that I'm fond of coming out."

Fiona owned a respected film production company, and they had worked together several times. Shortly after she started "dating" Tracy, that relationship came to an abrupt ending. Zuri always wondered if Tracy had lied about what she had with Fiona, but she never pursued it.

"I look forward to seeing what you've done. Your work is always enjoyable," Zuri said.

Rather than respond in kind, Fiona chuckled, but there was a bitter undertone to it. She pushed away from the wall to her full height. Zuri had forgotten how tall she was, almost 6 feet. Her size and masculine attire gave her a certain edge that never fit her overtly feminine first name. It was a fun contrast, and Fiona embraced it, never going by any masculine nicknames. Her proud butch persona was something Zuri had always admired, especially in their industry.

"I've always wondered what I would say to you once I got the chance, and now I don't even remember why I was so angry. You saved me," Fiona said, taking another puff.

"Saved you from what?" Zuri asked.

Fiona smirked as she shook her head. "She's got you good, huh? I can't say I blame you; I was the same way for a long time."

"According to Tracy, you two were just friends."

Fiona laughed, and this time it was genuine. "Is that so? Did she also mention that her "friend" paid for all of her plastic surgery, rented her apartments because she had bad credit, and got her auditions for all of those blockbuster movies? I made her a star because I was addicted to her." Fiona walked closer to Zuri. "Then she landed herself a bigger fish and forgot I existed. It's what she does."

Zuri swallowed over the lump in her throat. "Even if I

believe what you're telling me, she and I haven't even been in a committed relationship until now."

"Oh, baby girl, can't you see? You're the long game, and she's setting herself up for life." Fiona blew out another puff of smoke as she walked over to the balcony railing. She turned in Zuri's direction, her gray eyes dark with anger. "She kept you on a leash and had you wide open so that you wouldn't get bored with her. Now you're in love, and she has all the power."

Zuri's body vibrated with anger, but she remained calm. "If you came to see whether we were happy, we are. So you can make your way out the door knowing that I have what you couldn't keep."

Fiona walked up to her and bent down to speak directly into her ear. "Oh, when she wraps those chocolate legs around you and whispers sweet nothings in your ear, I bet you feel like a king. I should know; it was the same for me."

"Get the fuck out," Zuri said between gritted teeth.

Fiona smiled and nodded as if she expected that response. "You'll see for yourself, or maybe you won't until it's too late." She walked towards the balcony door, then paused with her hand on the handle. "Remember Sundance? You waited for her, and she never showed. Told you she got delayed because of her film? She was with me in Aspen the entire weekend. Even after she played me, I couldn't get enough of her."

Fiona licked her lips and yanked the door open, strolling over to Dana, an actress she knew well. Zuri remained outside, frozen in place. Of course, she remembered Sundance. She had begged Tracy to go with her and was so excited when she said yes. It would have been their first public appearance as a couple. When she didn't show, it hurt her; but she accepted it and moved on. Now Fiona was telling her it had all been a lie.

Zuri fixed her face and walked back into the party. Everything that had just been laid on her was too much to process.

"Is that Fiona?" Tracy said, coming up beside her. "What is she doing here?"

Zuri turned towards her and was going to respond, but she couldn't. She looked into the face she had loved for years and wondered who she was seeing. Was any of it real?

"Babe, are you okay?" Tracy asked.

"I'm fine," Zuri said, giving her a tight smile. "I just need another drink."

Tracy kissed her cheek. "I'll get you one," she said, bouncing off to the bar.

Zuri surveyed the guests in her house and realized just how much she disliked almost all of them. She didn't even invite her best friend Alma because she didn't care for Tracy. Now she was surrounded by fake people, and it looked like Tracy was among them. *What a fucking life.*

* * *

At work the following Monday, Zuri sat reading a script that had been on her desk for weeks. Elijah was sure it would be the next horror franchise a la the Conjuring series, and since those films were often cheap to make but brought in a good profit, it was something worth considering. While she was enjoying the story, her mind kept wandering back to Tracy.

That weekend they spent it as they had for the past several; yoga, a visit to the local farmer's market, an afternoon of reading or movie watching, and making dinner together. They usually made love as well, but Zuri couldn't get in the headspace to even try. Everything felt false. It pissed her off that she had allowed Fiona to get in her head.

A knock on her door jolted her out of her thoughts. Elijah and Reggie shuffled into her office. Used to the two of them joking around, she was stopped cold by the expressions on their faces.

"What's wrong?" Zuri asked.

"You need to see this," Elijah said, grabbing a remote.

He turned on the television that hung on her wall and clicked until he found one of the 24-hour news channels.

"Stunning accusations have rocked the film industry this morning. Executive producer Francis Beauregard has had several lawsuits lobbied at him claiming sexual misconduct and sexual abuse," said the blonde anchorwoman. "Most of the women starred in films by Sunshine Productions, a division of Ellis Films."

"What the fuck is this?" Zuri said, turning to her cousins.

Reggie switched off the television, and at that same moment, her phone buzzed. Zuri shoved it into a drawer and turned back to them.

"We are just as baffled as you," Reggie said. "I got a call from legal maybe twenty minutes ago. Shauna didn't contact you?"

"I've been busy all morning; I'm sure I sent it to voicemail," Zuri said. Her office phone rang, and she picked it up when she saw it was her assistant. "Yes, Stacy."

"Boss, the phones won't stop ringing. Everyone is asking to speak with you all," Stacy said, sounding panicked, which was unusual for her.

"I hate to do this to you, but just take messages. If any of them are reporters, please tell them we will release a statement once we have more information."

Zuri hung up. She got up sat on the edge of her desk and looked between Reggie and Elijah. "I'm speechless right now. What are you two thinking?"

Reggie shrugged and dropped into a chair. "With how

things have been in the industry since the MeToo movement, they will crucify Francis."

"It's what he deserves," Elijah said. "The only problem is that they could hold us culpable for his actions, since he committed his crimes in his capacity as our producer."

Zuri was quiet as she paced. "I just don't understand; Francis is..Francis. He's like my second dad."

The three of them sat quietly for a while and then began planning their next moves. The goal was to protect the studio, and the law firm they had on retainer would assist with that. She would open an internal investigation to find out who may have been complicit in Francis's actions.

Zuri was shocked to find out that a man she loved and respected had turned out to be someone else. That was sadly becoming a theme in her life.

Chapter Nineteen

"Babe, would you be mad if I didn't join you this afternoon?"

Zuri sighed; they had plans to attend a mini-festival of Blaxploitation films at the Palace Theatre. She bought the tickets months ago, and Tracy knew how excited she was about it.

"Seriously, Tracy? You've known about this forever; what is so important that you need to cancel at the last minute?" Zuri said.

Tracy came up behind her and massaged her shoulders. "Jessica phoned me a little while ago, and Dexter broke up with her. Plus, she just lost out on that part I told you she wanted. She's depressed. Cory and the rest of the girls want to cheer her up, and it would look bad if I didn't show up."

After Fiona's revelation at the party last week, Zuri felt like she was at a crossroads. A decision needed to happen soon on whether what she had with Tracy was something worth salvaging or if it was time to move on. She hated to admit it, but she had fought for so long to have her, it wasn't easy letting go.

Despite everything on her mind, she didn't want them to

have petty arguments. If she wasn't going to be with her, she had to decide not punish her in the meantime.

"It's fine; I'll find someone else to go. Maybe Alma's free," Zuri said.

"Thanks, baby, I'll make it up to you, I promise," Tracy replied, kissing her forehead.

* * *

Later that day, Zuri stood near the theater, waiting for her friend. Alma couldn't make it, and neither could the other two people she contacted. When she texted one last person, she got a yes.

"Hey, Z."

Zuri couldn't stop smiling as Genesis walked up to her. While they had remained in touch since arriving back home from Barbados, it was mainly through texts and brief phone calls. They met once for coffee and once for dinner, but then Zuri got so caught up in work that it was hard to find the time.

"Thanks for joining me," she said, wrapping Genesis in a hug. She smelled so good, Zuri was reluctant to pull away.

"Oh, it's no problem. I'm more than happy to get out of the house. My weekends can be bland, same old thing all the time," Genesis said as they got in line.

Zuri nodded. "Same here. I have a routine and stick to it."

Genesis gave her a look like she didn't believe her. "But at least you get to break the monotony with work."

Zuri laughed as she handed the usher their tickets. "That's true, but it's way more mundane stuff than you think. It's not all movie premieres and glamorous parties."

Genesis raised an eyebrow. "Sure." She looked around the lobby and pointed to the concession stand at the back. "I'm going to need a large popcorn, a slushie, and nachos stat."

"Well, come on," Zuri said.

"Which film are you most excited about seeing?" she asked.

"Friday, Foster. Everyone always talks about Foxy Brown, but Foster is my favorite Pam Grier film. What about you?"

"Black Caesar, for sure, it's just a phenomenal movie. It's also the first of that period I saw with my dad, so it's got a special meaning for me."

"It's cool that your parents introduced those movies to you. Mine limited our options as far as what we got to see. Most of my movie-watching started in college. I haven't seen the others."

Zuri's eyes lit up. "Oh, even better. You are about to have a great time."

At the counter, Genesis ordered her snacks. She turned to Zuri and asked, "Do you want anything?"

"So wait, all of that is just for you?" Zuri said.

"Yup, this girl does not share her movie snacks. Especially when we are about to be here for six hours. If you reach over, you might get your feelings hurt."

Zuri doubled over with laughter and let her know what she wanted. With everything going on between her and Tracy and at the studio, she had found little to smile about for the last week. Now she couldn't stop. It was looking like inviting Genesis out was the best idea she'd had in a while.

* * *

GENESIS

Six and a half hours later, Genesis and Zuri emerged and couldn't stop gushing over everything they had seen.

"Those movies are so much better on the big screen. I can't believe I've never seen them in this format before," Zuri said.

Genesis loved the child-like glee on her face; it was endearing. They had been chatting nonstop, even while watching the films, much to the annoyance of those around them.

"I agree, and the way they remastered them made it even better. If they do this again, we have to check it out," Genesis said.

Zuri looked pleased with her suggestion. "Yes, we should. I think I just found my new movie, buddy."

Genesis blushed and looked away. "Well, I'm parked in the lot down the street. Unless you want to get dinner or something like that."

"I have an appointment over on Rodeo Drive," Zuri said.

"Oh, ok, then nevermind. We can do it another time."

Zuri stopped her from walking away. "I can eat if you don't mind joining me. It's just to pick up a dress for an upcoming event."

Genesis smiled. "Yeah, I would like that."

* * *

Twenty-five minutes later, they arrived at their destination. After parking a couple of blocks away, Genesis followed behind Zuri and tried not to stare as they passed several famous faces. While she had lived in LA for years, Rodeo Drive was not a place Genesis ever bothered to visit. Shannon may have been one of the more popular players during her time in the WNBA, but she still never made a salary on the level of a male player. They were comfortable, but not wealthy. The Banana Republic was the most expensive store she frequented.

Zuri strutted along as if she belonged, and of course, she did.

"This is the store." Zuri stopped in front of a place called Les Vêtements and held open the door. "It's owned by a French designer named Touissant. I get lots of clothes from here for special events."

As soon as she entered the store, a glorious scent hit Genesis in the face. It was light, but she could smell the vanilla undertone.

"They pipe that stuff in every so often," Zuri said, entering behind her. "Toussaint says that vanilla is a scent that attracts women and lowers anxiety. It makes you more pliable for buying."

Genesis breathed in some more. "Well, whatever it is, I can feel it working."

A man with captivating gray eyes appeared behind them. "That would be our newest fragrance, Celeste. Quite the best-seller." He leaned over to Zuri and kissed both of her cheeks. "Zuri, I've got your dress all picked out. Do you need anything else with that?"

"Hi Marcus, I thought maybe I could get my friend here something as well."

"Excuse me?" Genesis said.

Zuri just looked at her and winked. "Trust me."

After introductions, Marcus led them upstairs. Genesis looked all around the sparse store. The display racks had limited clothing, and there were tall glass cases sprinkled throughout with singular dresses highlighted.

Marcus ushered them into a large room with seating out front and several individual dressing rooms.

"Have a seat, and I'll be back with some selections. Genesis, I'm guessing you're a size 12 in US sizes, correct?" Marcus said.

"Yes, how did you..."

"Oh, I do this all day. I can guess a woman's dress size in one glance. Angela's going to bring you some champagne."

Zuri sat back in her seat and crossed her legs, an amused expression on her face.

"So, what's the game plan here? Are we about to have a Pretty Woman moment? Because I'll have you know, my rates are pretty high," Genesis said in a whisper.

"First, why are you whispering? Second, I want to do something nice for my friend." Zuri smiled at the young woman who brought their champagne as she took the glass.

"Dresses here start at $5,000," Genesis whispered, holding up her phone, which displayed the information she had just googled. When she realized she was whispering again, she raised her voice to a normal level. "I appreciate the generosity, but..."

Her voice stuck in her throat when she saw the dresses Marcus wheeled out. There were five all together displayed on a rack. Each had rich colors and figure-flattering silhouettes. It was like he had read her mind because all of them were items she would have picked herself. Genesis felt Zuri's eyes on her as she put her champagne down and walked over to the dresses.

Zuri sipped her champagne. "You like them?"

"Like isn't the word. These dresses are gorgeous," Genesis said, letting the material of one glide over her fingers. "And luxurious."

"I tell you what. How about we make a trade? I buy you a dress, and you take over my taxes? Didn't you tell me you did that for several years before your current job?" Zuri said.

Genesis broke out of her trance and looked over at Zuri. "Yes, I did. I would have to brush up on some things, but I could do that."

"I keep meticulous records. It will be a piece of cake. Now please, try something on. I'm dying to see you in them."

Genesis didn't miss the lustful gaze Zuri shot her way, but it left just as fast as it appeared. She grabbed the first dress that caught her eye; it was dark blue and shimmered under the light. After finishing her champagne, she walked into a dressing room.

Several minutes later, she emerged, feeling the sexiest she ever had.

"Wow," Zuri said upon seeing her.

Genesis couldn't stop looking at herself in the mirror. Her hands slid down her hips as she turned to the side.

"This is heavenly, almost like a second skin. I don't know if I've ever been so comfortable in a dress before," Genesis said. "I don't even want to try on the others; this is the one."

"I agree," Zuri said. "You look amazing."

When she turned to face Zuri, this time, the desire she had seen earlier was bare all over her face with no attempt to hide it. She excused herself and escaped back into the dressing room.

"What am I doing?" she mumbled to herself.

Even if she gave Zuri services for the dress, it wouldn't be fair compensation. This one cost $7,500 according to the price tag. Zuri was being too generous, and Genesis felt weird accepting it. Yes, they were friends, but the fact remained, Zuri had a girlfriend, and Genesis was dating someone as well. Their relationship needed to stay where it was, in the friend zone.

Genesis exited the dressing room and placed the dress back on the rack.

"Hey, what's wrong?" Zuri asked, standing up.

"I can't accept this dress, but thank you for the offer. If you want my help with your taxes, then you can pay me." Genesis grabbed her bag from the chair. "I'll see you later, Z."

"Wait," Zuri called out, but Genesis kept walking.

For a moment, she let herself believe that she was over Zuri and could handle being her friend, but that one look told her she wasn't ready. The entire day had been surreal, as if no time had passed since leaving Barbados and returning to LA. Their previous get-togethers had been awkward, but this time every-thing just flowed. It felt good, too good.

Genesis reached her car and got inside. She gripped the

steering wheel and laid her forehead on it. It was silly to run away, but she had no choice. A tap on the passenger side window startled her.

"Gen, can I come inside?" Zuri stood there; her mouth turned down.

Genesis nodded and unlocked the door. Zuri opened the back and placed her dress down, then made her way to the front seat.

"Listen, I'm sorry if I made things uncomfortable back at the store. There is so much going on right now in my life, and you made me happy today. I was trying to return the favor."

Genesis sighed and released her grip on the steering wheel. "You're a kind person, Zuri, and it was a sweet gesture." She glanced in her direction. "But it's that, the way you're looking at me right now."

"What way?" Zuri said, averting her eyes.

"Doesn't matter, you're with Tracy," Genesis muttered.

"What if I wasn't?" Zuri said, turning to face her. "What if..."

"Don't," Genesis said, putting up her hand. "You have no right to make promises to me when there's another woman still in your life."

Zuri was quiet. "You're right; I don't know what I was thinking. I'm sorry." She pushed the door open, then paused. "Thank you for today. You don't know how much I needed it."

"You're welcome. I had a great time too," Genesis said sincerely.

After grabbing her dress from the back seat, Zuri waved goodbye and walked to her car. As Genesis got ready to drive off, she glanced in the mirror and saw a garment bag on her backseat. She knew Zuri took her dress, so this had to be the one she tried on.

Her phone vibrated with a text from Zuri. *I heard what you said, but that dress is meant for you. It's yours, no strings attached.*

Genesis couldn't help but smile and texted back, *Thank you.*

"That woman knows she's got me under her spell, damn it," Genesis said out loud as she started the car.

Chapter Twenty

I can still feel you on my lips...

Genesis looked down at the text message and tried to think of an appropriate response. She started seeing Olivia two months ago, and while things had been going well, she had yet to experience what she liked to think of as "the zing." The zing was when someone you're into made you feel all warm and tingly inside. Just being near them made your entire body light up. With Zuri, that feeling was immediate the moment they locked eyes. Ever since she met Olivia, there was nothing above a simmer.

"What are you frowning at?" Genesis's coworker Lucy asked as she placed a cup of coffee on her desk. She angled her neck to get a look at her phone.

"You are so nosy," Genesis said with a chuckle as she brought the phone close to her chest. "Don't you have important accountant work to be doing?"

Lucy sucked her teeth and backed up towards the door. "Oh, you're tryna be cute, so you must be talking to a woman. Which one is this?"

Genesis rolled her eyes but smiled. She and Lucy had been

friends for years. They both started at the firm around the same time and bonded over their love of music and Thai food.

"It's Olivia..."

"Ooh, she is a cutie. Don't tell me you're bored with her already?"

"Not bored... just not excited. I thought she was going to be a bit more; I don't know... something."

"Here we go with that zingy thing you're always going on about," Lucy said, leaning against the door frame. "In the real world, we don't get zings. Things just percolate at a satisfying heat level. That's the way it was with Keith and me, and you know how much I love that man."

Genesis nodded. Lucy was right, and she was acting ridiculous. Olivia was perfect wife material: 5'7, worked out, had an excellent job as an investment banker, and could cook like nobody's business. There was just no fire in her, and she was needier than she expected. The text she was looking at would be the first of many for the day. In the beginning, she found it flattering, but after dating for a couple of months, it was a bit much. They were both busy people; she didn't understand how Olivia was always so available to chat.

"It sounds like I'm being extra, but I want someone that I feel passionate about," Genesis said, leaning back in her chair.

"I'm not saying that you can't have passion, but most times, that will fizzle out anyway. Much better to build up to something; the passion will come.

Genesis twisted her lips. "So you're saying I shouldn't expect tingly feelings?"

"I didn't say that, but it wouldn't hurt to let it develop over time," Lucy said. "But let's be real, Olivia isn't the problem."

"What's that supposed to mean?"

Lucy sighed and sat in the chair across from Genesis. "We've been avoiding the elephant in the room, but we have to talk about it. It's been six months since you got back, and Zuri is still on your mind. That little date you had the other weekend proves it."

"That was not a date," Genesis said in protest.

"Right, except it ended with you two bonding over movies and her buying you an expensive dress."

"Whatever." Genesis grabbed a pencil so she could do something with her restless hands. "Yes, she is on my mind; how could she not be? But we agreed just to be friends. She's in love with Tracy, and I need to move on."

Lucy rolled her eyes. "I doubt she loves her as much as she thinks. Nobody would court someone as hard as she did with you if they were in love with someone else. My guess is Tracy picked up on the vibe and gave her what she wanted all along, which was a relationship."

She had a point, although it didn't make Genesis feel better. "Does it matter why they're together? The point is, she's not with me, and I don't want to be alone anymore."

"So you say, but don't even act like that kiss in Barbados didn't have you in your feelings."

Genesis sighed at the memory. "Lord, just the thought still has me in them," she said, fanning herself.

A call interrupted their fit of laughter, and Genesis showed Lucy the phone. "We mentioned Olivia too much, and now she's calling."

Lucy waved her off. "Girl, stop it and talk to your boo. You're the one who gave her your direct line." She mouthed, "be nice," as she walked out of the office.

Genesis chuckled and picked up the phone. "Hey Liv, how's it going?"

"Not bad. I had a busy morning, but I've been thinking about you. Wanted to hear your voice and see how you're doing," Olivia said.

Even though Genesis was complaining a few minutes ago, it touched her that Olivia always made sure she was okay. It was nice dating someone so concerned with her wellbeing.

"It's good to hear your voice, too. Are we still on for dinner tomorrow night?"

Olivia sighed. "That's the other reason I called. A work event changed days, and I have to attend. So I was hoping we could have dinner tonight instead."

Genesis wasn't a fan of them seeing each other two nights in a row. She was still on the fence and didn't want things to move too fast. Women were always quick to try to wife you up if you gave them too much access.

"I don't do last-minute dates, but I'll make an exception for you," Genesis said.

"Well, that makes me feel pretty special. Thank you, baby. I'll make us some reservations at Marmont."

"Will they even have an open table on such short notice?" Genesis asked.

Marmont was one of L.A.'s most exclusive restaurants, and you had to reserve far in advance to get a table.

"Oh yeah, my company has a standing table that brokers can use for business meetings."

"But I'm not a client," Genesis said, smiling.

"Weird, because I could have sworn you mentioned wanting to invest with the firm. Guess we will discuss that further over dinner."

Genesis laughed out loud at Olivia's boldness. They agreed on a time and signed off. Despite her reservations about their relationship, she did like Olivia. She was light-hearted and fun where Genesis could be serious, and she needed that balance.

After talking about Zuri with Lucy, it made Genesis wonder what she was up doing at that moment. Genesis opened up her Instagram account and looked up Zuri's handle, zurib. Her account wasn't public, which meant she had to make a friend request initially. Zuri accepted right away, but Genesis didn't want her to think she was stalking her online, so she rarely liked any of her pictures. However, she looked at her account often. The last post was a selfie from a week ago and featured her on a movie set. Her smile was radiant as she posed in front of a house in the film.

Genesis liked the pic, and less than a minute later, a notification popped up. She clicked on it, and there was a message from Zuri.

Zuri: Hi, Gen, how have you been? We haven't spoken since the movies.

Genesis: I've been doing okay. What, you miss me or something?

Zuri: Lol, or something...

Genesis wanted to ask what the or something was, but let it go.

Genesis: How are you?

Zuri: I've been better. Just have some crazy things going on at work. What's up with your account? You haven't posted a picture in weeks.

Genesis: Didn't think you would notice.

Zuri: It's the highlight of my time on the gram.

Genesis smiled like an idiot. Zuri always made her feel beautiful.

Zuri: I miss Barbados

Genesis: I miss it too—kind of over the grind here.

Zuri: Yeah, same.

Genesis: What do you miss the most?

Zuri: Our conversations.

Genesis paused. She had assumed Zuri was making a general statement about missing the country; it hadn't even occurred to her she meant their time together. It was still on her mind, too.

Genesis: That night on the beach was special.

Zuri: Yeah, it was, and it makes me think what if...

Genesis: What if?

There was a pause in Zuri's writing, and Genesis's heart was ready to beat out of her chest. She had no idea why Zuri's answer was so important, but it was.

Zuri: I shouldn't have said that. It isn't productive for either of us.

"You've got to be kidding me," Genesis said out loud.

That answer was a complete cop-out, and Zuri had to have known that. Genesis wasn't sure what irritated her more, that Zuri couldn't just say what she wanted or that she cared so much.

Genesis: Feelings aren't always meant to be productive; they just exist.

Zuri: I suppose you're right. Anyway, I have some stuff to take care of right now, but it was lovely chatting with you. Don't be a stranger and post some pics!

Genesis: Nice chatting with you too.

Then, just like that, she was gone. Genesis was about to log out and get back to work but then thought better of it. She pushed her chair closer to the windows behind her desk so the sunlight would highlight her face and struck a pose. The caption read: When the sun hits your skin just right.

After posting the picture, Genesis heard her phone buzz. She figured it was someone liking the picture, but when she glanced at it, she saw a text message had come through from Zuri. *I might have to save that for my private collection, Caribbean queen*, it read.

Warmth spread out from her chest and engulfed her. That

was what she had been missing with Olivia, and damn, it felt good.

* * *

On the drive home, Genesis wondered if she was a fool for humoring Zuri. She had avoided contact with her because she knew that if she got the smallest hint that she reciprocated her feelings, she would give in to her desires. But she didn't want to be anyone's rebound and get invested, only to be rejected. There was also the fact that she didn't know what Zuri's relationship with Tracy was at the moment. So even though she wanted to throw caution to the wind, she needed to be mindful.

As she pulled up to her house, an unfamiliar car sat in her driveway. The driver wasn't visible to her, but as she got closer, an all too familiar person stepped out to greet her.

Shannon waved as Genesis pulled up beside her. Her smile made Genesis remember why she had stayed away from her for so long. Her jet black curls surrounded her face like a frame, and she wore a monochrome black sweatsuit.

"Shannon, what are you doing here?" Genesis said as she got out of her car.

"Hello to you too. Sorry, I just showed up here, but getting in touch with you through other means has been impossible." Shannon grabbed the box of papers Genesis pulled from the back seat. "Bringing work home now?"

"It's been getting pretty hectic." Genesis opened the front door and turned on the lights.

"Thank you," she said, taking the box from Shannon's hand.

"The house seems empty," Shannon said, walking further into the living room.

"That's because I've sold a lot of the things you left behind." Genesis shrugged off her jacket and turned to find Shannon staring at her. "Oh, do not even start. You left me, and you left this house along with everything in it. I did what I had to do to pay the bills here."

"You're right; I'm sorry," Shannon said, sitting on the couch.

Genesis softened up a bit. "You want something to drink?"

"Sure, water is fine."

The moment Genesis stepped into the kitchen, she let out a deep sigh. Shannon popping up was the last thing she ever expected. After returning from Barbados, she had sent Genesis a few more messages, but since she never responded to any of them, they stopped. That she was there had her on edge.

When she got back to the living room, she handed her the water she requested and sat on the opposite couch. They both sipped on their drinks and waited for the other to talk. Since Shannon had been hunting her down for months, Genesis left it to her to say what was on her mind.

"So, I think the first thing I need to say to you is I'm sorry. I'm sorry for the way I treated you, and I'm sorry that I didn't give our relationship the respect it deserved." Shannon placed her water on the coffee table and leaned on to her long legs.

"When did she leave you?" Genesis asked, sitting back.

Shannon scrunched her face in confusion. "When did who leave me?"

"You expect me to believe that you divorced me, and it wasn't because of another woman? Maybe you forgot, but I remember what it was like towards the end. You didn't touch me and spent almost no time at home. You left before you were ever physically gone."

Shannon looked away; her shoulders slumped down. "It wasn't as simple as that. Our relationship wasn't the same anymore. There was no romance, no passion."

"It doesn't matter now. Why are you here?" Genesis said, trying to keep her voice calm.

"When I first started contacting you, it was to reconcile," Shannon said. "And since you didn't respond, I figured that was it. I was going to let you go, but..."

"Let me; I'm not yours anymore. You made that clear when you packed up your shit and filed for divorce. I can't even deal with this right now..."

"I'm sick, Gen."

Genesis stopped mid-sentence and looked at Shannon. Her appearance was the same on the surface, but now she noticed that her muscular build was more slender. A shadow of darkness was under her eyes, which made them appear more pronounced. If she hadn't known how she looked before the changes, it would not have been obvious.

"What's going on?"

"I have ovarian cancer." Shannon shifted in her seat. "I didn't know anything was wrong. I went for a check-up, and it turns out my ovaries have turned against me," she said with a sad chuckle.

"I'm so sorry, Shay," Genesis said. Her words were sincere. No matter how angry she was about how their relationship ended, she still cared about Shannon, and the thought of her being ill broke her heart. "Have you started treatment yet?"

"My surgery is in a month, but I couldn't go under without seeing you first." Shannon got up and kneeled in front of Genesis. "I am sorry for what I did, Gen. I didn't mean to hurt you."

Genesis teared up as Shannon broke down and dropped her head into her lap. Her sobs were so deep that her body shook from the force.

"I forgive you, Shay," Genesis said, kissing the top of her head. And she did because forgiveness was the least of what she could offer her.

Chapter Twenty-One

"Is this the worst idea ever?"

Genesis sat in her bedroom on a video chat with Andrea later that night. After talking with Shannon, they discussed what was going to happen after surgery. Chemotherapy was a possibility, which meant she would need help for several months. Her girlfriend, the person she left Genesis for, was out of the picture. Not interested in having to nurse her through illness, she left soon after her diagnosis.

The situation was so sad there was no room for gloating about the outcome. Had they still been together, Genesis would have taken care of her without hesitation. It seemed only natural to offer her to come back home if only so she wouldn't be alone.

"I'm not sure about this, Gen. On the one hand, it makes sense to help her out, but I'm concerned about you. Can you handle having her back in your space like that?" Andrea said.

"I have no interest in us getting back together. The fact is Kenzie, and I are her only family here; everyone else is back in Virginia." Genesis sighed and fell back on the pillow behind her. "She could die, Drea. I would never forgive myself if something happened, and I did nothing."

"You said they detected it early, so her chances of survival are higher. Don't let her guilt trip you into this."

"It's not guilt; she's still my family, even if she hurt me."

Andrea sighed."Well, all I have to say is, make sure you set boundaries. She can't come into your life again thinking that everything is going back to how it was."

Genesis pictured Zuri and shook her head. "No, that is not happening."

"You do you, but I will come over there and kick her ass if she hurts you again, sick or not. Anyway, how's it going with work?"

The accounting firm informed Genesis and several other associates that their positions were no longer secure. They were the last group hired, and since the company was downsizing, their jobs were the most vulnerable. At first, the thought of losing her job worried her, but it was looking like a blessing in disguise. There was money to sustain her for a year while she looked for more work or started a business for herself, which was something in the back of her mind for years. Thanks to Shannon, she had lucrative investments and a savings account.

"They still haven't told us anything, which is pissing me off. I swear companies have such little regard for their employees sometimes. Why even tell us you'll be letting us go if you plan to keep us in limbo?"

"It's a tactic, I bet, to weed out who will step up the most. Plenty of people will go above and beyond if they think their livelihood is on the line."

"You're right, but I'm not falling for it. I clock in when I'm supposed to and leave on schedule. And I have not taken on any of the different projects they keep throwing out at us. Let the old-timers handle that," Genesis said, sucking her teeth.

Andrea laughed. "That's what I'm talking about." She excused herself as she adjusted the phone and laid down on her bed. "When you called, I thought it was to talk about your boo thing, Zuri."

"Why? We talk at least once a week, but it's nothing mind-blowing."

"Wait, you haven't heard? I forgot you ignore celebrity gossip. Here, I'm going to send you the article I was reading."

The screen blanked out for a moment as Andrea texted her the article. Genesis skimmed it. There was mention of charges against Zuri's production company head for sexual misconduct, with a brief statement of how much damage the accusations and conviction could do to Ellis Films.

"When did this happen?" Genesis asked.

"I think the news broke a few days ago. Big names are coming up in this lawsuit. Your girl is going to need to do major damage control."

"Poor Zuri, that studio is like her baby. When we spoke over text, she didn't even mention it." Their conversation had been so light, and there was no sign she was in distress. "I wonder if that's why she was flirtatious."

"Excuse me?" Andrea said. "I'm sorry. Did you say she was flirting with you? Ever since Cruella Deville appeared, she has behaved. Perhaps there is trouble in paradise."

Genesis chuckled at the nickname. "Tracy is not Cruella. She was nice to me."

"It's the jawline, makes me picture her in a fur striking at dogs," Andrea said, making a sound like a whip. "From what you told me, Zuri sounds loyal. So if she was flirtatious, then maybe something is going on between her and Tracy. I'm not saying now is the time to strike, but..."

"So you're just going to ignore the fact that I'm seeing some-one?" Genesis pictured Olivia's smiling face. "Olivia is a decent woman."

"Ok, I didn't say she wasn't. But choose her because she is

the one that makes your heart sing, and if she doesn't, go for the one who does."

"Zuri and I are friends, and that's it," Genesis said, with a sly grin. "Which means if I stopped by her office and brought her homemade cookies, that would be within the boundaries of friendship."

"Oh, homemade cookies. I like the way you think. It's a sweet gesture; she will eat it up. And then you'll be next."

They both burst into a fit of laughter. Although Genesis was talking a big game, she had no ulterior motives. Her concern for Zuri was real, and she wanted to check on her. Now she just needed to get up the courage to go through with it.

* * *

ZURI

Zuri sat typing up a memo to be emailed out to all staff, making sure they understood recent events. They also scheduled a meeting the following day with the investigator she hired. The abuse had been going on for too many years, and there was no way other people didn't have a role in keeping things under wraps.

While she continued writing, Zuri answered her phone. "Yes."

"Hey Z, security just buzzed and said someone is here for you named Genesis. Should I allow them to come up?"

Zuri snapped out of her writing haze. Genesis there to see her? Now that was a surprise, but a pleasant one.

"Yes, please. When she gets here, you can bring her straight to my office."

As soon as she hung up the phone, Zuri dashed over to the

mirror and made sure she looked okay. Fridays were a dress-down day, so she had on jeans. Her t-shirt was retro and featured the poster for one of her favorite 80's movies, Big Trouble in Little China. She had a host of similar shirts that she liked to pull out, showcasing her movie nerd status. That didn't bother her; movies were her life.

Soon after she freshened up her lipstick and fluffed her locs, there was a knock on the door.

"Come in, please," Zuri said with a bit too much enthusiasm.

She didn't have time to reprimand herself before Genesis, who walked into her office with a burst of energy, enrapturing her.

"Hi, Zuri. This place is amazing!"

"Hey Gen," Zuri said.

She walked over to her, and they did that weird hesitant dance people do when they aren't sure how to greet each other. Part of her wanted to grab her into a hug and not let go, while the other wanted to maintain an air of nonchalance. So she compromised and offered a kiss on the cheek.

"I'm sorry to just bust in on you like this," Genesis said, taking off her jacket.

Genesis placed a box on Zuri's desk, which only briefly distracted her from what the other woman was wearing. She had on a dark gray skirt with a deep red blouse and red heels to match. Her outfit was sexy but professional and so different from her casual style.

As she bent over to place something in her purse, Zuri admired her legs. The heels she wore were high enough to cause that sweet tension, which made the calves flex. It was a delight to witness in action, but having experienced it herself, Zuri was aware of the torture it could bring. As practical as Genesis tended to be, odds were slim that she had worn those to work.

So the fact that she put them on to visit her pleased Zuri very much.

"I'm so happy you came by," Zuri said, pulling out a chair. "I think this is the most we've seen each other in months."

"Well, you're a busy lady, running your empire."

Zuri took a seat beside her and tried to stop grinning like an idiot. Up close, she smelled heavenly.

"So, how is the accounting business treating you?" Zuri said.

Genesis shrugged. "It's been fine; it's a job. We have heard rumors that the company might fire staff. They hired a bunch of people when there was a surplus of work, but things have slowed down in the last year."

"Does that worry you?"

"No," Genesis said with a laugh. "It might be the push I need to move on to something else. I'm not stimulated by what I do."

"Of course not; you're a creative soul." Zuri got lost in her eyes, then cleared her throat and turned to pick up the box she placed on her desk. "What is this?" she asked, shaking it.

"Uh, I made you cookies." Genesis placed her hands over her eyes and groaned. "I'm such a dork. I'm all like, 'heard that you're dealing with a sexual misconduct case, here are my cookies.' It's lame, but I just thought it might cheer you up, at least a little."

"You're funny. It just so happens that cookies always make me feel better," Zuri said while opening the box. She let out a squeal of delight when the smell struck her as she stared inside. "Homemade White chocolate macadamia nut?"

Genesis blushed and nodded. "It's a recipe from my mom. She made it all the time when we were kids. I perfected it when I had to make them for my sister; sometimes, they were the only thing that would cheer her up."

"Your mom's recipe? This was thoughtful of you, Genesis," Zuri said, reaching out to squeeze her hand.

"How are you dealing with all of this?" Genesis asked, her eyes pools of concern.

"I'm fine." Zuri paused. "Shit, no, I'm not. I don't even know why I said that."

"Because we're trained as a society to be polite and not burden others with our problems. Please, share with me. I want to know."

Zuri looked up at her with a sad smile. "I am still in shock. Francis is like a second father, and I never in my life expected any of this. I've lost all respect for him, yet I still love him and want answers. The thing is, I doubt that if I get one, it's going to change anything. He hurt other people, women, who I do my damnedest to protect because of how this industry can be. I meant the environment here to differ from other movie studios, and he made us just as bad if not worse than them."

It surprised Zuri when she touched her cheeks, and they were wet with tears. She hadn't even realized she was crying. These emotions needed release, and this was the first time it felt appropriate. With her cousins, it had been all business and figuring out how to fix things. Tracy tried to provide comfort, but her version of that meant making love, not talking about feelings.

Genesis stood up, took the box of cookies out of her hand, and hugged her into her body. Her warmth and the floral perfume she wore enveloped Zuri. The intimacy of it reminded her of their kiss. As if the same thought hit her, Genesis pulled back and rubbed her arm.

"I don't want to keep you from your work; you have lots to handle right now." Genesis grabbed her coat. "I suggest eating a cookie at least three times a day for the next few days. And call or message me whenever you need to talk."

"Thanks, doc," Zuri said.

Unable to take her eyes off of Genesis's curves as she put on her jacket, Zuri got up and sat at her desk, fiddling with items on it, as a distraction.

"Hey, um, would you like to hang out tomorrow night? I mean, Tracy will be there and some friends, but it's a get-together to kind of get my mind off of things. It's a club over on Sunset called After Dark. We bought out the VIP section," Zuri said as she sat down.

Genesis stood there with her face scrunched up in thought.

"Sure, why not? Maybe my friend Lucy wants to come and Olivia," Genesis said.

"Yeah, invite your friends. That's fine because there will be plenty of space."

Genesis hesitated to speak, then said, "Well, Olivia is someone I'm dating."

"Oh, you're seeing someone?" Zuri said, her voice sounding too high and chipper.

The comment had her mind spinning. Of course, Genesis was seeing someone. A woman like her would not be single forever.

"It's fairly new, not sure where it's going just yet, but I like her."

"Good, good," Zuri said.

Genesis pointed towards the door and said, "So, it's time for me to leave. Text me the details about tomorrow night."

"Of course, see you then," Zuri said, waving goodbye.

The smile on her face dropped once Genesis closed the door. She didn't know what had possessed her to invite her out. Things would be awkward with Tracy and now this other woman who Genesis was dating, but she hoped they would spend some time together, no matter how short.

Chapter Twenty-Two

Zuri sat in the VIP section of After Dark, happy that she didn't have to mingle with the masses. In the past, she refused to pay for VIP because she found it pretentious, but now it was the only way she could tolerate visiting night clubs.

Her best friend Alma sat beside her, swaying to one of the top 40 songs they were spinning. She was shocked when she accepted her invite since Alma hated this scene, but she was grateful to see her.

"God, I hate this place more and more every time I visit," Alma said, sipping on a Sprite.

"Seems like you're having fun to me," Zuri said with a smirk.

"Why, because I'm moving my head to a song? It's Kelani; I'd love her music wherever it's playing. This place makes my skin itch."

"Okay, so then why did you agree to come out?"

Alma rolled her eyes and let her head drop back. Her jet black hair fanning out on the couch behind her. "Because if I have to spend another Saturday night curled up with Sy watching classic movies, I'll die, literally."

Sy was Alma's elderly neighbor, an older Jewish man she befriended after moving into her complex. Alma got Sy's mail by accident, and when she returned it, she discovered that he lived alone. His wife had died several years ago, and while his kids visited, they lived in other states. Alma took it upon herself to watch out for him, and they became the best of friends.

"You realize that you could date, right? Kirk broke up with you two years ago, and if I recall, you weren't all that fond of him."

"Oh, he was a total asshole, but he gave me something to do outside of work. Now I have to rely on my friends for company, and the two I have are always busy," Alma said, squinting her eyes at Zuri. "Anyway, you'll never believe what Sy said to me the other day? 'A nice oriental girl like you could have any man she wants. You need to put yourself out there.' Oriental? I was like, what the fuck Sy, am I a rug?"

Zuri burst into hysterical laughter. "Seniors have no filter. I had an old woman at the nursing home where I used to volunteer say to me that I was a nice colored girl and a credit to my race."

"Well, Sy knows I have a mouth on me, so I corrected him on that oriental nonsense."

Their assigned server stopped by and took orders from everyone. Zuri invited some people she worked with, plus a few other associates. Her friend circle was pretty tight, to begin with, but being busy with work played a part in that as well. Alma was an old friend from middle school, and they had been in each other's lives off and on for years. It was nice having someone around that wasn't a part of the film industry.

"I missed you at my party the other night," Zuri said.

Alma chuckled. "I was not going to one of your industry get-togethers. Everyone always asks who I am, and once they learn I'm a nobody, they slither away like the snakes they are."

Zuri laughed, but she was right. "I don't fault you for staying away."

She thought about telling Alma what Fiona had revealed to her, but she was reluctant. Tracy had always left an unpleasant taste in Alma's mouth, and she didn't want to add fuel to her dislike. Especially when she still hadn't decided whether she wanted the relationship to continue.

"You have been staring at the front door for over an hour," Alma said with a raised eyebrow.

"I'm just waiting to see when Tracy gets here."

Alma smiled and nudged her. "You are such a liar. Don't act like you aren't looking for a certain someone."

"Okay, then I won't act like I'm not looking for her," Zuri said, sticking her tongue out at Alma.

"Z, how long is this going to continue?"

"Is what going to continue?"

Alma put down her drink and turned to Zuri with a serious face. "Are you happy with Tracy?"

Before Zuri could answer, the woman in question entered the VIP area with a few of her friends.

"Hey baby, sorry we're late. Cory took forever getting ready," Tracy said, bending down to kiss her lips.

"It's no problem, honey. Hey ladies," Zuri said, waving to Tracy's friends.

"Alma, it's been a minute. Where have you been hiding?" Tracy said.

Alma stood up and hugged Tracy. "I like my space to myself, and I wanted to let you two lovebirds have yours."

Tracy waved her off. "Don't be silly; you're always welcome at the house." She called over the server and placed an order.

"Two bottles of Dom Perignon, please? Thanks. So, ladies, what were you talking about?"

Alma and Zuri looked at each other. Zuri shrugged and said, "Nothing, just how crowded this place has gotten."

"Oh my God, right? It's like they just let anyone in now," Tracy said.

Alma mouthed at Zuri, "We'll talk later."

* * *

GENESIS

"Thanks for the invite, Gen. I haven't had a night out in ages," Lucy said as they strolled up to the club. "So, Olivia is meeting us here?"

"Yeah, she should be here soon." Genesis sent Olivia a text. "And you're welcome; I'm glad you could make it on short notice."

"Girl, Keith rushed me out of the house. His friends are coming over for one of their game nights. I'm glad not to be there listening to the hooting and hollering coming from the basement."

"Hey, ladies," Olivia said, appearing beside Lucy.

"Olivia, right on time," Lucy said, leaning in for a hug.

"Damn, Genesis, you look amazing."

"Thanks, Liv," Genesis said, blushing. "You look good too."

Olivia wore a fitted black henley shirt that showed off her muscular physique and black jeans and boots. She had a fresh haircut as well.

Genesis had worn an outfit she hoped would turn heads, and it was. She had on a black, sleeveless bodycon dress that hit just above her knees. It showed off her curves in the best way possible, and while she didn't wear it often, it seemed appropriate for the night. Around her neck was a thin diamond necklace Shannon bought her years ago, and she loved to wear it when she had any sort of cleavage. The way it sparkled against her skin was lovely.

As she was getting dressed, she tried to convince herself that she was dressing up for Olivia, but that was far from the truth. The day before, when she visited Zuri, she had noticed how the other woman was admiring her body. She wanted more of that.

"So, we don't have to wait on this long ass line, do we?" Lucy asked.

"Nope, follow me," Genesis said, leading the way to the bouncer. "Hi, we are guests of Zuri Baker."

The bouncer asked for their names, and when he found them, lifted the velvet rope. It had been years since she experienced that treatment. When Shannon first hit the league, and was a big deal, they could get into any venue. It was nice, but she had never been in to the club scene, so the novelty wore off fast.

Once inside, Genesis looked around and saw the area where Zuri sat with Tracy and a group of other people. She hadn't lied. They had not one but two VIP areas cordoned off for them. They walked over, and Zuri jumped up to greet them.

"I'm so happy you could make it." Zuri pulled her into a hug.

Maybe it was the tightness of her dress, but she felt bare as the warmth of their bodies melded. When Zuri pulled back, she looked into her eyes and could tell she wasn't the only one who noticed.

"Um, this is Olivia and Lucy," Genesis said, stepping back.

After introductions, Olivia excused herself and headed to the bathroom. Tracy jumped up as soon as they entered the area and hugged Genesis.

"Gen, how are you? It's been ages," Tracy said, kissing both her cheeks.

Genesis didn't miss the false note in her voice, but she brushed it off. Tracy's opinion about her presence didn't matter. Zuri wanted her there.

"It's been hectic for everyone, I'm sure. This is my friend, Lucy, she's a big fan," Genesis said, stepping aside.

She left Lucy to gush over Tracy, who she was sure would eat it up. After grabbing a glass of champagne off of a tray, she settled next to a pretty woman who was texting on her phone. The woman looked up when Genesis settled in the seat beside her.

"You're Genesis, right?" she asked.

Genesis finished taking a sip of her drink and nodded.

"I'm Alma, Zuri's friend. I've heard a lot about you, so it's nice to put a person to the name," she said, putting out her hand.

"Nice to meet you, too. So, Zuri's been talking about me. Good things, I hope?" Genesis said as she took her hand.

"Oh, all the good things, trust me," Alma replied with a grin.

The two of them got deep into conversation, and it surprised Genesis to find out she wasn't in the film business. She had assumed everyone in Zuri's world was from the industry, but she realized that was a silly assumption. As they talked, she caught Zuri looking over at her, and they smiled at each other.

Olivia returned from the bathroom and gulped down a glass of champagne. Her eyes were bright as she dropped onto the couch beside Genesis. She introduced herself to Alma, then set back, her leg moving with nervous energy. Olivia loved to talk, but she was quieter than usual.

Genesis turned to her and said, "Is everything okay?"

Olivia smiled a bit too wide. "I'm great," she said, smoothing down her shirt. "I love this song; you wanna dance?"

"Of course." Genesis excused herself to Alma and followed

Olivia to the dance floor.

They had to fight their way through a sea of people to find a space of their own. Once they did, Genesis let the music take her away. While she hated clubs, she loved being engulfed by the loud music. Olivia pulled her into her body and moved with her, which was nice but not as nice as the hug she shared with Zuri.

Was this what she had to look forward to every time they interacted? The simplest gesture taking on a meaning all its own because they continued to deny what they both wanted; each other.

After dancing through several songs, they headed to the bathroom. The line wasn't as long as she expected. After washing her hands, she stood to the side and waited for Olivia. As she stood there, she heard sniffling coming from Olivia's stall.

When Olivia came out, she smiled at Genesis and wiped at her nose. She watched her wash her hands and tried to convince herself that what she was thinking couldn't be right.

"Liv, are you good?" Genesis said as she leaned against the sink.

"Of course," Olivia said with a grin.

"You just seem...off."

Her smile faltered for a moment; then she smiled again. "I'm good, Gen. Just sometimes on the weekend, I need something to take the edge off. Work can get crazy."

Genesis stood up straight and stepped back. "Is this new?"

"No, it isn't. I laid off for a while when we started seeing each other. It's not like I'm an addict or anything like that; I just indulge sometimes."

Genesis couldn't keep her face neutral, and she saw Olivia's expression change along with hers.

"I'm just having some fun; it's no big deal," Olivia said, throwing her hands up.

The bathroom filled up again, so they walked back out front. They navigated through the bodies until they were near the VIP area. Genesis figured they could finish the conversation after they left the club, but Olivia stopped her before they walked up the steps to VIP.

"Listen, I'm sorry I never mentioned it, but it's personal, and I don't think it's relevant to our relationship. We haven't gotten that serious just yet," Olivia said.

"We may not be serious, but don't you think this is something I should know about?"

Olivia shoved her hands in her pockets. "Not really."

"Not really? Are you kidding me?"

"Can you lower your voice?" Olivia asked, stepping closer to her. "Everyone is looking."

Genesis laughed out loud but lowered her voice. "So it's okay to sniff coke in a public restroom, but you're embarrassed about me being loud? I was ready to let this drop until we were alone."

"I don't get why you're so mad. You're acting like I'm an addict on skid row," Olivia said.

"It's not about how often you use it," Genesis said. "If you think using hard drugs is okay, then that means you and I have a fundamental difference in how we live our lives." Genesis sighed and rubbed her forehead. "Listen, I just want to go back upstairs and try to enjoy the rest of the night. We can talk about this later."

"Wait," Olivia said, reaching out for her.

Genesis ignored her and continued walking until Olivia gripped her arm tight enough to make her cry out.

"Olivia, let go," Genesis said, attempting to yank her arm away.

"Don't walk away from me when I'm talking to you," Olivia whispered into her ear. Her voice vibrated with anger.

The change in her demeanor was so quick; it took Genesis by surprise. They stood there staring at each other for a couple of uncomfortable minutes until Olivia dropped her arm. Genesis continued to stare her down, refusing to allow the fear inside of her to show.

"Gen, are you okay?" Lucy said as she leaned over the balcony at the top of the stairs.

"Is everything okay?" Genesis asked Olivia as they continued to stare each other down.

Olivia looked away first. "I think I'm gonna head out," she said, her voice dejected.

"I think that's for the best," Genesis replied.

It wasn't until Olivia left that she allowed her body to relax. Lucy walked up to her, concern written all over her face.

"What was that? You two looked like you were arguing?"

Genesis sighed and put her hand out. "Can I have one of your cigarettes, please?"

"A cigarette? You haven't smoked in years."

"Can I have one or not?"

Lucy opened her purse and dug out her pack of Virginia Slims. She handed one to Genesis but held onto her hand. "You sure you're okay?"

"I'm fine, sweetie. I just need some air and to think," Genesis said, patting her arm for reassurance.

As soon as she stepped outside, Genesis took a deep breath. It was baffling how fast what she had been building with Olivia unraveled. If this is what she had to look forward to in the world of dating, she was ready to take a step back.

She placed the cigarette in her mouth, then realized she hadn't asked Lucy for her lighter.

"Fuck," she screamed.

A group of people standing nearby looked over at her, but she didn't care; she was all out of fucks to give.

Chapter Twenty-Three

Zuri noticed the tension between Genesis and Olivia, but didn't think it was her place to intervene. The last thing she needed was to end up in an argument with Tracy because she appeared too concerned about something that was none of her business. Still, she kept an eye on them and was about to get up when she saw how Olivia grabbed Genesis's arm, but Lucy had already gone to check on them.

"Hey Lucy, is Genesis okay?" Zuri asked as she walked back to where they were all seated.

"Yeah, she went out for a smoke," Lucy said, settling back into her seat. She leaned into Zuri and, in a lowered voice, said, "Maybe you should check on her."

Zuri took the hint and got up. "Tracy, I need to make a phone call. I'll be back."

"Sure, babe," Tracy said, returning to the conversation with her friends.

Zuri made her way through the crowd and breathed a sigh of relief once she reached the outside. The noise level in the club was irritating her more than she realized. Not sure which direction to go, she walked down the block and turned the corner. Genesis was at the end, leaning against the building.

Unable to stop smiling, Zuri walked over to her and leaned against the wall beside her. Out of the corner of her eye, she saw Genesis glance over at her, but neither of them said anything. When Zuri looked down, she saw the unlit cigarette and fished in her pocket for the lighter she carried.

"Looks like you need this," she said, handing the lighter to Genesis.

"Thanks," Genesis said. She lit the cigarette and took a deep drag as she handed it back to Zuri. A cloud of smoke surrounded her as she breathed out and said, "God, I needed that." Her eyes flicked back over to Zuri. "You smoke?"

"Nope," Zuri said, shoving the lighter back in her pocket. "I just carry it around so I can light cigarettes for pretty ladies."

Genesis laughed and took another drag. "Of course you do."

"In all seriousness, I got in the habit of having a lighter and some cigarettes on me in case I run into someone of importance in the business. So many actors, directors, and others smoke and yet always run out of one or both. Strike up a conversation and," Zuri snapped her fingers, "suddenly I'm working with Scorsese. Or someone like that, you get what I mean."

"Sure, it makes sense. Clever," Genesis said. She pushed away from the wall and began pacing.

"Looks like your night isn't going so good," Zuri said. "I'm sorry."

Genesis didn't respond, but she chuckled at the statement. This was the first time Zuri had seen her so serious and she wasn't sure what to say. So she grabbed her hand and made her do a twirl.

"This outfit is to die for," Zuri said.

She wasn't lying; the outfit Genesis had on was sexy, and

when she saw her enter the club, it took everything in her to keep her mouth from dropping open. This was a side she hadn't seen yet, and she liked it, and she liked her. Genesis was someone with layers, and she loved that she still had more to learn about her.

"Thank you." Genesis flicked the cigarette on the ground and put it out, then picked it back up. She saw Zuri look at her funny, and she shrugged. "I hate littering," she said as she threw it in a garbage can near them.

"Um, do you want to take a walk around the block?" Zuri asked, not ready to go inside.

"Sure," Genesis said, walking ahead.

They walked the first block without speaking, the silence only punctuated by the patrons of various bars out and about. Their hands brushed against each other a few times, but she stopped herself from reaching over and holding on.

As they rounded the corner of the second block, Genesis spoke.

"I can't do this with you anymore, Z."

"Do what? Walk on the street?"

Genesis didn't laugh and stopped short. When she turned to Zuri, her eyes were ablaze with something she couldn't quite decipher.

"What do you want from me?"

Zuri looked off to the side. "Uh, friendship, and... Hey, where are you going?" Zuri ran after Genesis, who was speed walking away.

"You are so full of shit," Genesis said without stopping. "One thing I learned tonight is I need to stop waiting for something to happen and go after what I want."

"Okay, I hear you but can you slow down," Zuri said, jogging to catch up to her.

Genesis stopped and waited for Zuri. "Are we not two grown women?" Genesis said.

"We are."

"So explain to me why we're playing these childish games?"

Zuri rubbed the nape of her neck. "I wasn't aware we were playing a game."

Genesis sighed. "Zuri, I like you. So much that I have allowed myself to continue this charade. I don't want to do it anymore; I can't." She walked closer to Zuri and took hold of her hand, placing it on her chest. "Do you feel that? Whenever I'm near you, when we speak, or even just messaging each other, it's this way. It's been years since someone affected me like this."

Genesis's heartbeat was strong against her hand. She closed her eyes for a moment, and they were in sync. When she opened them again, Genesis was just watching her. She had said her piece and was waiting for Zuri to respond.

She didn't know what to say. Things with Tracy were still up in the air, but it wouldn't be fair to commit to anything before that was over. How easy it would be to just fall into Genesis's arms, but she deserved more than that.

Zuri let her hand drop. "I'm sorry."

Genesis's face looked pained. "Yeah, me too," she said, stepping back. "Goodbye, Zuri."

As she watched her walk away, Zuri forced herself to stay put and not run after her like she wanted. Genesis deserved someone who could give her everything, and until she could do that, it was best to stay away.

* * *

2 Weeks Later

"Well, that was a fun night out," Tracy said as they entered the house.

Since Tracy was leaving at the end of the week for London, she convinced Zuri to go out and celebrate with her friends. Zuri obliged her like she had been doing, but her heart wasn't in it. Ever since she and Genesis parted ways, her mood had been off. She kept telling herself she was doing the right thing by staying committed to Tracy, but how was it right if she still yearned for someone else?

"It was an excellent suggestion. I would have never gone out otherwise," Zuri said, dropping on the bed as soon as they got upstairs.

"That's why I said we should do it. You need to get your mind off of all of that nonsense at the studio. It'll blow over soon." Tracy slipped on a robe after getting undressed and climbed on the bed. She moved Zuri so that her head was in her lap. "Once it's proven that your godfather acted on his own, you all will be off the hook."

"Simple as that, huh?"

"Yeah, simple as that."

Zuri closed her eyes as Tracy massaged her temples. "I think I'm going to visit Francis," Zuri said. It had been on her mind to do so already, but talking about him made the idea concrete in her mind.

Tracy stopped massaging her. "Why would you do that?"

"I want to know why he did what he did." Zuri sat up on her elbows. "It's important to me."

"What difference does it make why Z? The fact remains, he did it. You know, he knows, and now the world knows. The only thing this will do is possibly bring more unnecessary attention to you and Ellis Films."

Zuri sat up. "That may be, but I've been doing what I can to ensure it won't happen again. I've already started working on rooting out any other questionable people on our staff and we are going to implement new policies."

Tracy sucked her teeth and climbed off of the bed. "I just don't understand why you would jeopardize us for a pervert."

"Jeopardize us? Last time I checked, my cousins and I own the studio," Zuri said.

"I am well aware of that, but any future you and I have depends on it," Tracy said as she went into the bathroom.

Fiona's comment about Tracy treating her as the "long game" for her future popped into her mind. She wanted to believe that most of what she said was just the talk of a bitter ex, but maybe not. Perhaps their relationship had felt too good to be true because it was.

"Were you in a relationship with Fiona?" Zuri asked.

"What?" Tracy called out from the bathroom. She appeared in the doorway, brushing her teeth. "Why are you asking me about Fiona?"

"Just answer the question, Tracy. Were the two of you in a romantic relationship?"

Tracy stepped back inside to rinse her mouth out, then reappeared in the doorway. Zuri could see by her expression that she was deciding how much to tell her.

"We had a transactional relationship. She did things for me, and I would accompany her to premiers and parties. Sometimes we would have sex, but there were never any emotions involved. Whatever she told you, I never led her on."

"So you were what, an escort?"

"Don't be crass," Tracy said, stepping into the bedroom. "We were dating, but she wasn't someone I saw myself with long term, so I kept things casual."

"You mean you used her?"

Tracy threw her hands in the air. "Call it what you like, but she was aware of the parameters of our relationship ."

Zuri quieted as she tried to process what Tracy was telling her. "Why have you never told me this?" she asked.

Tracy sighed as she sat next to her."Didn't seem relevant."

"So you were never with her after you got with me?"

"No, of course not. I would never do that..."

Zuri stared at her. "So when you stood me up for Sundance, you weren't in Aspen with her?"

Tracy froze like a deer in headlights. She didn't think Fiona would tell her that little tidbit, but whatever hold she used to have on the other woman appeared to have ended.

"That was so early in our relationship..."

"One year, we were together at that point, not that early." Zuri got up and stood in front of her. "Why did you decide that now was the time to commit to me?"

"Does the time matter? I love you and want us to be together," Tracy said, reaching for her.

Zuri stepped back and shook her head. "It took me a while to figure out what was going on, but when Fiona spoke to me, it all clicked. You're in your mid-40s, roles are changing for you, and soon the calls are going to slow down to a trickle. You're still beautiful, but with each passing year, your light dims."

"Stop it," Tracy said, a slight quiver in her voice.

"You would have never considered a tv role back in the day, but now the movie roles are few. This last shoot is what, your first film role in over a year?"

"Zuri..."

"I'm your insurance plan. With my connections and money, you would never have to worry again. There would be roles and if you stopped, it would be on your terms. All the while, you got to screw around with whoever you wanted while I panted after you like a dog in heat." Zuri dropped to the balls of her feet so they would be face to face. "Are you even in love with me?"

"I love you, Z, I do," Tracy said, raising her hands to cup her face.

"That's not what I asked," Zuri said. She pressed her hands on top of Tracy's. "I said, are you in love with me? If you care about me, please be honest."

Tracy pursed her lips together. Tears fell from her eyes as she said, "I love you so much, but no, I'm not in love with you."

Zuri's head spun as she stood and moved away. Her body jerked as she sobbed. Tears wet her shirt.

What did she expect? All the questions she asked were leading to this, and everything inside her told her it was true. That's why she kept putting off having the conversation. Now, for once, Tracy had been honest with her. Somehow she hadn't expected it to hurt as bad as it did.

Tracy followed her. "Please, baby. Falling in love takes time. I'm sure it will happen eventually..."

"Time? What the hell do you think I've been doing these past five years?" Zuri screamed. "I gave up someone wonderful because of an obligation to you, and you stand there and say you could fall in love? After everything I've sacrificed of myself to love you?"

"Someone? Do you mean Genesis? You can't be serious; she's not in your league," Tracy said, her voice dripping with venom. When she saw the look on Zuri's face, her face dropped again. "Baby, I'm sorry. Please don't do this."

Zuri swiped the tears from her face, her mouth tight with anger. "You can stay here until you leave for London, but I am done. I'll be in the guest room."

Tracy followed behind her, but Zuri slammed the door to the guest room and locked it. Tracy would get tired and retreat.

Zuri sat down and breathed in and out slowly. She needed

to calm herself so that she could think rationally. A getaway would be useful, but she didn't want to go to Barbados. There, she would have too much time alone and memories of her time with Genesis were sure to plague her. So she picked up her cell and dialed a number she hadn't used for far too long.

"Hello? Z, is everything okay?"

"Mom, I need you."

Chapter Twenty-Four

Genesis grabbed a couple of boxes out of Shannon's car and brought them into the house. She expected her to only bring a couple of suitcases with clothes, but she had forgotten the number of things she owned. As long as it all fit into the spare bedroom, she figured it would be fine.

"This is so awesome," Kenzie said as she bounced into the house with a box.

Days after Genesis agreed to let Shannon stay with her, she got a call from Kenzie. Of course, her sister assumed that this was a clear sign they were getting back together. No matter how many times she told her that wasn't happening, she continued to insist, to where Genesis had to let it drop.

"Thanks again, Genesis, seriously," Shannon said as she walked into the house.

"You don't have to keep thanking me. I know you would do the same," Genesis said, squeezing her arm. "So, what's going on with your condo?"

"I did a short-term rental. So I have someone staying for the next three months."

"That sounds perfect. Oh, and I took Monday off so I can go

with you to your first appointment. I'll need the dates for your other visits, and Kenzie and I can trade off on times we'll be able to go with you."

Shannon nodded her head, and Genesis could see she was tearing up.

"Okay, you big baby. Don't go getting all emotional on me."

"I'm sorry," Shannon said. She laughed and wiped her eyes. "You two mean so much to me, and I'm grateful for this. You'll never know how much."

"Well, you can show it by letting our little sister know that we are not getting back together."

A look of guilt passed over Shannon's face, and Genesis smacked her arm.

"Please don't say you told her we were?"

"No, I didn't say that explicitly, but I might have said something like never say never," Shannon said with a shrug.

"Shay, you can't get her hopes up like that."

"I know, but," Shannon took Genesis's hand in hers, "it's not impossible, is it?"

Genesis wished she could outright say no, but after what happened with Olivia and Zuri, Shannon's familiarity didn't seem so bad. She would need to make amends for how she ended their marriage, along with other changes, but Genesis was no longer opposed to the idea. If Zuri could choose the easier route, why couldn't she?

"How about we get you moved in and save that discussion for later?"

Shannon grinned. "You didn't say no," she said with a wink.

Genesis laughed. "That's right; I didn't say no."

* * *

A couple of days later, Genesis got called into her manager David's office. She could tell by his demeanor that he didn't have good news. Instead of tearing up or getting angry as he informed her they were letting her go, she felt free. When he gave her a date for her last day, she told him she wanted to leave at the end of the week. He didn't argue with her. There was no point in dragging it out any longer than it had to be.

That Friday, as she exited the building, she took a deep breath and happily skipped to her car. Anyone who saw her would have assumed she had gotten a promotion, not a pink slip. Lucy had offered to take her out for drinks. She felt terrible for being so happy about staying on earlier in the week, but Genesis declined. Rain had been in touch and wanted to see her, and she figured that would be a less sad affair.

When she pulled up to the Ellis Studio movie lot, her mind automatically went to Zuri. She knew she might see her, and she wasn't sure how she felt about it. They had not spoken since that night at the club. At first, Zuri's response hurt her when she told her how she felt. Still, after thinking about it, she appreciated the fact that Zuri was loyal to Tracy. It showed what type of character she possessed, and even though the outcome wasn't what she wanted, she respected her choice.

"Hey sweetheart," Genesis said, running up to Rain.

"Gen, I am so happy to see you. Seriously," Rain said as she hugged her.

"You okay?" she asked.

"Yeah." Rain nodded yes, but her body language said otherwise. "I just need a break away from set life. It's been intense. Let's go; I already made reservations at Ravi's."

Genesis followed behind Rain in her sports car. Ravi's was a popular Indian restaurant that had opened up only a few months ago. Like many new upscale places in Los Angeles, the buzz before it opened meant insane waiting lists to get in. Of course, that didn't apply to people like Rain. So when she called only that morning for a table, they found one.

"So they hold tables for celebrities, right?" Genesis asked, looking around to see who else might be there.

"Weekends are super busy, but they always leave some tables open." Rain ordered them a bottle of wine. "The menu prices are ridiculous, but don't worry; I got it."

Genesis glanced at the price of the meal she was interested in, and her eyes bugged out of her head. "People pay these prices?"

Rain laughed. "Of course, so they can say they ate here. Look at them; half of the people here aren't even eating; they're just taking selfies and pics of their plates," she said.

When Genesis looked around, she realized that Rain was right. Most people were documenting their time there instead of enjoying it.

"God, that must be tedious," Genesis said, turning back to Rain. "Why aren't you doing the same?"

"Because I don't give a fuck," Rain said with a boisterous laugh. "My agent hates that I'm not more engaged with my audience. But guess what? They love that I'm a mystery. When I post on social media, it's shit I care about and the occasional pic. You should see the likes I get. I've got a ridiculous amount of followers. I post when I feel like it, and they eat it up."

"You know what? You are a mess, but I love it."

The server came back with the bottle of wine, poured some out for them, and then sat it on ice.

"So, what's new with you?" Rain asked after taking a sip.

"Well, I am officially unemployed," Genesis said with a grin.

"Wait; what? Oh my God, I'm so sorry." Rain's face scrunched up in confusion. "Why do you look so happy about it?"

"Because I am. For the first time in my life, I don't have a plan. I don't have to worry about how my choices affect someone else, and I can do something that I want. It's an amazing feeling." Genesis felt herself tearing up. "I'm sorry, but I had to sacrifice so much after my parents died and honestly, even before them. I don't regret it at all, I did what I had to do, but man, does it feel good to be selfish for once."

Rain raised her glass for a toast. "Well, here's to being selfish."

"I can drink to that," Genesis said as their glasses connected. "So, how are things going with Jackson?"

Rain rolled her eyes. "I don't want to talk about him. Things have been awful, but we are making it work. When you see the final cut of the film, you will believe we are in love, and that's what matters."

"I'm sorry, Rain, I know how much you like him."

Rain sighed and said, "It is what it is. I'm sure he won't be the last man to break my heart."

Although she wasn't wrong, it made her sad that someone her age had already given up. "You're too young to be so pessimistic."

Rain made a face. "You call it pessimistic; I call it realistic. Anyway, what's going on with you and Zuri?"

The abrupt change to talk of Zuri threw Genesis off. "Um, nothing at the moment."

"I spoke to her before she left for France, and she was all cryptic. Something about mistakes and hurting people. She didn't elaborate, so..."

Although it didn't change how she felt about what happened between them, it felt good to hear that Zuri had regrets.

"It's nothing, we decided, or rather I decided, that it would be better if we stopped communicating. Things were getting confusing, and I just didn't want to put myself through it anymore."

"Hmm, interesting," Rain said.

The waiter brought over their meal, and they were quiet for a while as they ate. Even though the food seemed overpriced, Genesis had to admit it was delicious.

"You mentioned that Zuri went to France?" Genesis said.

"Yeah, a couple of weeks ago. It's not like her to just leave on short notice, but she said she needed to see her parents. I don't know if it was to get advice about this sexual misconduct thing or what, but she hasn't come back yet," Rain said, pouring dressing on her salad.

Genesis drank some wine. "That doesn't sound like her at all."

"Yeah, but Reggie and Eli are smart, so they'll hold it down, I'm sure. I know the staff is concerned about their jobs because of the scandal. No one is sure how this is going to affect the studio."

"Did you know about what was going on?"

"About Francis? Oh, I knew he was a creepy old man. He was always shaking your hand and holding it just a touch too long, lingering looks and off-putting suggestive jokes. But I thought that was the extent of it; I didn't know he was forcing women to have sex with him. There are plenty of men who will borderline harass you, but he took it to another level."

"I'm sorry you had to deal with this at your age. Why didn't you tell anyone?"

Rain stopped eating. "Are you serious? Gen, you are told not to say anything in a not-so-subtle way. So you keep your head low and try to avoid the pitfalls. Men like Francis can make or break a young star's career. The Me Too movement has made strides, and some people are being held accountable. Still, it's going to take quite a while before this ends."

"I didn't even think of that. Has anyone ever...?"

"Tried to get me to screw them for a part?" Rain picked up her glass and took a long sip. "How much time do you have?"

"Awww, Rain, that's awful."

"Don't worry; I never said yes, and the damage was minimal."

"Did Zuri know what was happening to you?"

"No, but she guessed at it with a few roles I didn't get. She had some words for certain people," Rain said with a smile. "She's always protected me as much as she could, but it's a cold world out here."

"Well, you've got one more protector in me. I might not have any pull in Hollywood, but I can teach you some mean self-defense moves."

Rain laughed. "Thanks, Gen. That's sweet. Maybe I'll take you up on it," she said, doing a karate chop in the air.

They both broke into laughter and continued to eat and laugh late into the night.

* * *

As she drove home, Genesis reflected on her conversation with Rain. It was heartbreaking to hear what she had to go through to make it in the industry. Had Zuri not taken her under her wing, there was no telling what direction her story would have gone.

Thinking of Zuri made her wonder what was going on with her. They hadn't spoken because she kept her word and refused to reach out, but that didn't mean she stopped caring. Zuri was many things, but impulsive wasn't one of them, so she hoped everything was alright.

When Genesis walked into the house, she was greeted by the scent of cinnamon. That meant Shannon had made a pot of a delicious concoction she created using almond milk, cinnamon, vanilla, and nutmeg. It was a delicious alternative to hot chocolate, and it had been a long time since she had any.

"Hey beautiful, how was your last day?" Shannon asked, turning away from the television.

"Kind of great," Genesis said, walking into the living room. She sat down and laid her head on Shannon's shoulder. "I am a free agent."

Shannon laughed. "That always sounded way better than it was back in the league. Scrambling to find a team, hoping people still wanted you around."

"Yeah, but the freedom to decide where you want to be? That's priceless."

"True, true. You want a glass?" Shannon asked, raising her empty mug. "I'm about to have some more."

"Yes, please. It's the perfect way to end this week."

"Okay, coming right up," she said, kissing Genesis's forehead.

The gesture brought back memories of their time together. Was this what she wanted? It felt good; it felt familiar, but did she want it to be her future?

Chapter Twenty-Five

Zuri sat on the balcony of her parent's guest room and sipped on a coffee. Even though she would have loved to stay indefinitely, her trip had gone on two weeks too long. With no notice, her departure baffled her cousins. To appease them, she was using her time there for work. They were thinking of shooting an upcoming film in Paris, so she was doing the location scouting. It gave her something to do other than stare at the walls in the room.

When she first arrived, her parents tried to get her to talk, but she wasn't up to it, and she wasn't sure where to begin.

There wasn't much in her life that hadn't gone according to plan. She attended the right schools, hung around the right people, and even though owning a studio wasn't easy, she never doubted it would be a success. Her pedigree and that of her family almost guaranteed it.

Now, with the allegations against her godfather, everything was in limbo. There was no guarantee that Ellis Films would make it out unscathed, and although the private investigator she hired had yet to find any other evidence of misconduct, they weren't off the hook.

The situation with Tracy was just an added stressor. Zuri had been so sure that she was doing the right thing, giving her the benefit of the doubt and committing to a relationship. Now, to find out it was all a lie had broken her, but she didn't blame Tracy for that. She had gone along with it out of loyalty to the woman she had loved, but the reality was those feelings had changed long ago. They were both playing a part, so it was no wonder it had all gone to shit.

"Zuri, you awake?"

The sound of her mother's voice startled Zuri back to the present. Her parents were respecting her space, and even though they could tell something had to be wrong for her to reach out, they still had left her alone. She figured before she departed, she owed them an explanation.

"Yeah, mom, I'm up. I'll be down in a few for breakfast."

Her parents lived in a top-floor apartment in an old Parisian apartment building. It was a three-bedroom, two bath, with a spectacular view of the Seine, a river that flowed through Paris. Multiple rooms opened onto the continuous balcony that she had been sitting on, and light flowed throughout the apartment. It was a gorgeous place they purchased back in the early '90s at the height of both their careers. When her mother started working less, and her father became pickier about the films he directed, they retired there. Retire was a strong word since they both still worked, but it was only on projects that inspired them.

"Nice to see you've graced us with your presence," her father said, glancing up from his newspaper.

"Morning, dad," Zuri said, leaning down to kiss his cheek. "I've been in such a mood in the morning that I'm sure you wouldn't have wanted me around."

"Maybe we miss your surly early morning behavior," her mother said, kissing her forehead. "Reminds us of your teen years, right Fred?"

"Oh yes, we miss those days of you sitting and shoving cereal in your mouth while scowling at us," Frederick said with a smirk.

Zuri pretended to scowl, and her parents laughed. Such lighthearted interactions with them were still new. Years of reprimanding and judgment had trained her to expect their disapproval, but now they seemed indifferent to it all. It was jarring.

After pouring more coffee, Zuri settled at the table, and her mother handed her a plate with scrambled eggs and a croissant.

"So, are you going to talk to us about what's going on with Francis?" Veronique asked, sitting down.

"I know about as much as you do. Investigators have been to the studio and spoken with us, but we aren't privy to what information they have."

"I can't believe he would do that to you, our child," Frederick said, slamming his paper down in disgust. "I'm the reason that man even has a career, and this is how he repays me?"

"Dad, this isn't just about us. He hurt women, quite a few of them, and it was going on even before he was at Ellis Films."

Veronique reached out and rubbed Zuri's hand. "We understand, sweetheart, we're just hurt. With us being here, we thought it was wonderful that Francis was working at the studio. He was like a second father to you, and we thought he would watch out for you, not use your company as a hunting ground."

Zuri pushed the salt shaker on the table between her hands. "Have either of you spoken to him?"

Veronique looked at Frederick, and he nodded. "I did, but it wasn't a productive conversation."

"I think I want to see him when I get back." She could see the disapproval in her parents' faces. "I need answers."

They were both quiet for a moment, then Veronique patted her hand. "You do whatever you think is best, my darling."

* * *

A couple of hours later, Zuri strolled along the Promenade Plantée. An old railway turned park; it featured greenery flanking the sides and multiple iron archways throughout. It was full of people on a typical day, but the chilly March air meant far fewer visitors.

Zuri snapped pictures as she walked, capturing the stunning architecture that surrounded the area. The spot was perfect for the romantic comedy she had in mind.

"Seeing you with that camera reminds me of when you were in grade school."

Zuri turned to see her mother standing not too far away. With the sun peeking out from behind the clouds, hitting her just right, Veronique glowed. Even in her 70s, she was still gorgeous. At 5'10, she was tall and just as slender as she had been in her youth. Her skin was a magnificent cocoa brown that Zuri used to envy; she had inherited her father's reddish-brown complexion. When she was a teen, she could remember feeling ugly standing next to her statuesque mother with her dazzling smile and perfect skin. Now, most people said she looked like her twin.

"Mom, what are you doing here?"

"I wanted to make sure we had time to talk before you left for LA. You were hiding away most of your time here, so I figured you needed that space," Veronique said. She walked up to Zuri and placed a gloved hand against her cheek. "Talk to me, sweetheart."

Zuri leaned into her hand, and tears fell. It wasn't often that she needed comfort, but this time, she did, and from her mother in particular.

"Oh, Zuri." Veronique pulled her to a nearby bench and let

her cry into her shoulder as she whispered soothing words to her.

After a few minutes, the tears subsided, and Zuri calmed down enough to speak.

"Mom, have you ever regretted a decision right after you made it?"

Veronique smiled. "More times than I care to admit."

"I ended things with Tracy," Zuri said. She brought the camera from around her neck. "Things seemed perfect, but it was all a lie."

"I'm sorry to hear that Z, I know you cared for her very much."

Zuri caught the tone in her mother's voice. "But you didn't?"

Veronique folded her hands in her lap. "Tracy reminded me of many actresses I've known over the years. Very good at selling themselves, but not willing to let anyone into their inner life. She was nice, but I didn't think she was all that into you."

"Why didn't you ever say that to me?"

"Darling, would you have listened to me if I did?"

Zuri shook her head no. It was true; anything she might have said to her would have fallen on deaf ears.

"So, you regret breaking up with her?" Veronique asked.

"No, the regret was from choosing her. I met someone else in the summer, but Tracy made me believe that we could have what I always wanted. So I rejected the unknown out of loyalty to Tracy; it was undeserved."

"You did what you believed was right with the information you had. As much as this might surprise you, you're human."

Zuri chuckled and leaned against her mom. "That might be true, but I hurt Genesis in the process."

"Genesis? I'm intrigued already."

Zuri told her mom about how they met and their time in Barbados. As she was recounting everything, memories came flooding back along with the emotions. She had wasted the last several months when she could have been enjoying them with Gen.

"Well, she sounds lovely, and if you think she's someone you could have a future with, then go after her. If she cares about you, she'll give you a chance."

"You think so?" Zuri asked.

Veronique caressed her cheek. "I know so, my beautiful girl." She sat back and looked out over the horizon. "I've been waiting for this type of conversation for years. Forty years old, and this is the first time you've come to me for advice."

"I'm sorry, mom, I am. It's just; you made it clear that you didn't care for my choices in many areas of my life, including my love of women."

"I didn't say that expecting an apology." She turned back to Zuri. "Your father and I should apologize to you, but since I'm here, I want to say I'm sorry. We put a lot of pressure on you as our only child, and it wasn't fair. Even with women, I thought it would make your life harder, but it was me doing that. You carved your path despite us, and you're amazing. I hope that from this point forward, we can make up for the lost time."

Zuri grabbed her mother and hugged her close. "Of course, mom, you don't even have to ask."

They sat a bit longer chatting and talking about many of the things Zuri had kept to herself over the years. It was nice being able to share with her mom with no judgment.

Veronique stayed with her as she took more pictures and met with some people to inquire about using the promenade. Then they walked arm in arm to have lunch in a small cafe.

* * *

ONE MONTH LATER

Zuri stared at the clock on her office wall. She wanted to leave, but was less than enthusiastic about going home.

After pulling out her phone from her bag, she tapped on Genesis's name, something she had been doing for the past couple of weeks. Their last set of messages from the night at the club were still there.

She missed her, and their lack of contact had made everything that much harder. *Text her.* Her hand hovered over the keyboard, but she couldn't bring herself to do it. If she didn't respond, it would devastate her. But, if she wanted Genesis, she would have to fight for her, which would not happen by sulking.

That's why an hour later, she found herself in front of Genesis's house. It was larger than she expected and did not fit Gen's style at all. Her ex must have chosen it. After giving herself a pep talk, she got out of the car and sauntered towards the front door.

After ringing the doorbell, she patiently waited. There was always a chance Genesis wouldn't be there, but she hoped she was. A dog began barking on the other side, then the door opened. Instead of the woman she had been daydreaming about for weeks, another very tall one opened the door. It took her a moment, but then she recognized who it was.

"Shannon Colbert?"

"Yeah, that's me. Can I help you?" Shannon said, narrowing her eyes.

"I'm sorry, uh, I'm a friend of Genesis. I stopped by to say hi; my name is Zuri," she said, sticking out her hand.

"Oh, ok, Gen is at the grocery store but nice to meet you." Shannon shook her hand. "You want to come inside and wait for her? She should be back in a few."

Zuri's instinct was to say no, but she needed to stay and tell Genesis what was on her mind or else she might talk herself out of it. So she followed Shannon into the house and took a seat in the living room.

"Can I get you something to drink?" Shannon asked.

"Sure, some water, thanks."

She looked around the home. It was spacious and modern, a bit too pedestrian for her tastes, but it was open and inviting. The dog whose barking she heard padded up to her and stared for a bit. A gorgeous Siberian Husky. Her size was intimidating, but her presence was one of calm. Zuri put her hand out, and after a minute, she walked up to her and sniffed it. Apparently, she thought she was okay because she nuzzled her and indicated she wanted to be petted.

As she happily rubbed the dog's gorgeous fur, the front door slammed and caused her to turn around. Her breath caught in her throat when she saw Genesis, who had placed her bags down and took off her coat.

Done with her, the dog ran to greet its master. "Hello, my baby. How are you?" Genesis said, dropping to scratch behind her ears. "Shay, do you have company? There's a car parked out front."

Genesis stood up and turned, their eyes meeting for the first time in over a month. A myriad of emotions played out on her face; joy, anger, confusion.

"Zuri, what are you doing here?" Genesis said.

Zuri stood up and strolled over to her. "What I should have done seven months ago." She placed her hand over her heart. "I'm hoping you'll go on a date with me."

Genesis didn't respond as Zuri stood in front of her and picked up her hand. Shannon reappeared, but they were so caught up in staring at each other, neither looked away. She cleared her throat, and they turned to her.

"Uh, here's that water you wanted," she said, handing a glass to Zuri.

Shannon excused herself, and Zuri noted that Genesis still had not let go of her hand.

"Let's go to the backyard and talk, okay?" Genesis said.

She walked towards the back of the house, still holding Zuri's hand. Happier than she had been for a while, Zuri followed behind, grinning from ear to ear.

Chapter Twenty-Six

Genesis tried her damndest not to look back at Zuri. The heat from her eyes followed her as they walked to the back of the house. That she was even in her home had Genesis flustered, but she tried to keep her cool.

"I hear you were in Paris," Genesis said as she slid open the doors to the backyard.

"Yeah, went to visit my folks for a bit. Had to work some things out." Zuri gestured towards the house. "So, Shannon, huh? Are you two back together or..."

"You care about that after asking me out in front of her?" she said with a raised eyebrow.

Zuri smiled. "I wasn't thinking straight, but you're right. No doubt I would not be here right now if that were so."

"She's staying here because she isn't well and can't be alone while getting treatment. We've talked about the future, but I'm not sure what I want right now."

Zuri looked at the ground. "You seemed sure a few weeks ago."

"Yeah, well, you made it obvious you didn't feel the same."

Genesis led her to the patio, and they sat opposite each

other on the benches. Neither said a word and since she wasn't the one seeking forgiveness, Genesis stayed quiet. Instead, her eyes roamed over Zuri as she sat across from her, looking fine as ever.

Zuri's locs were down and fuller than usual, which meant she wasn't maintaining them as often. They framed her face in such a way that they reminded Genesis of a lion's mane. It seemed fitting, and it only made her look sexier.

"So, I realize that I came out of nowhere appearing here." Zuri rubbed her hands on her pants. "I should explain myself."

"That's an understatement. Last time we hung out, you told me in no uncertain terms that nothing was going to happen between us."

Zuri looked down. "I did."

Genesis folded her arms. "I care about you, Z, but I deserve better than being stuck in an emotional limbo."

"I broke up with Tracy," Zuri said.

"Oh, when did that happen?" Genesis said, unfolding her arms.

"A month ago, around the time I left for Paris. I needed time to get my mind right."

"I'm sorry to hear that. Breakups are hard when you've given years to someone," Genesis said, standing up, "but I can't do this with you."

Zuri furrowed her brow. "What do you mean? That's over with; I came here because I want to be with you."

Genesis scoffed and threw her hands up. "I don't want to be a rebound, okay? You need to want me, not settle because Tracy didn't give you what you wanted."

"Tracy and I had something, but it changed a while ago. I was in love with the idea of us, but not the reality. That's what kept me blind for so long."

Zuri appeared sincere, but their last exchange was still fresh in her mind. She had already rejected her twice.

"I'm glad that you figured the situation out for yourself, but I don't know if you're ready for me."

"Genesis." Zuri reached out and grabbed her hand, pulling her until they were close to each other. She stood up to her full height and ran her hand through Genesis's hair. "I was going to give it time, but I realized I didn't want to any longer. I want you. Genesis, please."

"Don't do that," Genesis said, her voice barely above a whisper.

"Do what?" Zuri asked, moving closer.

"Say my name that way."

"What way?" Zuri let her free hand trail down to her hip while she kept her other hand in her hair. "I swear these curls drive me crazy."

Genesis wanted to be strong enough to push her away, but it was hard to think straight with her so close. *Don't say my name like you're in love with me. Don't break my heart.* She refused to say what was on her mind out loud. Not that it mattered, anyway; she was gone over her already.

"Have dinner with me," Zuri said, her lips dangerously close.

"What if I say no?"

Zuri looked into her eyes and said, "Please, have dinner with me."

"I like hearing you beg," Genesis said, biting her lip.

"Well, in that case, please, please, please," Zuri said, kissing her way down Genesis's cheek to her neck.

The kiss she placed on her neck was so tender that she had to shut her eyes against a flood of emotions. "Yes," she said. Genesis opened her eyes to find Zuri staring at her.

"Okay," Zuri said, stepping back. "I'll pick you up here tomorrow night at 8. Is that good for you?"

"That's fine," Genesis said, startled by the abrupt change.

After sending for a cab, Genesis walked Zuri to the door. They kissed each other's cheeks and waved goodbye. It was so polite after what had been a sensual exchange, but that was for the best. She had been on the verge of dragging her upstairs ever since she laid eyes on her.

Genesis padded into the kitchen and poured herself a glass of water. After gulping it down, she stood there in the dark and reflected on what had just happened. She never believed Zuri would choose her, and she had come to terms with that. Now they had a date, and she was excited but nervous.

Tracy was nothing like her, and if that was who had held Zuri's attention for so many years, how was she supposed to compete?

Genesis was well aware of the reasons she liked Zuri. The other woman was worldly, smart, comfortable with who she was, and a gentlewoman in every sense of the word. Not just because of her social standing and class, but in her behavior. When they were around each other, Genesis felt taken care of in a way she never had with Shannon.

Shay showed she cared by controlling everything so that her loved ones wouldn't have to think about it. Instead of a sense of security, it had left her feeling voiceless and ignored.

Genesis looked into the living room and saw Shannon was watching an NBA game. While she seemed to enjoy her post-basketball career, there was a part of her that still missed playing. How could she not? It had been her life since they were teenagers.

"Looks like another blowout for Denver, huh?" Genesis walked over to the couch and leaned on the back.

"Yeah, looks like it," Shannon mumbled.

Already able to tell that she was in a mood, Genesis turned to head upstairs. "I'm gonna get ready for bed," she said, waiting for a response.

Shannon continued to stare at the television with her jaw clenched. Not interested in indulging her attitude, Genesis called to Kuma and headed upstairs. As soon as she saw Zuri in the house, she was positive it would be an issue, but had hoped her ex would at least give her time before throwing a hissy fit.

Kuma climbed into her bed as Genesis undressed, went into the master bath, and started the water. After covering her hair in a shower cap, she shut the door and breathed in the steam. She let the hot water cascade down her back. Her entire body relaxed, and she placed her hands against the shower wall as she leaned into it.

With the steady pressure of the shower against her lower back, she thought about Zuri's hands on her earlier. Her touch was unobtrusive but firm and so sexy.

It made her wonder what those hands would be like on her naked body. Was she the same when she made love? She clenched at the thought, and her hand followed the path of the water, skimming her thighs.

"Hey Gen, are you almost done?" Shannon called out, knocking on the bathroom door.

Startled, Genesis let out an irritated sigh. "I'll be out in ten."

Fantasy interrupted; she grabbed her washcloth and bathed. When she finished, she exited the bathroom and found Shannon sitting on her bed, scrolling through her phone. She wrapped her towel tighter around her body.

How many times over the years had she been naked in Shannon's presence? Yet she was uncomfortable. She would have made a joke about it if there wasn't so much tension in the air.

"You startled me," Genesis said as she dug through her drawers for something to wear.

"Sorry, the game finished, so I figured maybe I should come up and talk." Shannon placed her phone down. "So, who is Zuri?"

Genesis stepped into the walk-in closet to change and apply some lotion. She left the door ajar so that Shannon could hear her. "We met while I was in Barbados. She owned the house I stayed at and was there at the same time."

"You never mentioned her before, but she came in here like she knows you well. Not just as a house guest."

Genesis rubbed lotion on her arms and chose her next words carefully. "We became friends while we were there, and there was something between us, but she had a girlfriend until recently."

Without seeing Shannon's expression, Genesis judged her response by her words or lack thereof.

After a couple of minutes, Shannon said, "I thought you and I were going to try again."

Genesis pulled her shirt down over her head. The sadness in Shay's voice made her feel bad, but there was no point in sugar-coating the situation. She walked out of the closet and placed her towel on the closest chair. "I never told you it was definite."

Shannon jerked her head back. "Wow, okay. I guess I deserve that." She got up and began pacing. Her face looked pained, as if she was struggling to find the words she wanted to say. "I fucked up, but I wanted to make it right."

Genesis took her spot on the bed and curled her feet underneath. " I don't owe you another chance, Shannon."

"When you said I could come back here..."

"Before you even say it," Genesis said, cutting her off, "I said for you to come back here while you were getting your treatments. Between you and Kenzie, I'm sick of my words being twisted and ignored."

Shannon dropped to her knees and grabbed hold of Genesis's hands. "It's obvious you're still mad at me; I get that. But if you give me a chance, things would be even better than before."

Genesis pulled her hands away. "You don't get it. The day you left me, you broke my heart, you broke us, and there's no way to repair that. I'm ready to move on."

Looking defeated, Shannon stood up and rubbed the back of her neck. "So, that's it, then?"

"Yeah, that's it."

"Alright, I guess I'll let you get to bed."

Genesis watched as she shuffled away. If Zuri hadn't shown up, over time, she would have let Shannon back in because it was easy, but it wasn't what she needed from her.

"What was so great about our relationship, anyway?" Genesis asked.

Shannon stopped in the doorway and turned around. "What do you mean?"

"I mean, you were controlling in every sense of the word. It never felt like you valued my opinion about anything. Even this house. I hated it when we attended that open house, and you said I would grow to like it. You didn't even let me have a say in where we were going to live." Genesis scoffed at the memory. "Is that what you liked? That I accepted my place without question?"

Shannon walked back into the room. "You were my wife, and I felt one of us had to be the head of household, so I took on that role. If you hated it so much, why was I the one who left?"

"You were all I knew," Genesis said, raising her voice. "And we could have run our home together. It didn't have to be your way or no way. I didn't hate it, but I was not happy. I was just too weak to leave."

Shannon flinched and ran her hand over her head. "You weren't weak, Gen, never have been. You're one of the strongest people I know. Why do you think I'm here? I'm truly sorry I ever made you feel anything other than special because you are. You deserved better, and I came back because I wanted to love you the way I should have before."

Genesis got up and walked over to Shannon. "We can't change the past, Shay, and our time is over, but that doesn't mean we can't be there for each other. You and Kenzie are all I have."

"And Zuri now too, it seems," Shannon said with a sad chuckle.

"Yeah, so it seems. That doesn't change what you've meant to me."

Shannon reached out, and she walked into her arms. It felt like home, and she understood that this is what they needed from each other. Not romance, but the love of family, and that was just as important.

Chapter Twenty-Seven

"Ooh, wear this," Alma said, holding up a pants suit. "It's screams power lesbian."

Zuri laughed and gave her best friend the middle finger. "I am powerful, and I don't need a suit to say that for me. Besides, that's for work. Tonight is all about sexy and carefree."

Eyeing the three outfits she had laid out on her bed, Zuri tried to guess what Genesis would like. Each dress was sexy without being over the top, but none of them felt right.

"Forget all of this." Zuri went back into her closet and came out with a pair of slim dark Levi's, a plum silk button-down shirt, and heels.

"Um, that doesn't scream I want to sleep with you, but okay," Alma said, with an eye roll.

"Good! I want to sleep with her, but I also think it would be nice just to hang out." Zuri thought about their trip to the film festival a few months back. "We've had a fancy rooftop dinner. I just want to be near her and have fun. Every interaction doesn't have to be about trying to impress her."

Alma pretended to gag. "Ugh, that was almost sweet enough to give me a cavity."

Zuri leaned into her vanity mirror. "Whatever, you're the one who's been advocating for me to leave Tracy and get with Genesis. So all of this sappiness is your fault," she said, turning to point her eyeliner pen at Alma.

"This is true," Alma said. She dropped on Zuri's bed after moving her clothes. "But I'm happy you did it. It was time to move on from Tracy."

Zuri's chest constricted at the memory of their confrontation. " I cared about her and thought what we had was real. Instead, she was just biding time until she got a ring."

Alma got up and walked over to Zuri. She hugged her from behind and looked at her in the mirror.

"It's okay to be sad about what could have been, but you are going to be fine. I may have only met her once, but from what you've told me, Genesis is a good person."

Zuri leaned into her: "Thank you, Alma."

"So, since we're talking about new relationships, I have a confession to make."

"You're dating someone," Zuri said.

Alma's eyes opened wide. "How did you guess?"

Zuri raised an eyebrow and said, "You asked to borrow Metropolis. It's a wonderful movie, but I knew you didn't suddenly develop an interest in German silent films."

"That is 100% true. Anyway, his name is Nathaniel, and he's a film buff. He mentioned the movie, so I thought I would impress him." Alma dropped back down on the bed and sighed. "I like him."

Zuri grabbed her clothes. "And that's a bad thing because…"

"He's so damn nice and polite. I'm always afraid I'm going to say something to turn him off. You know me, Z, I have a reckless mouth."

Zuri laughed out loud. It was true, Alma was brash and brutally honest, but she always found that to be a part of her charm.

"Listen, if he's the guy for you, then he'll like you, regardless."

Zuri excused herself as she went inside the bathroom to get dressed. After putting her hair up, Zuri stepped back into the bedroom.

"Damn Z, I was wrong about the outfit. Are those jeans painted on?" Alma said with a wink.

"I told you it's not the outfit. It's the one wearing it," Zuri said, snapping her fingers. "Now, let's go. I don't want to keep my lady waiting."

* * *

Zuri thanked the server as she sat at a reserved table. She chose a small bistro that was casual but still upscale.

Genesis seemed pleased when she told her that there was no need to dress too fancy. She also wanted something more low-key. As long as they got to spend time together, Zuri would do whatever she wanted.

Her eyes were on the menu when she looked up and saw Genesis walking towards her. Even after knowing her for almost a year, she still took her breath away.

"Hey," Genesis said when she got to the table.

"Hey," Zuri replied, trying not to smile too hard. "Let me get that for you."

She jumped up and helped Genesis remove her short leather jacket. Their outfits were similar, jeans and heels, but Genesis wore a soft pink sweater that was a nice contrast against her skin.

"Thanks. Sorry, I'm a bit late. Traffic was insane."

"I don't mind; it was worth it just to see you walking towards me like that. You look beautiful."

Genesis dipped her head down and smiled. "Thank you, so do you. I love your hair that way." She grabbed her menu and started looking over the options. "Any suggestions?"

"I've been here several times; almost everything is good. Their seafood dishes are my favorite."

"You don't own this place, do you?" Genesis asked, a twinkle in her eyes.

Zuri chuckled and shook her head. "Sadly, no, I don't."

The waiter stopped by with the bottle of wine she ordered. He poured some into their glasses and left the bottle on ice. Zuri lifted her glass for a toast, and Genesis followed suit.

"Here's to getting to know each other better," Zuri said.

Genesis stared into Zuri's eyes and said, "I can drink to that."

After they took their first sip of wine, they talked about any and everything. While their conversations had always flowed, this was different. They discussed everything from their favorite colors to which character from the sitcom Martin they most identified with and why President Obama had such effortless swag. It was sweet and what Zuri had hoped it would be.

For dessert, Zuri took her to a shop a couple of blocks away that made their ice cream on site. When they got their orders, they took a stroll in Grand Park.

"This is so good," Genesis said as she took a bite out of her cone.

"You bite your ice cream cones? Damn, I guess we can't be together. I'm a licker myself." Zuri took a long swipe at her ice cream and didn't miss the lustful gaze Genesis sent her way. "Also, your favorite flavor is vanilla?"

Genesis averted her eyes and went back to watching the passersby. "It's a classic, and I have never had bad vanilla, but with other flavors, it's hit, or miss and licking takes too long. If I like something, I want to devour it."

Zuri threw her head back in laughter. "That was subtle, Gen."

Genesis gave her an innocent smile. "I wasn't trying to be dirty. I was just stating a fact."

They took a seat on the first empty bench they found and did some people watching. After talking nonstop for the past couple of hours, Zuri appreciated that they could also enjoy quiet time together.

"This is nice, "Genesis said. "By the way, I lost my job last month."

"Oh man, I'm so sorry. How are you doing for money? Do you need anything?" Zuri said, leaning towards her.

"That's nice of you, but I'm okay. I have a cushion in my savings, and Shannon is helping right now. I'm taking this time to figure out what my next move is going to be. I'm thinking about opening an accounting firm."

"That's ambitious." Genesis gave her a side-eye. "I didn't mean to sound unsupportive. What I meant was, it may sound easy, but going into business for yourself is always more complicated than the average person realizes."

"Well then, good thing I'm dating a successful business-woman," Genesis said with a smirk.

"Are we dating? Will there be more of this?" Zuri said, pointing between the two of them.

Genesis bit her lip. "What do you think?"

Zuri shifted forward until she was close to Genesis. She lifted her hand and placed it on the back of her neck, nestled in her curls. As she brought the other woman to her, there was a crackle of energy between them that intensified the moment their lips touched. It may have been months since they first kissed, but it took her back to that night as if it happened yesterday.

This time there was no hesitation from either of them. Genesis sighed and raised her hand, brushing her thumb against Zuri's cheek. The scent of her shampoo, tropical and fruity, further evoked memories of the islands. If not for the occasional sound of traffic coming from the street, it was as if they were once again on her private beach.

"How do you feel so good?" Genesis whispered against her lips, breaking the kiss for a moment.

Zuri didn't answer. Instead, she tilted her head and kissed her again. This time she slipped her tongue past her lips, and Genesis rewarded her with a moan as she reciprocated. The sweetness of the ice cream they had just consumed still lingered in their mouths and made the kiss even more delicious.

Time meant nothing as they got lost in each other. When they finally pulled apart, they both wore the same self satisfied grins on their faces. Zuri stood up and offered her hands to Genesis and pulled her off the bench.

They strolled back to the garage where they were both parked, their hands linked. Zuri wasn't ready for the night to end, but she knew it was best if it did. They had plenty of time to spend together now. Everything would happen in due time.

Genesis parked on a higher floor, so they took an elevator up to her section.

"I had a great time. This was fun," Genesis said, leaning against the hood of her car.

Unable to resist, Zuri stepped in between her legs and held her head in her hands. She kissed her forehead, eyes, and nose. "Today made me happy," Zuri said.

Genesis opened her eyes and smiled. "It made me happy too."

Zuri got inside the car so that Genesis could drop her off on the level where she was parked, but the car wouldn't start.

"Are you kidding me?" Genesis turned the key several times, but nothing was happening. She slammed her hand on the steering wheel. "I missed my last inspection, so anything could be wrong with it."

"There's a garage I like not that far from here. Let me call them and see if they can get the car." Zuri called and spoke to the owner. They let her know someone would be over shortly to get the vehicle.

Genesis gave her a wary look. "How much is it going to cost?"

"Well, they won't have an estimate until they see what's wrong. Let's get whatever you need out of here, and we can take it to my car."

After they transferred the items, they waited for the garage to pick up the car. Zuri greeted Javier, who she knew from using the shop off and on. They chatted in Spanish, and he let her know that he would get her an estimate the next day after they looked over everything.

Traffic was lighter on the drive to Genesis's home, so they reached in a short length of time. Although they were prepared to separate earlier, suddenly Zuri didn't want to let her leave, and Genesis appeared to be feeling the same way. She unbuckled her seatbelt but didn't attempt to leave the car.

"So, you speak Spanish?" she said, turning in her seat towards Zuri.

"Fluently, my nanny was from Mexico. My parents wanted me to learn, so she only spoke to me in Spanish from birth." Zuri leaned back and smiled. "It's always entertaining to see how people react when I use it. For some reason seeing a black person speak another language throws them off. Never mind the millions of black people who live in Spanish speaking countries."

"You must encounter things like that often, being in your industry and growing up among the wealthy."

Zuri sighed. "Yeah, and it can be infuriating, always being underestimated. But, then I remember the sacrifices my grandmother made to have the privileges I do. So I always hold my head up high."

Genesis mumbled something as she settled back into her seat.

"What did you say?" Zuri asked, leaning into her.

"Nothing, uh, that wasn't supposed to be out loud." Genesis turned back to her, leaning against the headrest. "I really like you."

Zuri felt her face heat up at the sentiment. "I really like you too."

"Would it be weird if I ask you to come upstairs with me? I just want to feel your body next to mine."

"No, that's not weird at all," Zuri said as her hand clenched in her lap. "I'll behave if you will." *Please don't behave.*

Genesis bit her lip and let her heated gaze sweep over Zuri. She didn't have to do much to stoke the desire inside of her, but something about Genesis's eyes penetrating her with unbridled lust made her feel breathless.

"Well, you'll just have to come up and see, won't you?"

Zuri knew she was going to say yes about going upstairs no matter what. Shannon's presence gave her pause, but if Genesis was comfortable with it, she saw no reason not to be as well.

When they got inside, the house was dark and quiet. Zuri expected her ex to be up, but then she looked at her phone and realized it was after midnight. Time with Genesis always seemed to pass by far too quickly.

In her room, Kuma laid beside her bed, sleeping. Genesis bent down and gently woke her to let her know that Zuri would be spending the night. Their exchange was adorable. Kuma padded over to her and nudged her hand delicately. Zuri pet her and was surprised that she seemed to remember her from the night before.

Once Kuma was done getting affection, she walked back over to her bed and assumed her previous position. Genesis passed Zuri a pair of shorts and a shirt to sleep in, then went into the bathroom. While she was gone, Zuri admired her bedroom as she changed. It felt like Genesis throughout, unlike the rest of the house.

The walls were painted a calming blue and lined with several bookcases overflowing with books. Sparsely decorated, the bed and her library took up most of the room. A queen-size bed was the centerpiece with a floor to ceiling panel head-board in a rich cream color, a nice contrast against the blue. A beautifully upholstered chair sat diagonally in a corner across from the bed. She decided to sit there and wait for her to come out.

After fifteen minutes, Genesis emerged in her pajamas, a cute purple camisole with matching leggings.

Zuri pointed to her books. "You like to read?"

Genesis laughed. "I went a bit overboard buying books. Now I limit myself to a couple a year and read the rest as ebooks."

"Such a voracious reader. I find that incredibly sexy," Zuri said with a smirk.

Genesis climbed on her bed and did a slow crawl across until she was near the edge closest to the chair. Zuri licked her lips and admired the glimpse of her breasts as she bent over.

She sat back on her knees and said, "Well then, get ready to drop your panties because I read every book on those shelves. Some more than once."

Zuri placed her hand over her heart. "Oh my, I think I just had an orgasm."

Unable to contain herself, Genesis fell back with raucous fits of laughter. Kuma was startled and let out a small bark, likely not appreciating having her sleep disturbed. Genesis whispered an apology but continued to laugh, although much quieter.

Zuri laughed as well and excused herself so she could freshen up and change. While in the bathroom, she noticed that Genesis had put out a towel, washcloth, and toothbrush for her. It was such a simple gesture but thoughtful, and it made her smile.

When she finished and reentered the bedroom, the lights were already off, and Genesis sat up in bed, scrolling through her phone. Kuma had repositioned herself and fallen back asleep. Zuri took a moment to appreciate the scene in front of her. She hoped it was the first of many nights that ended this way.

Genesis looked up and beckoned her to the bed. While she put her phone away and turned to her side, Zuri slid under the sheets and snuggled up to her back. She heard Genesis mumble something before settling.

"What was that you just said?" Zuri asked.

"It was a prayer," she replied, yawning.

Zuri was surprised to hear that. "You're still religious?"

Genesis shook her head. "No, but I never stopped believing in God. I just had to develop my own relationship with them."

"Them? I like the gender neutrality of that," Zuri said.

Genesis yawned. "Well, it's men who said God was a man. I don't think they were impartial when they made that designation."

"That's so true." Zuri loved the way her mind worked. "I swear I could listen to you talk for hours."

With her arm draped over Genesis's waist, Zuri pressed closer and moved in for a kiss, but then heard the soft sound of Genesis lightly snoring.

"Even her snores are cute," Zuri said, laughing to herself. She laid her head on the pillow beside her, brought Genesis in tighter to her body, and drifted off to sleep.

Chapter Twenty-Eight

Three Months Later

Zuri stood in the Vincent Hotel's lobby and tried to talk herself out of turning around and walking back out. While she had been talking nonstop about confronting her godfather, she had yet to do so. When he reached out, she decided it was time to face him.

A small, unassuming boutique hotel, The Vincent was the place big names went to hide. It was still upscale but had few amenities. It served its purpose as a nice place to lay your head or whatever else you wanted to get up to during your stay.

Zuri already knew which room Francis was in because she contacted his assistant, Bella. It shocked her that the woman still worked for him, but she was loyal. Francis was a generous man and treated his employees with the utmost respect, a sharp contrast from the allegations against him.

It didn't surprise her though, one of the first things he taught her was to endear herself to people to garner their allegiance. He said it was beneficial in the long run, and now she saw in action what he meant.

As she entered the elevator and pressed the button for his floor, Zuri contemplated how she would approach him. There were so many questions, but the main one was why.

When she got to his room, she knocked, almost hoping he wouldn't be there. Then she heard his voice from inside asking who it was. Of course, even though he was staying at an inconspicuous location, anyone who looked hard enough could find him there.

Zuri cleared her throat and said, "It's me, Francis. Zuri."

He yanked the door open, and before she could react, Francis had her in a tight hug. His cologne, which she used to find comforting, was overpowering, and she had to take a step back. She didn't miss the distinct smell of alcohol on his breath as well.

"I'm so happy to see you, Z. Come in, please," he said, ushering her inside.

Her eyes swept over him as he walked past her. He looked the same but disheveled. His beard had grown in with gray hair sprinkled throughout, and his hair had grown out as well. Even his outfit, a sweatsuit, was not something she could ever remember seeing him wear. Suits and slacks were his everyday attire.

Francis pointed to a chair stacked with newspapers. "Have a seat. Let me just clean this off for you," he said, grabbing the papers and tossing them onto the television stand.

The room was small but efficient. Along with the flatscreen television were a king-sized bed, a desk, side tables, and a large closet. The bathroom was around the corner. It wasn't the Four Seasons, but it was adequate.

Francis watched her, and she felt the anxiety coming off

him in waves. "How have you been? We haven't talked in a couple of months."

He appeared uncomfortable, and that made her less so. "I'm fine, everything's fine. I'm not here to talk about me."

"Of course not," he said, sitting on the edge of the bed. "You have questions about these charges."

"Yes," Zuri said, her voice barely above a whisper.

"Listen, Z, none of this is what it seems, ok? I can be flirtatious sometimes, but I haven't raped anyone. Those women are liars." Francis stood up and ran his hands through his hair. "You know me. If something happened, it's because they wanted it to happen."

Zuri's lip curled up in disgust. "I'm going to need more than the standard; she asked for it, Francis. For God's sake, do you even understand what you've done?"

"I'm a powerful man in Hollywood, Zuri; everyone knows that. So many women have thrown themselves at me for a role or a bigger part. Fuck, invites to exclusive parties even."

"This isn't about incidents like the ones you've mentioned. Plenty of men who can get any woman they want still use their power to hurt them."

Francis raised his head and looked at her, his face crestfallen. "Is that what you believe I did?"

Zuri fought the urge to look away, but she needed to see him for who he was, not who she wanted him to be. His smooth brown skin looked aged, with an increase of worry lines running along his forehead. Even his eyes, bright and engaging, appeared tired. This was a man on the verge of losing everything, but she was all out of sympathy; it was what he deserved.

"We created Ellis Films as a tribute to my grandmother. That you would defile it with your disgusting behavior makes me sick to my stomach." Zuri stood up . "Yes, I think you did it.

You have always been a self-centered show-off, but I looked up to you. I saw you as larger than life, but you're just an asshole."

Francis's demeanor changed after she spoke. He stood up straight, and the sad old man vanished. She had injured his ego, and he wanted to strike back.

"I didn't force anyone to do anything. They were aware of what it was when they came to my hotel room. Pay to play, that's the game in Hollywood, and they paid with what they had."

Zuri balled up her fist. "They are human beings who did not deserve that treatment. And most of them were women of color. Black and Latina women already have it so hard in our industry, and you used that to take advantage of them. How can you live with yourself?"

Francis brushed past her and walked over to the minibar, and poured himself a drink. He downed the glass and refilled it. He pointed at Zuri and said with a sneer, "You were always a spoiled little bitch. Even when you were an awkward and unattractive teenager, you walked around like your shit didn't stink. I worked for everything I have, and you had it handed to you, but you think you can judge me?"

Zuri backed up at the anger in his voice. Never in her life had Francis spoken to her that way, and his demeanor flipped so fast it was scary. This was the man those women had met, and he was hiding underneath there the whole time. It broke her heart.

Tears fell as Zuri walked to the door. "I hoped that you would be remorseful, but now I don't know why I ever thought you were capable of that." She turned with her hand on the doorknob. "This spoiled little bitch loved you since childhood, but this is unforgivable. Don't call me, don't write to me, we're done. The next time I see you, it will be at your trial."

Not interested in giving him another chance to speak, Zuri

hurried out of the room. She composed herself enough to get downstairs and exit the building. As soon as she entered her car, the floodgates opened, and she cried. For the women he hurt, for her negligence, and for losing the man who at one time meant the world to her. It was a loss she wasn't sure she would ever get over.

Chapter Twenty-Nine

Zuri ran around doing last-minute fixes on her house's decor. Genesis was at her place often, but she still worried that something would be out of place. She told Alma that she didn't want to worry about impressing her anymore, but it was always on her mind. Genesis had given her a chance to be in her life and it made her so happy. She just wanted to get everything right.

After her confrontation with Francis, she threw herself back into work. She got what she needed from their conversation which was confirmation that the accusations were true. Hearing how he felt about those women and what he had done propelled her to start working on how to change the work atmosphere at her studio and beyond.

She shared with Genesis what happened. At first, she didn't want to because even thinking of what he said to her made her feel ill, but like always, Genesis was understanding and gave her practical advice. Guilt for feeling complicit, with or without knowledge, wasn't going to solve anything. So, Zuri came up with a plan that she worked on with her cousins to implement new measures at the studio to help curb future issues.

That included anonymous reporting of harassment, more women in positions of leadership, and stringent screening of all staff regardless of prior affiliation with any of them. She felt ashamed she hadn't deemed any of that necessary before, but now she understood where her blind spots had been.

When she saw Genesis pull up to the house, Zuri stepped outside. It had been a rough couple of weeks, so having her there offered a nice mental break. They were having dinner at her place, and Genesis was bringing the food. She wanted them to cook together, to bond. Zuri was down, even though breakfast was the only meal she had ever bothered to get a handle on.

"Hey beautiful," she said, greeting Genesis.

Genesis gave her a bright smile as she climbed out of the car. "Hey yourself. You're looking mighty fine today, Ms. Baker," she said, walking up to her.

Zuri wrapped her arms around her waist and bit her lip. "Not as fine as you, Ms. Malone. It looks like that food will not be the only thing on the menu."

"You better stop," Genesis said with a smile.

They had been dating for three months, and while she was not one to rush into anything; her desire for Genesis kept her up some nights. No one had ever made her feel this way, not even Tracy.

The first couple of months, things were burning hot, and they had done everything but have sex. Then Genesis cooled off and wanted to take things slower. She feared perhaps she had done something wrong, but in every other area, things were going well.

Zuri let her go and grabbed the bags from the back seat. "What did you bring for us to make?"

"A meal-kit from that company Good Stuff. It was easier than coming up with dinner ourselves," Genesis said as she grabbed one bag.

"I missed you." Zuri took her hand as they walked to the house. "How are things going with Reggie?"

Genesis squeezed her hand. "I missed you too, baby, and I'm sorry I've been MIA. His finances are a mess, so I have my work cut out for me, but I'm getting through it. Once I'm finished, he is going to be in a much better place."

"I'm happy that you're the one helping him; I appreciate it. He and Elijah are like my brothers, so I want to make sure they're good."

They put the bags down in the kitchen, and Zuri started taking out pots. She owned the latest gadgets and tools for cooking, so she was excited to finally use them.

Genesis began unpacking the groceries. "Your love for your family is heartwarming. I sometimes wonder what it would have been like if I had those relationships growing up. My family on both sides is quite large."

"Have you ever thought about reaching out to them?" Zuri asked, leaning against the counter.

"Kenzie and I have talked about it, but something always comes up. I'm not going to lie; I fear they won't want anything to do with us."

Zuri walked over to Genesis and pulled her by the waist into a hug. "They would be crazy not to want a chance to get to know you. You're an amazing woman, and if they can't see that, then it's their problem, not yours."

"You are so good for my ego," Genesis said, kissing her chin.

"Oh, I'm good for lots of things." Zuri pressed her into the island and placed a kiss on the pulse point of her neck. A spot she knew would get her wet.

Over the last few months, she learned so much about what Genesis liked and what she desired. She knew the scars on her body, the beauty, and birthmarks. That her night time routine usually involved a book and tea. That she got up at least two times a night to use the bathroom. And yet, this one thing was out of reach.

Genesis let out a gasp. "We have to make dinner."

"Dinner can wait," Zuri said. She looked into Genesis's eyes, and instead of reluctance, there was something else. It was the same look she gave her when they first kissed in Barbados. *She wants me.*

"You're right; it can," Genesis said, her hands moving up her back.

Zuri's body was full of tension. Genesis's hands relaxed her in a way nothing else could. "That feels so good, baby," Zuri said, pressing her lips against her ear.

Genesis turned and kissed her with no hesitation. Zuri did not know where this change of heart had come from, but she was more than happy to give in to what she wanted.

She was desperate for her to know just how much she cared for her. That no one else mattered, and she was hers, mind, body, and soul. Everyone else had been a temporary stop on her way to loving her.

But that was too much to place on Genesis the first time they made love. So instead, she gripped her the way she knew she liked and kissed her deep and slow. Their tongues slid against each other, and a shudder ran through her body.

These kisses were different. They promised more than they ever had before.

"Let's go upstairs," Genesis mumbled against Zuri's lips.

They walked with Genesis leading her by the hand. As they ascended the stairs to her bedroom, Zuri licked her lips and tried to calm herself. That wasn't easy with her eyes hungrily taking in every inch of Genesis's curves. Her hand acted with a mind of its own as she reached under her skirt to touch her thigh.

Genesis paused at the top of the stairs and held the banister.

"I can't move with your hand there," she said in a breathy whisper.

"Maybe I don't want you to move." Zuri kept her hand under her skirt as she made it to the top. She pressed into Genesis as her back hit the wall, eliciting another gasp as she brushed their lips together. "What if I wanted to take you right here? Would you let me?"

Genesis nodded yes. Her response surprised Zuri, but she didn't give herself time to second guess it. Instead, she brought both of her hands down and lifted her skirt. She filled her hands with her bottom and pushed forward with her knee, opening Genesis's legs.

As she squeezed and caressed, Zuri couldn't resist going in for another kiss. While she had always been tentative in their interactions before, now she felt like she didn't need to hold back . It was an honor to be only the second woman Genesis had given herself to, and she wanted to show her what that meant to her.

Zuri's hand drifted to the front, and she felt the heat coming from Genesis as she stroked her. "You're so wet for me," she said, pressing her fingers against her underwear.

Genesis ground against her hand, the fabric soaked with her juices. No longer able to wait, Zuri slid her hand inside and sighed at the slickness that coated her fingers as she neared her entrance.

"Please," Genesis whispered. She brushed her lips along Zuri's jaw, sending chills down her body. "I need you."

Genesis bore down and brought Zuri inside of her. They both groaned as she slid in as deep as her fingers would go. Her strokes were gentle but firm as she let Genesis get accustomed.

"Fuck, you feel so good," Zuri said into her shoulder as she kissed all over her bare skin. Her senses were in overload as Genesis's wetness pulled her in, and her moans filled her ears.

They found a rhythm as Zuri moved in and out, and Genesis's hips followed her lead. Each brush of her thumb against her clit made Genesis shudder. Not wanting to lose momentum, Zuri kept at it, and Genesis's soft pants became grunts of pleasure.

Zuri placed her free hand against the wall to brace herself and leaned closer to Genesis. "I want you to come, just like this," she said. "Then I'm going to take you to my bedroom and make you come again. Would you like that?"

Genesis gasped in response and grabbed ahold of Zuri's back. She angled her head to kiss her, and as their tongues played with each other, Genesis's body tensed up. Within minutes, Genesis threw her head back and clenched on her fingers, crying out with Zuri's name on her lips.

They stumbled into the bedroom a few minutes later and began removing their clothes. She froze as Genesis climbed onto the bed. While they had been in various states of undress around each other before, the last glimpse she had of a naked Genesis was in Barbados.

"Are you okay?" Genesis asked, sitting up on her elbows.

Bathed in moonlight, Genesis looked like a goddess come to life. Her breasts sat high, and while not large, they were round and full. Her nipples stood dark and erect against her honey brown skin. They had yet to receive the attention they deserved, but she would remedy that.

The rest of her was just as delectable, from her sensual lips to her thick thighs. "You're so beautiful," Zuri said, standing at the edge of the bed as she finished removing her clothes.

Genesis looked embarrassed and threw herself back. "Stop. I've got stretch marks, twenty pounds I can never seem to lose, and my butt is nonexistent."

"So you don't look like a surgically enhanced video vixen, you mean?" Zuri climbed on the bed, kissed the top of her foot, and then began making her way up her leg. "Please continue because I have yet to hear anything that makes you less than sexy to me."

"I can't... I can't concentrate with you doing that," Genesis said, writhing beneath her.

"Then let me give you something to concentrate on." Zuri kissed the coarse hairs on her mons as she parted her legs. Delicately, she opened her up with her tongue and savored her essence. They both moaned as she pressed further. *She tastes like heaven.*

With her fingers splayed wide on her hips, Zuri brought her in close and sucked her into her mouth. Genesis's hands found their way into her hair and held her in place. The pressure from her grip spurred her on. Intoxicated with lust Zuri's only thought was to make Genesis come.

Her wish came true moments later, as Genesis bucked against her and arched off the bed. "Oh God, Zuri...yes...yes...yes."

The sound of her name as Genesis climaxed was the most beautiful thing she had ever heard. Her mind was already racing with all the ways she could make that happen again and again.

Genesis loosened her grip as she ran her hands over her hair. Zuri wanted more but was content to rest for a while. She moved up Genesis's body and laid beside her, wrapping her in her arms.

They were quiet for some time, listening to the trees surrounding her property sway in the breezy night air. The coolness swept over their bodies, and Zuri was on the verge of drifting off to sleep when Genesis slipped out of her arms.

When she opened her eyes, Genesis was on her elbow, looking down at her. Her face was so serious that for a moment, Zuri thought she was going to tell her she regretted what just happened. Instead, once she saw she was awake, she climbed on top of Zuri and looked her in the eye.

"Show me how to please you."

Chapter Thirty

Genesis was nervous; there was no doubt about that. While she longed for Zuri, she had underestimated how uncomfortable she would feel being with someone else sexually. Despite her relationship's length, she was inexperienced and feared Zuri would be turned off by it. So she waited as long as she could, but it was impossible to deny their chemistry.

Shannon was controlling, but in the bedroom, this was even more true. She liked to give but wasn't interested in receiving. Since she was the first and only woman she had been with, Genesis took it in stride. Whenever she tried to switch things up, Shannon put a stop to it. So she came to accept that it was all she would know.

From the first day they met, Genesis noticed a difference in her interactions with Zuri. There was give and take instead of her having to play the role of pillow princess. She liked their dynamic and wanted it to continue. So now she sat, butterflies floating in her stomach, ready to learn how to satisfy her.

"Having you in this position is pleasing," Zuri said, gripping her hips.

She loved when she grabbed hold of her that way. Zuri's grip was firm but never oppressive. It made you aware that she was in control, but she could take as good as she gave, and that made Genesis want to surrender to her even more.

Genesis ground against her and watched her playful expression change to unbridled lust. Zuri bit her lip and gripped her even harder, pushing up as she pushed down, making for some pleasant friction. The heat between them left her unable to catch her breath.

"You can do whatever you like, baby. If it's too much, I'll let you know." Zuri brushed an errant hair from her face. "I'm yours."

Those were the words she yearned to hear. It was possible for this beautiful woman beneath her to have anyone, and she had chosen Genesis. Her big dark brown eyes stared up at her, drinking her in, and all she wanted was to lose herself in her.

She lowered her head to Zuri's breast and took a nipple into her mouth. As they had moved across the bases like a pair of horny teenagers, she discovered just how sensitive Zuri was there. In response, Zuri cried out, arching into Genesis's hand. She cupped her, basking in the evidence of her arousal. Her wetness tempted her to dive inside to its source, but that needed to wait. What she desired most was to taste her.

Zuri let out a small cry of protest as she abandoned her breast but settled into a new set of moans as she kissed her way towards her lower body. When she looked up and saw the state of Zuri, hands fisted in the sheets, a sheen of sweat covering her body, she knew there was no need to second guess herself anymore. She wanted this, and she wanted her.

Genesis's tongue flicked at Zuri's clit, then plunged inside of her. Zuri trembled as she slid over her drenched center. Even though it was her first time, Genesis followed Zuri's cues and discovered what she liked. Not too much pressure, circular movements followed by focused licks. When she hooked her arms on either side of her legs to get closer, Zuri groaned in appreciation.

Time passed like nothing, and Genesis would have stayed longer, savoring every bit of her, but soon, Zuri's body tensed then released, her juices coating her tongue. Her moans reached a crescendo, and she bucked up as she cried out, pinning Genesis in place. No need; nothing could have pried her away from Zuri's sweet spot.

They both collapsed, breathing hard and unwilling to let go of one another. The chilly breeze coming in from the windows spurred Genesis to move. She draped her body across Zuri's and sighed at her warmth.

"All of this was so good and unexpected," Zuri said, her voice raspy from her cries of passion.

Genesis took a deep breath and snuggled into her neck. "I'm sorry."

Zuri pulled up the sheet from the edge of the bed to cover them. "Don't be; this was worth the wait."

She smiled and wrapped her arm around Zuri's waist as she leaned in for a kiss. Her mind was still analyzing everything that transpired between them, and she was proud to be able to bring Zuri pleasure. It was another way to show her just how much she meant to her when words weren't enough.

"Are you okay?" Zuri asked, lacing their fingers together.

Genesis licked her lips, tasting the traces of Zuri still there. "Never better," she said with a sultry smile.

* * *

Later in the evening, they finally got around to preparing dinner. It was quick; salmon with red potatoes and broccoli rabe. Zuri listened as she showed her how to season and cook each item. Everything came out perfect.

"See, I knew you could do it. Once you can cook one item, it's easy to branch out," Genesis said as they sat at the table.

"That was fun. I might have to get those kits for myself. It takes the guesswork out of cooking." Zuri placed a piece of salmon in her mouth and savored it. "Delicious, just like you," she said, giving her a wink.

Genesis winked back and drank some wine. She began eating, but every once in a while looked in Zuri's direction. Zuri continued to grin from ear to ear.

"Are you going to stare at me like that all night?" Genesis asked, raising an eyebrow.

Zuri shrugged. "Haven't decided yet, but I just have to say you're amazing."

"She says after, how many orgasms? I lost count." Genesis gave her a toothy smile as she picked up her glass.

"Oh, look at you. Talk that talk, baby. I might learn a few things from you," Zuri said, laughing.

Genesis got quiet and placed her fork on her plate. "I know I made you wait, and I don't want you to think it was because of anything you did. I'm just not the most experienced in pleasing someone in that way, and it was always on my mind. It's a conversation we should have had by this point."

"So what made you change your mind? Not that I'm complaining."

"I wanted you," Genesis said matter-of-factly. "And it was long overdue."

Zuri watched her, and Genesis saw the wheels in her mind turning. "So you never did that with Shannon?"

Genesis pursed her lips. "Nope, wasn't her thing. She loved to give pleasure, but she never allowed me to do the same. But when I look back on it, it wasn't all her fault. We never spoke about what we did in bed; I just accepted it. That's not the way to have a relationship. It's no wonder she left."

Zuri got up and walked over to Genesis, crouching beside her chair. "Or she needed to leave so you would find your way to me."

Genesis caressed her cheek. "That sounds much better."

"Whatever experiences you've had or didn't have don't matter to me. We're together now, and we can deal with anything that comes up as a team. Don't be afraid to talk to me, ever, okay? Even if it's something, you think I might not want to hear." She hugged Genesis close to her body. "Now, let's hurry and finish this food so I can show you more of my tongue tricks."

Genesis laughed out loud and kissed her. For the first time in years, she was experiencing pure unadulterated joy, and it was the best gift anyone had ever given her.

Chapter Thirty-One

A couple of weeks later, Shannon went in for her scheduled surgery. Although there was no reason to believe it wouldn't go well, she made sure beforehand that things were in order. She asked Genesis's permission to designate her as a health proxy just in case anything went awry. Genesis agreed without hesitation. Living together for a second time had allowed their relationship to develop in an unexpected way, and she was more than happy to be there for someone she once again considered a true friend.

Genesis knocked on the door to Shannon's hospital room and raised the bag in her hand. "I brought treats."

Shannon grinned and waved her into the room. "See, that's why I love you. Get your butt in here."

Genesis laughed as she walked in and placed her things down in an empty chair. She handed Shannon the bag of candy after grabbing a Snickers bar.

"Ms. Colbert, how are you?"

Shannon's doctor, Richard Howzer, walked into the room and greeted Genesis. His bedside manner impressed her, and she felt at ease upon meeting him. His kind hazel eyes and silver hair only added to his charm.

"Hey, Doc, I'm great. Only slight pain where you entered, but otherwise, I'm good already." Shannon flexed for him, and he chuckled.

"Well, my wife would never forgive me if I injured one of her favorite basketball players. I'm glad to hear you're good. I'll be leaving soon, so contact the nurses if you need anything." Dr. Howzer turned to Genesis. "And for you, Ms. Malone, I have a folder here with information on aftercare and what Shannon might need. My number is there as well."

Genesis took the folder and thanked him. When he left, she slid it into her bag and poured Shannon a cup of water.

"Here, remember they said you need to stay hydrated."

"Thank you, doctor," Shannon said with a wink.

After their conversation about where their relationship was not going, things had been better than Genesis expected. Shannon backed off and made sure things remained platonic. She would flirt on occasion, but never in a way that made her uncomfortable. Genesis was grateful that they could still be friends because she loved her, even if it wasn't romantic. There was still much she wanted to discuss to move past their previous issues, but that could wait until after she was cancer free.

"So, are you ready for New York? I was never a fan, but it's cool to visit," Shannon said, sitting up.

Genesis was more than ready. When Zuri invited her for a weekend away, she had been reluctant to leave since it fell around the time of the surgery. It was Shannon who insisted she get Kenzi to stay with her. "I've always wanted to visit, so I am more than ready." Genesis sat beside her and turned on the television. "Kenzie should be here soon."

When they spoke, Kenzie didn't sound pleased that she was

leaving, but she said yes. The inevitable conversation they were going to have about it had her stomach in knots.

Although Genesis had yet to tell Kenzie about Zuri, she had hinted that she was aware there was someone in her life. With the hope of her and Shannon getting back together gone, Genesis was sure she would make her feelings known. It was time for her to put her in her place, something she had put off for far too long.

"Ugh, she's going to come in here and destroy my entire mood," Genesis said, massaging her temple.

Shannon reached over and patted her arm. "Don't worry too much about her, Gen, okay? I'll talk to her. Our relationship is between us."

"Yeah, well, she decided it involved the three of us a long time ago." Genesis folded her arms. "It's my fault for thinking that I shouldn't discipline her just because we lost our parents. Then when we broke up, I wasn't honest with her about how it ended."

Shannon raised her eyebrows. "You didn't tell her I left to be with someone else?"

Genesis sighed and rubbed her face. "No, because I didn't want her to be angry with you. She looks up to you so much, and I didn't want to take that away from her. I just let her think we both moved on."

"Gen, just because your parents died doesn't mean you have to be a martyr. Kenzie is going to love you regardless. Don't beat yourself up. You did what you thought was right. We became parents with no one to guide us," Shannon said. "Your parents passed, and mine disowned me. We all were orphans."

Genesis looked over at Shannon and saw the sadness that washed over her face. She didn't often talk about her parents. Their dismissal of her from their lives still hurt. If not for other family members, one aunt, and a few cousins, she would have been alone. It was something that had brought them closer together.

"I don't doubt I would have gotten the same treatment from my parents. The sanctified are always the most judgemental." Genesis let out a deep sigh. "At least you were brave enough to come out to yours."

Shannon scoffed. "Yeah, after we were thousands of miles away in school. I figured the rejection wouldn't hurt as much, but that wasn't true. Thank God I had you," she said, reaching out for her hand. "We were an awesome pair once, weren't we?"

"Yeah, we were," Genesis said, squeezing her hand.

"Knock, knock. I come bearing gifts." Kenzie entered the room with balloons and a giant stuffed teddy bear.

Genesis moved her hand back to her lap; happy the balloons blocked her sister's view. She didn't need to add any fuel to her delusion.

"Hey, sis," Kenzie said, bending down to kiss Genesis's cheek.

"Hey, Kenzie. Fancy balloons," Genesis said, pointing to the shiny globes floating to the ceiling.

"Right? I got them at the gift shop; they seemed perfect for Shay. How are you?" Kenzie asked, hugging Shay close.

"I'm good, little sis. The doctor said they removed all of the cancer and expect that I'll make a full recovery. Anything is possible with an illness like this, but I hope that this is the last time I'll be wearing a gown with my ass out for the time being."

They all laughed, and Kenzi gave her a high five.

"Well, I made you a huge pot of chicken soup. Genesis gave me our mom's recipe, and it's delicious."

"Word? Oh, I'm looking forward to that," Shannon said, rubbing her hands together. "With my two favorite ladies by my side, I'm gonna be good."

Genesis's phone buzzed, and her heart skipped a beat when she saw Zuri's name on the screen.

"I'll be right back. Shay, drink more water," Genesis said, nodding towards the pitcher.

Once she had some distance from the room, she answered the phone.

"Well, you took long enough to answer," Zuri said.

"Oh, you're clocking how many times I let it ring?" Genesis said. Her cheeks hurt from grinning so hard.

"Well, I think I've earned a second ring pick up at the very least."

"Oh, at the very least," Genesis said sarcastically. "I'm very excited about our trip."

"Good, I have lots of fun things planned for us. I figure when we get there, we can drop our bags at my apartment and..."

Genesis cut her off. "You own an apartment there?"

"Of course, New York is expensive. I bought it years ago in Brooklyn before the real estate became so in demand. I could sell it and make some good money, but it comes in handy."

Genesis remained silent and listened to her talk.

"Shit, did I sound bougie just now? Because you got quiet."

"Just a little, but it's not that." Genesis sighed as she leaned against the wall and pressed the phone closer to her ear. "I like listening to you talk."

"Is that so? Well, I've got so much to talk to you about, baby."

"Mmm, and I love it when you call me baby," Genesis said, gripping the phone.

Genesis heard her name and turned to Kenzie, walking towards her.

"Z, I have to call you back."

"Okay, call me back when you can."

Genesis hung up and slid the phone into her pocket. "What's up, Kenzie?"

"I got everything ready at the house, and I looked over that folder about what to pay attention to after her surgery. I just don't get why you're choosing now to go away. Shannon needs you."

"I didn't plan on leaving right now; it just worked out that way. The trip is only for a weekend. I'll be back by Tuesday morning. Shannon is fine with it." Genesis started back towards the room.

"But what if I wasn't available? You would have left her alone?" Kenzie asked, following behind her.

"Then, a friend would have stayed with her; she has plenty of those."

"But you're her wife," Kenzie said

Genesis stopped and turned around. "Ex-wife. And enough with the games, Kenzie. Things have been over for almost three years between Shannon and I."

"Yeah, well, if you were a better wife, you two would still be together."

"How dare you?" Genesis realized how raised her voice was when a few nurses turned in their direction. "Come with me," she said, grabbing Kenzie's arm.

They walked until Genesis found an accessible staircase, and she pushed Kenzie into the stairwell.

"I've had enough of this shit from you. Shannon and I are over, and we are never getting back together. Since you can't get that through your thick skull, understand this; she cheated and left me. There is no coming back from that for me, and I have moved on; you need to do the same. I should have told you from the beginning."

"I know she's the one who left," Kenzie said. "You both tried to hide it from me, but I'm not stupid. Shay had a girlfriend right away, and you didn't. You walked around, looking miserable for months, and she was happy. It was obvious."

Genesis threw up her hands. "Then why do you keep pushing this?"

Kenzie looked away and clenched her jaw. She turned back to Genesis and said, "Because you guys are my family. You're all I have."

Genesis softened up when she noticed Kenzie's mouth trembling. "We are still family. Shannon would never abandon you, and she hasn't. It's time for me to move on, Kenzie. I need to find happiness."

Kenzie nodded and swiped at a tear rolling down her face. "When she moved back in with you, I thought we would all be together again like before. It was stupid."

"It's not stupid; you just miss mom and dad." Genesis pulled her sister into a hug. "I miss them too."

Kenzie held her close, and Genesis smiled. It had been a long time since they shared any genuine affection. Sometimes she wondered if that's why Kenzie favored Shannon. They had a decent relationship, but their interactions were weighed down by things left unsaid. That needed to change.

"I have my regrets," Genesis said, stepping back to look into Kenzie's eyes. "I'm sorry we never had time to bond the way we should have. One minute we were sisters, then the next I was your guardian, and I had a hard time navigating that."

"You did your best," Kenzie said with a shrug. "We were young and alone in the world. I acted like a brat, but I appreciated everything. You gave up dancing to take care of me, and it meant a lot to you. I'm sorry too for being so hard on you all the time."

"Thank you for saying that. And I would do it again because I love you, Kenzie."

Kenzie looked down and smiled. "I love you too. It's been a

while since we said that to each other."

Genesis smiled. "Well, we should change that."

"Yeah, we should." Kenzie wiped her face. "I think this whole cancer thing with Shay is getting to me. I'm worried about her."

"Yeah, but our girl is a fighter, and we'll do what we can for her. We may not be together, but I'll always have her back, and I know she'll have mine."

They left the stairwell and walked back to the room. Kenzie nudged her.

"So, is Zuri Baker your girlfriend now?" Kenzie said with a smirk.

Genesis glanced at her. "How did you hear about that?

"Online, there were pictures of you two at dinner the other night. You'll need to get used to that again."

"Yeah, I can't say I missed it, but I'm willing to put up with it for her."

When they reached the room, Kenzie turned and said, "You look cute together. Not as cute as with Shannon, but..."

Genesis rolled her eyes and laughed. "Thanks, I think."

"Maybe when you get back, I can meet her."

Surprised, Genesis shook her head yes. "Of course, I'm sure she'd like that."

"Cool."

Genesis watched her sister as she went back inside and dropped into the seat beside Shannon. She had to admit, seeing them together reminded her of their time as a family of three, and she understood why Kenzie yearned for what they had. It brought normalcy to their lives when everything else was out of control. While she couldn't give that same experience to her anymore, it was time to move forward and create something new. The love shared between them meant that it was more than possible.

Chapter Thirty-Two

They arrived in New York on a Friday evening and took a cab to Zuri's apartment in Park Slope, a Brooklyn neighborhood. Genesis had only ever been in Manhattan, so she wanted to explore the area. It was near Prospect Park, a sprawling oasis that rivaled the more well-known Central Park, albeit smaller.

The cab dropped them off around 6 pm and, while tired, Genesis wanted to go out.

"Over the weekend, can we go to Times Square? Ooh, and the Statue of Liberty? I have to go to the top of the Empire State Building. One of my favorite movies has a scene there." Genesis couldn't stay still.

Zuri laughed as she unlocked the door to the apartment. "I've never seen you this excited; it's adorable."

"That's me, as cute as can be," Genesis said, kissing her cheek. "Wow, this place is so nice."

Unlike Zuri's home in California, the apartment was smaller and more traditional in style. Other than upgrades to the kitchen and bathroom, she left most of the original features intact. The building had been around since the 1930s, which in

New York was a plus because the apartments were often larger than their modern counterparts.

"My dad was the one who convinced me to buy this place when I used to come to New York more often. He figured it would be an excellent investment, and it has been." Zuri put their bags down in the living room and went to see what was in the fridge.

"How do you maintain the apartment? It feels lived in," Genesis massaged the fabric on the couch then sat down.

"I visit a few times a year, and I let family and friends stay whenever they're in the city. So it sees activity for at least six months out of the year. Also, a good friend of mine who lives here checks in every so often," Zuri said. She handed Genesis a glass of Cranberry juice with ice and sat beside her. "My cousin left behind juice."

Zuri pulled out her phone and looked for a local restaurant to have dinner. She remembered a fantastic Italian place not too far from the apartment.

Genesis placed her hand on Zuri's leg and turned to face her. "Thank you for bringing me here."

"It's my pleasure, baby, and I hope we have more adventures together," Zuri said, squeezing her hand. "On that note, I'm starving. There's a superb Italian restaurant a couple of blocks away."

"Well, that isn't happening," Genesis said as she finished the juice. "We are not staying in the city with one of the largest Caribbean populations outside of the islands and getting Italian."

Zuri laughed at her unexpected outburst. "Okay, so what do you suggest?"

Genesis pulled her phone from her pocket. "I'm glad you asked. I already looked up places near here, and there are quite a few with great reviews."

"Give me a minute." Zuri got up and dialed a friend of hers. After catching up, she got off the phone and gave Genesis a name. "That was my friend Daphne, and she recommended a place called Island Sun. It's small and no-frills but has the best food, according to her."

Genesis pouted and held up her phone. "But what about the places I found?"

Zuri chuckled and grabbed their bags. "Never trust reviews online because they can come from people who aren't familiar with the cuisine. Much better to ask the people who know what's up. Daphne's family is from Jamaica, so her suggestions are legit."

Genesis got up to help her. "That's excellent advice. I remember a coworker took Lucy and me to this place that supposedly had amazing soul food. It was basic at best."

Zuri entered the bedroom and placed their bags in a corner. "So here's my room. It isn't anything fancy but..."

Genesis put her fingers against her lips to get her to stop speaking, then placed the bag in her hand on the bed. Zuri waited with bated breath as Genesis brought her close and kissed her. Sometimes she wondered what she had been doing with the other women in her life because their kisses were not the same.

"What time does the restaurant close?" Genesis asked in between kisses.

"Um, 11." Zuri trembled as Genesis's hands made their way under her shirt.

"Well, that sounds like just enough time to thank you for this trip. How about we take a shower?"

Zuri nodded in response, unable to do much else, and followed behind Genesis as she took her hand and led her to the bathroom.

* * *

Flatbush Avenue on Friday night was a sight to behold. Typically crowded and bustling, the coming of the weekend seemed to give it even more kinetic energy. Although it was after eight, there were plenty of stores still open and people roaming up and down the streets.

Reggae music spilled out into the warm and humid night air. Zuri kept glancing over at Genesis as they walked. The smile on her face had yet to leave as she took in their surroundings. Her excitement was contagious and reminded her of their time in Barbados.

Island Sun was an unassuming restaurant tucked in between a beauty salon and a clothing store. They almost missed it, but the smell of the food wafting out the front door led the way.

Daphne was not exaggerating when she called the place small. That was an understatement. The decor was clean and evoked the Caribbean with its colors and wood in the design, but it could barely fit the few tables they had. Zuri was pleased that there was a backyard space, although that was tiny as well.

The food was pre-made and displayed buffet style, with staff dishing it out from behind the counters. After they ordered and paid, they walked to the backyard and found a small table available.

Genesis dug in right away and did a merry dance in her seat. "This food is so good; I don't even care that people have elbowed me ten times. Tell your friend thank you for the suggestion."

"I will; she always knows the best places to eat . I swear, hole in the wall places almost always have the most authentic food."

Genesis popped open her ginger beer and took a swig. "How do you know her?"

"Oh, we go way back. Her father is a theater producer here in New York, and he worked with my mother on a few plays. Our families used to travel together and the whole nine." Zuri paused and could see that Genesis was waiting for more. "Are you trying to figure out if we were an item?"

"Now that you mention it, sure," Genesis said.

"Jealousy, now that is something I didn't expect. Have sex with a woman a few times and she thinks she owns you," Zuri said with a smirk. Genesis threw a napkin at her, and she caught it. "In all seriousness, she's straight as an arrow. I had a crush on her when we were teenagers, but that's it."

"For the record, I'm not jealous. Just want to know more about you," Genesis said.

"I think jealousy is healthy, as long as it doesn't become all-consuming." Zuri sat back and looked her in the eye. "For instance, I hate the fact that Shannon is staying at your house."

Genesis stopped eating. "You've always said it wasn't a problem."

"Realistically, who would want their girlfriend living with their ex? Of course, it bothers me, but I'm mature enough to realize that it's not about my feelings. You're doing the right thing by helping her."

"Hm, that's the rational side of you. What does the irrational side think?"

Zuri began humming the melody from the Jazmine Sullivan song, Bust Your Windows. Genesis laughed and threw her hands up.

"Fine, you made your point. Yes, there was a twinge of jealousy when you mentioned Daphne, but I always do whenever you mention the women in your life. Knowing that they were intimate with you makes me feel..."

"Vulnerable," Zuri said, finishing her sentence.

"Very vulnerable. Does that ever change?"

"It's hard not to compare yourself to someone's prior partners. The fact is, they aren't with them anymore, so why stress yourself," Zuri said. She reached over and took Genesis's hand in hers. "And baby, I can guarantee you that none of them made me feel the way you do. So they never saw this side of me."

"You are such a smooth talker," Genesis said, kissing the top of her hand. "But I like it, tell me more."

* * *

Saturday, they visited as many tourist spots as they could fit in the day. Genesis insisted on taking the subway since she had never been inside an underground station. Her childlike glee was contagious, so Zuri obliged her whatever she wanted.

The following evening, she had plans for them but didn't inform Genesis until that afternoon. After they had lunch at a Thai restaurant, they discovered on a walk; she took her shopping on Fifth Avenue.

The avenue stretched the length of Manhattan but had a shopping area in midtown known for its luxury stores. Zuri took her into Bergdorf Goodman, a department store in business for over 100 years. She had already chosen the outfits they were going to wear, so they made a brief stop to pick them up, then headed a few blocks away to Tiffany and Co. The famed jewelry store was busy, so Zuri had Genesis wait for her while picking up her item.

Genesis said nothing, even though her face spoke volumes. When they walked several blocks west, and Zuri told her they would be staying at a hotel nearby, she broke her silence. They found rose petals scattered about and in the shape of a heart on the bed of the hotel room. A box of truffles sat in the center.

"Z, what is all of this?" Genesis said, walking over to a bottle of champagne on ice.

Zuri brought her to sit on a chaise lounge by the window. "We met almost a year ago, and it was the best thing that could have happened to me. You make me so happy, and I want to give that back to you. Trust me, you'll be happy that I kept the surprise from you until the end."

"You're so sweet, but I feel lame not having anything for you in return," Genesis said.

"All I need is you," Zuri said, kissing her softly. "Although that move you do with your tongue is pretty nice. Perhaps that could be my gift."

Genesis snickered and ruffled her hair. "You got it! I'm going to get dressed. You said we have to be there by 8 pm, right?"

"Yes, but it's a block away from here, so we have time."

After they both showered and got dressed, they took turns viewing their outfits in the full-length mirror beside the bathroom. Genesis wore a floral wrap dress with cream heels to match. It flowed over her body. Zuri had on black cigarette pants, a black bustier, and a fitted suit jacket.

"Are you trying to give me a heart attack?" Genesis said, coming up behind her. "I swear you can wear anything, and it works."

Zuri kissed her cheek and picked up the jewelry box. "Put out your hand."

Genesis did as she was told, and Zuri placed a rose gold tennis bracelet surrounded by diamonds on her wrist. She gasped as she admired the piece and wrapped her arms around Zuri.

"So this is what you bought at Tiffany's," Genesis said, turning her wrist. "It's gorgeous. Thank you."

After Zuri put on her jewelry, they headed out. As they

walked down the street, Zuri was eager to see what Genesis would say once they reached their destination. As they neared the building, Genesis gasped and froze in place, her hand over her mouth. When she lowered it, her lip trembled.

"Is this...?"

Zuri smiled as she pulled her closer. "What does it say?"

Genesis's eyes watered as she stared at the name across the front of the building. "Alvin Ailey American Dance Theater."

Zuri gave her a moment to compose herself as she continued to look at the building in awe. Then she turned to Zuri and cried into her shoulder. She was sure they were tears of happiness, so Zuri tamped down the protective side of her that wanted to make it stop. She needed to let her emotions out.

A few minutes later, Genesis lifted her head and got a tissue out of her purse. "Thank God I didn't put on a ton of makeup."

Zuri took it from her hand and dabbed at the wet spots. "So, was it a pleasant surprise?"

Genesis gazed at her as if seeing her for the first time, then nodded and looked away. "This is the best surprise I've ever gotten. You outdid yourself."

Zuri presented her arm, and Genesis hooked hers through it as they walked inside.

Chapter Thirty-Three

On Monday, Zuri had some work to catch up on, so Genesis visited the Brooklyn Central Library, which wasn't too far from the apartment. While it wasn't as large as the main library in Manhattan, which they visited over the weekend, it was impressive in its own right.

When she was young, before she fell in love with dance, Genesis used to dream that she would one day work in the publishing industry. It always sounded so glamorous compared to her life in Virginia. There was also the fact that she loved books. Reading was her way of escaping the oppressive presence of her parents and the church.

After an almost two-hour tour of the building, she took a stroll through the neighborhood and ended up at a small cafe. She sat by the window with a croissant and latte, watching the activity on the street.

New York was an exciting place. The hustle and bustle were real, but she liked the intense energy. She had spoken to Zuri earlier about making the trip a yearly ritual.

Already planning the future. She smiled to herself as she sipped her coffee. Zuri was everything she had hoped she would be, and sometimes she felt overwhelmed by just how good things were between them.

The evening before their visit to the Alvin Ailey event space, there had been an honest apprehension that maybe the relationship was progressing too quickly and she needed to slow things down. Once Zuri surprised her, she knew without a doubt that she was in love with her. Unabashedly, head over heels, crazy in love. She almost said it out loud, but she forced it back down.

Her phone buzzed in her pocket, and she was ecstatic to see it was Lucy. They hadn't spoken in a few weeks. She missed their daily talks at work, even though she didn't miss the job.

"Girl, aren't you supposed to be working?" Genesis said.

"Of course, but I've earned my break. And it's not like you're here anymore for me to chat with, which sucks, by the way. God knows I can't stand most of the other people here." Lucy told her to hold on, then returned shortly after. "Sorry about that, nosey Paul was sniffing around. I swear he hates it if we aren't busy every second of the day."

Genesis pictured his widow's peak and scowl. "Yeah, I'm still convinced that he's a spy for the company."

Lucy laughed. "So, how have you been?"

"I'm good, in New York. It's been so fun." Genesis filled her in on everything they had done. When she mentioned the visit to the Alvin Ailey theater, Lucy squealed with delight.

"See, that woman is a keeper. She listened and had the forethought to get tickets to that show. I'm impressed."

"You? I started bawling my eyes out. I'm still in shock. She's so great," Genesis said, her voice going soft. "Anyway, I've been meaning to tell you I'm going into business for myself."

"That doesn't surprise me. You were brilliant at your job, and we are poorer for not having you here."

Genesis smiled. "Thanks, friend. I already started working

with my first client. Zuri's cousin Reginald needed a new accountant because the last one screwed him over. So I'm looking over his financials now."

"Oh, okay, so your boo is helping you out. I like that; it's better than just handing you money."

"Believe me, she has tried, and it's sweet. But I prefer this because I can build something on my own and not run to her with my hand out."

Lucy agreed. "So, I'm waiting on you to spill the real tea."

Genesis raised an eyebrow. "What tea might that be?"

"Don't even play; I'm trying to find out if you wiped out those cobwebs from between your legs," Lucy said with a cackle.

Genesis laughed so hard she almost choked on her latte. "I can't believe you just said that."

"You're the one trying to be all coy. It's been almost three years since you got some. We all need some loving. Unless I'm wrong, but you never had sex with Olivia, right?"

Genesis turned up her lip. "Ugh, no, and I'm glad. She still texts me, apologizing and asking for another chance. Even if Zuri weren't in the picture, that would be a hard pass."

"When red flags happen early, thank God. There is nothing worse than falling for someone and having to deal with their issues. Did that once, never again."

"If you must know, we have connected in that way," Genesis said, her cheeks burning at the memory.

"About time. The tension between you two was getting to me," Lucy said. "Are you happy? You sound like it."

Genesis thought about the question. Happy sounded so basic, but then she thought about what Zuri said the day before, about how she made her feel and wanting her to experience that as well.

"Yes, I am thrilled. I just worry that it might end. Like I'm waiting for the other shoe to drop. I was so in love with Shannon, and it fell apart. I don't know if I have it in me to go through that again."

"I understand, but Gen, you can't let one relationship change how you behave with someone else. Zuri is Zuri, and she has shown you nothing but kindness. I know that situation with her ex didn't feel that way, but she made the right choice. When it came down to it, she came to you when she could be the woman you needed."

"You're right. I have to stop worrying so much and enjoy what I have," Genesis agreed.

It sounded good, but she hoped she could take her own advice.

* * *

That evening, they ordered in from a local Indian restaurant. After the flurry of activity, it was nice to have a chill night. Their flight was early, so they planned to settle in after a marathon of the Netflix series for Spike Lee's She's Gotta Have It.

"So what's the verdict? Yay or nay," Zuri said as she fixed them a drink.

"Decent show, but DeWanda Wise was the highlight. Without her, I don't think it would have worked."

"Very true. I Love Spike Lee, but some of his directorial choices are not my favorite. Regardless, what I wouldn't give to work with him." Zuri handed her a glass of rum and coke as she sat back down on the couch.

Genesis raised it for a toast. "Here's to a wonderful weekend and many more to come."

Zuri clinked their glasses together. After she took a sip, she grabbed her phone, unlocked it, and handed it over to Genesis. "What do you think of this?"

Genesis took the phone and let out a whistle. The image was of a red Audi Cabriolet, one of their newer coupes. "It's gorgeous. Did you buy this?"

"I did, but not for myself," Zuri said as she took the phone back. "It's yours."

Genesis swallowed and had to make sure she had heard her right. "You bought that for me?"

"Yeah. You've been driving around that old car, and even though we got it fixed a few months ago, it's about time to get something new. It's expensive but paid in full, so you only have to worry about gas and insurance."

Words kept flowing out of Zuri's mouth, but all she could think about was Shannon. This was how it started once she made it into the league—expensive gifts, choosing where they should live, not including Genesis in significant decisions.

Taken aback, Genesis spit out, "I don't need another car. The one I have is old, but I bought it."

Zuri gave her a quizzical stare, her smile faltering. "It's a gift, honey."

"Okay," Genesis said, getting up from the couch. "In your world, you can afford to give these things out like candy, but that's a major purchase. One you made without my input." She took her glass to the sink and washed it, then turned to lean on the kitchen island. "If I want a new car, I can get one for myself."

Zuri got up and walked over to the other side of the island. "I'm sorry. I drove by a car dealership last week and thought you would love it."

Genesis sighed. "It's a beautiful car, but that's not the point."

"Then what is the point? I'm confused right now because you're mad at me, and I don't understand why."

Her thoughts were all jumbled, and she couldn't figure out

what she wanted to say. How do you tell someone that your compass for what is acceptable in a relationship is off because you only ever had one destination? That you didn't need someone to take care of you, just love. *Say it.*

"I need to take a walk." Genesis grabbed her jacket from the hook by the front door.

"What do you mean? It's almost 10 pm," Zuri said, following her.

She could see the conflict on Zuri's face, her concern for her fighting against not wanting to make her more anxious.

Genesis placed a tentative hand on her arm. "I just need a moment to myself. I'll stay in the front of the building, promise."

Zuri nodded but still looked displeased. Genesis felt lighter when she heard the click of the door after she stepped into the hallway. Since they were only on the second floor, she took the stairs down.

The security guard at the front desk greeted her. "Good evening, ma'am,"

"Good evening," she replied.

The cool air washed over her when she got outside. It was raining, so she remained under the awning that extended from the main entrance. There weren't many people out, and she appreciated the peace. The steady drip of the rain put her at ease.

Genesis knew it was wrong to run away from Zuri, but she hated confrontation. It put her on edge, and the last thing she wanted was to jeopardize what they had because she couldn't express herself. There was no room for repeating the mistakes of the past.

After twenty minutes, she headed back upstairs. As soon as she entered the apartment, Zuri jumped up from the couch; her face etched with sadness.

"Whatever I did, I'm sorry. Just tell me how to fix it..."

Genesis cut her off with a kiss to calm her down. She could feel Zuri's heart racing as she pulled her in close.

"I'm sorry too," she said, placing her hand over her heart. "Let's sit down and talk."

Genesis hung up her jacket and joined her back on the couch. The anxiety was gone, but she was still nervous.

"I told you about my parents and the way they dominated so much of my young life. It's something that I accepted as normal because it was for me. Until recently, I didn't see how that seeped into my relationship with Shannon. She had many wonderful qualities, but she didn't know how to be a partner to me. There were many times in our relationship when she would take control and decide without me. I hated it, and I came to resent her. Our divorce devastated me. I sacrificed for someone who didn't value me. I can be honest with myself now and say she did the best thing for us when she left."

Zuri took her hand in hers. "That doesn't sound like it was a healthy situation."

"It wasn't, and I spent too long suppressing myself for her. Then when I figured out that therapy might help, she shut me down on that too. If we had learned how to communicate, things could have gotten better, but that never happened." Genesis folded her legs and leaned forward. "I felt irrelevant in that relationship, and I never want that to happen again. I won't let it. You are a kind woman, but you also have a dominating personality. It's sexy as hell, but it has its place."

A smile crept up on her face. "So you think I'm sexy?" Zuri said with a grin.

Genesis laughed and caressed her face. "Very much so, and funny, intelligent, strong and so thoughtful. Bringing me to that show yesterday is going to be the highlight of my year."

Zuri's eyes lit up. "So, you want more of that and less material stuff."

"I like nice gifts," Genesis said, holding up her wrist. "But that's not why I'm with you, and you don't need to shower me with things. I just want you."

"I want you too," Zuri said, bringing her in closer. "In the future, I will consult with you on any major decisions and do my best to curb my alpha energy."

Genesis pushed forward and climbed on top of Zuri. "No need to curb it, remember I said it has its place." She ran her hands through Zuri's locs, and she closed her eyes, leaning into Genesis's touch. "I promise I won't run away anymore. When something is wrong, I will talk to you about it."

Zuri squeezed her waist and kissed the top of her breasts. "I'm down with that, especially if it ends like this," she said with a twinkle in her eye.

Genesis kissed her, then hugged her close. Whatever they experienced, they would do it together, and that was all she ever wanted.

Chapter Thirty-Four

Genesis walked out of her first business class, feeling like a brand new woman. The city of Los Angeles offered the classes for free to everyone, and it was a great way to get familiar with the basics of ownership.

Zuri found the information for her almost as soon as she mentioned a desire to open an accounting firm. She was happy that instead of telling her what to do, Zuri encouraged her to learn independently. It was clear she believed in her and what she was capable of, something she needed.

Genesis checked her phone for the time and jumped into her car. Zuri asked her to visit her non-profit Beacon when she finished with the class. She planned to expand their offerings and wanted her input. Genesis wasn't sure what advice she could give other than financial, but she was more than willing to help.

After turning on the radio, she began the drive to Inglewood. She was excited to learn more about the other parts of Zuri's life outside of being a movie executive. While her work ethic was impressive, there was so much more to her as a person, and Genesis enjoyed peeling back those layers.

Her phone rang, and she glanced to see who it was. She smiled when she saw Andrea's name pop up.

"Hey girl," she said, turning on her blue tooth.

"What's up with you? We haven't talked in a minute."

"I'm sorry, it's been pretty hectic," Genesis told her about the trip to New York and her argument with Kenzie.

"I am so happy you put her behind in her place. She has always been a spoiled brat. I can't pretend like I know what it is to lose your parents at a young age, but you and Shannon gave her a good life."

"It's my fault for not nipping it in the bud when she was younger. But I didn't know how to discipline her, so it was easier to let her have her way."

"So, Shannon has gone back home?"

"Yes, her aunt Katie is retired and offered to stay with her indefinitely."

"You mean to tell me she could have asked for that help from the beginning? Now I'm sure she was trying to get back with you. She knew you wouldn't say no, and had Zuri not been in the picture; you might have fallen for it."

Genesis hated to admit it, but Andrea had a point. "You're right, I'm sure that was her plan, but I'm glad it happened. It allowed us to make amends."

"That's true, but she might have put it on you with her sex game, and you would have been down for the count."

Genesis burst into laughter. "Whatever, it was good, but not that good. Not after what I've experienced with Zuri." The memory of them together the last time they made love had tingles running all over her body.

"Oooh, you nasty, but tell me more," Andrea said with a chuckle.

"A lady doesn't kiss and tell Drea."

"Good thing I'm not talking to a lady."

They continued going back and forth with jokes. Genesis missed the hell out of her friend and was about to ask her if she was free for a visit soon when she got even better news.

"So, Natalie and I are getting married."

Genesis let out a little scream of joy. "Are you kidding me? Natalie tamed you?"

Andrea scoffed at the comment. "No one can tame me, honey, but I've decided that I'm getting too old for the games. She's a wonderful woman and makes me happy."

"That's beautiful, Drea. I'm so happy for you both. When is the ceremony and everything?"

"We're thinking this summer since that is the warmest time of year here in Denver. Will you and Zuri be able to make it out here?"

"You don't even have to ask. I'll make sure we're both available."

Genesis pulled up to the area by Beacon and looked for parking. She ended the call with Andrea, excited for her friend and her future with Natalie.

Once she got out of the car, she walked up to the building and admired it for a moment. Decorated with bright colors and murals that intermingled with the colored tiles, it stood out in the right way.

She found the entrance around the corner and made her way inside. A young woman sat at the front desk. Genesis waited for her to look away from her phone and acknowledge her. Once that didn't happen, she cleared her throat, and the girl snapped to attention. She half expected her to have an attitude since she interrupted her phone time, but the girl gave her a dazzling smile.

"Sorry, I got caught up on the 'gram. How can I help you?"

"No worries, social media gets us all in trouble."

The young woman shook her head. "Right? But there's this

one dude, in particular, I'm following, and he responded to my messages."

Genesis remembered how she used to wait for Zuri to post pictures. "Girl, say no more. Get your man."

They both laughed. Ariel, as she introduced herself, looked for Genesis's name in the guest book and tapped on it.

"You're Ms. Zuri's girlfriend, right?"

Genesis wasn't keen on telling their business, but Ariel seemed harmless. "Yes, I am."

"I knew it. She was way hype when she mentioned you stopping by," Ariel said.

Genesis blushed and tried not to smile too big. Ariel gave her directions to the gymnasium, which was down the hallway to the left.

As she walked, Genesis admired the artwork that adorned the walls. Most of it didn't look like the work of teens, but artists that had been painting for years. The opportunities that Zuri was providing for the young women who attended Beacon was admirable.

The sound of sneakers streaking across the floor was a familiar refrain as she pulled open the door to the gym. Memories of her high school days playing with Shannon for fun came rushing back.

Genesis spotted Zuri across the room, talking to another woman who was standing a tad too close. She laughed at something Zuri said and reached out to hold her arm as she doubled over. *What she said could not be that funny.* Genesis had never been insecure; she got used to disrespectful women when she was with Shannon. It was something she always handled with grace, except for pushing that overzealous groupie in the pool. That was out of character for her but warranted.

Now, as she stood there watching whoever this other

woman was flirting with Zuri, she reminded herself of what they had.

"Z," Genesis called out, walking towards them.

Zuri's face lit up as she excused herself and jogged over to Genesis.

"Hi baby, I'm so glad you're here." Zuri hugged her close and kissed her on the lips. "I'd love to give you more than a peck, but we're being watched."

Genesis giggled as she noticed the girls had taken a break from playing basketball and huddled together, whispering. No bad vibes were coming from them, just curiosity.

"Well then, I'll save my proper kiss for your office," Genesis said, biting her lip.

"Hello there." The woman talking to Zuri made her way over, a fake smile plastered on her face. "My name's Lea; you must be Genesis. I've heard so much about you."

Genesis shook her outstretched hand. "Oh, okay, I'm afraid I've heard nothing about you."

Zuri stifled a laugh. "Lea is the director of the program. She runs the day-to-day operations."

"Oh, I may run the day-to-day, but Zuri does so much here. It's refreshing to have someone doing philanthropic work that is so involved," Lea said.

Genesis rolled her eyes as Lea gazed into Zuri's face. Obviously, she harbored a crush, and while she had no chance with Zuri, it was still annoying.

"Well, that's Zuri; she's very hands-on with everything she commits to," Genesis said, slipping her hand into Z's.

Lea noticed the move and looked a bit flustered. "Well, I'm going to get back to my coaching duties. Pleasure meeting you, Genesis. Zuri, we can finish our chat later," she said, her blond hair bouncing behind her as she sauntered over to the girls.

"Hmm, wonder what she needs to chat with you about," Genesis said as they walked to Zuri's office.

Zuri smirked at her. "Beacon stuff. Why, are you jealous?"

Genesis tilted her head to the side as Zuri opened her office door. "Me jealous? Stop."

After she shut the door, Zuri grabbed her around the waist and pressed her against the nearest wall.

"It's obvious you are, but I don't mind; it's kind of cute. The way your left eye was twitching made me think I might have to break you two apart."

"You wish," Genesis let out in a breathy whisper. "Sounds like a fantasy to me. Two women fighting over you."

"That sounds nice, but you bent over my desk is something I'd be more interested in seeing." Zuri stepped back and took her hand, leading her to the seat in front of her desk. "But, before we talk about that a bit more, I asked you here for a reason."

Genesis tried to shake off the lustful feelings running through her body and concentrate on what Zuri had to say.

"After what you just mentioned, whatever it is, the answer is yes," Genesis said.

Zuri smiled and leaned against the edge of her desk. "I'm going to give you the grand tour, but I am working on something that I want to run by you. We have talked about having a dance program here for years, and we even have a few studios. There just hasn't been anyone who fits our mission. Having someone like you at the helm would go a long way towards creating something sustainable."

Genesis sat back. "Okay, are you asking for suggestions or...?"

"I'm asking if you would be that person, Gen. Your love for dance is still so strong, and you would be an asset to us. The young women who come through these doors need someone who knows what they will go through as women of color in the world of dance. Plus, I can trust you."

Stunned, Genesis sat there, trying to take in everything she said.

"I am beyond flattered, but it's been years since I danced in any sort of real capacity."

Zuri pushed off from the desk and squatted beside her, taking her hand. "You don't have to teach the classes if you don't want to. It can be an administrative role, but you would be in charge of vetting the teachers and setting up the program and how it will run."

Genesis thought about the years she spent telling herself she had moved on from dance because she believed it would never be a part of her life again. Zuri wasn't just offering her a job; she was offering to give her back her first love.

"This is so overwhelming. I'm not sure what to say."

Zuri stroked her hand. "Say, yes. And if not, yes, that you'll think about it. This is my gift to you. I heard you back in New York, and I want to support you in the things that are important to you."

Genesis looked at the sincerity on Zuri's face and said, "The answer is yes. A thousand times, yes."

"This is going to be an awesome experience, baby." Zuri kissed her softly. "I already got approval from the board for salary and all of that. It's in the offering letter on my desk."

Zuri jumped up and handed Genesis the folder. She opened it just to glance at the letter, and her eyes widened when she saw the salary. "This is a generous amount."

"You're going to be implementing an essential department here, plus it's a temporary position. After six months, you get to decide in what capacity you want to stay on. That gives you flexibility since you have your accounting business on the horizon," Zuri said.

"And it puts money in my pocket."

"You have your investments and savings, but you're going to need capital for your business venture as well."

"This is so thoughtful of you, Zuri, seriously."

Zuri held out her hand. "Let me show you something else."

They walked back out in the hallway, and Zuri led her down a set of staircases. On the lower level, she could hear music spilling out from behind some doors.

"Quite a few of our students come here to practice, even when there are no classes. We give them free rein to use any of the empty spaces. This way," Zuri said, holding open a pair of double doors. "Now this section is unused. We have some ideas for it, but most of it comprises dance studios."

Zuri opened the door to one room, and it was beautiful. Wide-open and pristine, it even had a new smell to it. The windows covering the opposite wall allowed for an abundance of light, and Genesis imagined it warming some young dancer's skin as they lept around.

Unable to resist, she wandered towards the middle of the room. She pointed the toes on her right leg, slid forward, and then moved the leg backward, bending her knee. It caused her to twirl, and while it was a simple move that she had not done in years, the muscle memory came flooding back. Soon she was gliding across the floor.

Once she stopped, she opened her eyes and found Zuri staring. Her face was beaming with pride. She clapped and cheered as if she were at a sporting event. Genesis blushed but bent over into a bow.

"You're amazing." Zuri walked towards her. "How did I get so lucky? Just when I think I couldn't love you more."

"Love?"

Hearing Zuri say the words should not have been so surprising.

Zuri held onto her hands. "It's okay if you aren't ready to say it. I just needed you to know."

Genesis was unsure where the reluctance was coming from, but she couldn't bring herself to say it back. So she kissed her instead and hoped that for the moment, it would be enough.

Chapter Thirty-Five

Zuri stood with her cousins at the wrap party for Rain's latest picture. With the early buzz that "Dream a Little Dream" was getting, they expected it to exceed their initial box office predictions. It was something the studio needed. Although the scandal with her godfather didn't seem like it would affect them as much as they thought, that didn't stop Zuri from worrying. His trial would happen soon, and with it, more details about his deeds.

"Z, what's with the sour face? It's a time to celebrate," Elijah said, doing a little dance.

"Bad dancing is no way to celebrate, just saying, bro." Reggie mocked his moves. "Like how do you do the two-step wrong?"

Zuri laughed and brought them both into a hug. "Leave it to you guys to make me smile. I'm sorry, just thinking about the future of Ellis Films."

Elijah squeezed her arm. "Future, which means not right now. Enjoy the present; good things will most be coming our way. Look, your someone good is heading over here now."

Zuri looked in the entrance's direction and lost her breath.

Genesis had entered the party, and she was wearing the dress Zuri gifted her a few months ago. It looked even better than she remembered. A pair of sapphire earrings surrounded by diamonds that Zuri bought her to wear that evening set the whole outfit off.

"You're right, Eli; I have so many reasons to be grateful. Now, if you two will excuse me." Zuri made her way over to Genesis and met her halfway. They hadn't seen each other for over a week, and it felt like an eternity. "How is it possible that you look better and better every time I see you?"

Genesis smiled and shrugged. "Oh, I don't know, just blessed, I guess."

The corner of Zuri's eyes crinkled as she gazed at her. "Only you could say something so arrogant and make it sound sexy. Come here."

Their lips touched, and the room and everyone in it disappeared. Whatever spell Genesis had her under, she was more than happy to succumb.

When she told her she loved her at Beacon, it stung a bit when she didn't say it back, but she realized that it didn't matter. Genesis made her feel loved by her actions. Tracy had said the words, but they meant nothing to her. They were just that, words. She knew that when she was ready, Genesis would say it. Until that time, she was fine saying it as often as she could.

Zuri wrapped her arms around Genesis's waist. "The first time you put this dress on, it floored me. I almost followed you back into that dressing room."

"Oh, I remember that look you gave me. Had me running out of the store." Genesis placed her arms around her shoulders. "I'm glad I don't have to do that anymore."

"Get a room," Rain said, sidling up to them. "It's like watching my parents make out."

Zuri ignored her and kissed Genesis again. "No one told you to come over here last time I checked."

"I'm bored and over this movie. Glad it's done." Rain stopped talking and scooted behind Genesis. "Damn it; I think he saw me."

"Who are we talking about right now?" Genesis asked.

"Jackson," Zuri whispered in her ear.

Genesis searched the room. "You're kidding me. So now you don't want to see Jackson?"

"Yeah, what's up with that?" Zuri asked.

Rain popped out once he was on the other side of the room. "During the shoot, he charmed me, and we kind of hooked up again."

Genesis gave her a side-eye. "Kind of?"

"I know, I'm an idiot," Rain said, covering her face. "Anyway, as soon as the movie wrapped, he stopped taking my calls. It's so embarrassing. I don't know how I fell for his lies twice."

Genesis looked over at him with barely concealed disgust. "It's clear he was never taught to respect women. With someone like that, you have to sever ties, or they'll keep hurting you."

She excused herself, and Zuri watched as she headed across the room to where Jackson stood with other cast members. She pulled him to the side, and they huddled together as they talked.

"What is she doing?" Rain asked.

"If I know Gen like I think I do, making sure he leaves you alone," Zuri said, her voice filled with pride.

After a few minutes, Genesis walked back towards them, leaving a confused looking Jackson in her wake.

"He won't be bothering you anymore," Genesis said, rubbing Rain's arm.

Rain was stunned. "What did you say to him?"

Genesis grabbed a glass of wine from a passing waiter. "I

might have told him that if he doesn't leave you alone, I know someone who could make his face not so pretty anymore."

"You threatened to beat him up?" Zuri laughed out loud. "Oh my God, that is hilarious."

Rain hugged Genesis close. "Aww, thank you, big sis. That is the sweetest thing anyone's ever done for me." She turned towards Zuri. "See, I told you she was a keeper."

Zuri looked at Genesis and sighed. "Yeah, she is."

* * *

Genesis

Genesis's eyes followed Zuri as she walked around the room, speaking with various cast members and staff. She was reluctant to leave her side, but Genesis insisted that she needed to make the rounds. If she had learned anything during their time together, it was how meaningful building and maintaining relationships were in the film business. There was also the bonus of getting to admire her from afar. She was sexy on the regular, but watching her in work mode was something else.

After hanging out with Reggie, Elijah, and Rain, Genesis went to find Zuri.

"Hey, you think we could go down to your office to talk?" she asked.

"Of course. Is everything okay?"

Genesis didn't answer and grabbed her hand. A few people attempted to stop them to speak with Zuri, but she declined and promised to return.

The rooftop of the principal office building on the studio lot was the site for the party. Zuri's office was a couple of levels down.

"So what was so important that you just had to pull me away?" Zuri said as they entered the elevator.

Instead of responding, Genesis did what she had been imagining all night. She pushed Zuri against the elevator wall. As they stared into each other's eyes, Genesis tried to convey what was so hard for her to put into words. Their lips were mere inches apart, and when she pressed against Zuri's, her body melted into hers.

Had kissing always been this way? The intensity left her feeling out of control. She couldn't get enough of it.

The ding of the elevator broke the spell, but neither rushed to leave the confined space. Genesis separated from Zuri and followed her into the hallway. They walked a few doors down to her office, and Genesis waited while she unlocked it.

Zuri threw her clutch onto her desk. "So, Ms. Malone, you got me all to yourself. What now?"

Genesis turned and shut the door. Her core clenched at the sound of the lock being engaged. While she was eager to get her hands on and inside of Zuri, she allowed herself a moment to calm down.

She leaned against the locked door and gazed at the vision that was Zuri as she sat against the edge of her desk. Although Genesis loved her dress, the one her lover wore was equally beautiful. Form-fitting like a bandage dress, it was jet black and flattered Zuri's athletic figure. Her right arm was bare while the left was covered from neck to wrist with a sleeve that extended from the dress and bared just the right amount of skin on her chest. It wasn't something that everyone could wear, but on her, it was flawless.

"I've missed you," Genesis said, her voice only slightly above a whisper.

"I missed you too. We've both been busy. It looks like we need to learn how to balance that." Zuri waited for her to speak, but Genesis remained quiet. "What's going on baby, you're all broody. It's cute, but tell me what's wrong."

Genesis shook her head. "There's just so much I want to say to you and…"

"And?"

"Maybe it would be better if I showed you."

Zuri's eyes never left hers as she walked towards her, kicking off her heels. The moment she reached her, Genesis ran her hand over her cheek and down her neck. Zuri closed her eyes and trembled as her hand drifted lower, brushing against her breasts.

Genesis nuzzled her neck, and Zuri let her head fall back, leaving it exposed. She gasped as sweet kisses turned into sensual bites. Yearning to move slower but desperate to touch her, Genesis pushed her dress up and over her hips. Zuri's thighs dropped open as she pressed forward.

"You're taking to being the dominant one, I see," Zuri said, with a lazy smile.

"I just love making you feel good." They both moaned when Genesis's hand stroked her and pressed against her clit.

Genesis used both of her hands to pull off her thong and let it drop to the floor. With so many thoughts running through her mind, she wasn't sure what she wanted most. Zuri decided for her when she took her hand and led it back to her center.

With a slow and delicate touch, Genesis pushed forward, eliciting a sigh of pleasure from Zuri. She captured her lover's lips as she stroked her. Their tongues slid against each other, and she added another finger, reveling in the way she drenched her hand.

This was what she had been missing when she allowed Shannon to make her a spectator in their lovemaking. The ability to bring about this sort of response in another. To see them bend to her will, knowing that her hand, her mouth, was the reason they were writhing in pleasure. It was exhilarating, and she couldn't get enough.

Enveloped in her heat, Genesis curled her finger and dragged along the tender spot she knew would send Zuri over the edge. Zuri cried out in ecstasy as she rode out her orgasm against Genesis' hand.

"That was amazing, "Zuri said, bringing Genesis in for another kiss. "Please tell me I get to return the favor."

A naughty grin appeared on her face as she grabbed some tissues and cleaned her hand. "Oh, I've got a few things in mind, but I need to say something." She smoothed down Zuri's dress and looked into her eyes. "You make me happy in a way that I've never known. The thought of opening up and losing you is scary to me, but I don't want to be afraid anymore. I didn't realize how much I was holding back until you told me you loved me. The words were right on the tip of my tongue, and I couldn't say them."

"Baby." Zuri brought her in closer. "Thank you for opening up to me. It means so much."

Genesis held her face in her hands. "I would do anything for you, Z. I love you."

Zuri looked surprised, then pleased. "I love you too."

Hearing the words again, and saying them herself, broke that last barrier between them. There was no more wondering if what they had was real. This was the woman she had longed to find, and she wasn't going to let her go.

Genesis leaned into her, and Zuri kissed her forehead. She was safe and loved, and it was everything she needed.

Chapter Thirty-Six

Zuri watched as the screenwriter of their latest acquisition, Stewart Macintosh, signed the contract to give them rights to his film script. He had done like Zuri asked and returned to them once he fleshed out his ideas. She liked that he listened, and it showed in his presentation this time around.

"So Mr. Macintosh, is Get Out meets Rosemary's Baby still how you would describe this film?" Reggie asked as he picked up the signed contract.

Stewart laughed. "Yeah, but I can explain what it means when I say that now. Thanks for giving me another chance."

"Your success is our success. We want to make sure that we always give a chance to people who might not get one otherwise," Zuri said. "Besides, I read that script, and it is going to make us tons of money."

They all laughed and shook hands. Zuri watched Stewart walk out with a slight bounce in his step. She sensed they would work with him again.

Reggie dropped into the seat across from Zuri. "Weird how

things come full circle, huh? A year ago, he was in here, scared and unable to articulate his concept. Today he came in prepared and poised. I love to see it."

Zuri got up to pour them both coffee. "That's how it is, cuz. Most of our business is about having the audacity to believe in yourself and your abilities. Once we told him his idea was worthwhile, that made him feel confident."

Reggie agreed and took the cup of coffee from her hand. They sat chatting about work when Elijah burst into the room. He wore a manic grin on his face as he slammed the door shut and vibrated with excitement.

"You're not on that stuff, are you, bro?" Reggie said with a raised eyebrow.

Elijah rolled his eyes. "Hell no. I only tried that one time."

Zuri almost spit out her coffee. "Wait, how do I not know about this? Auntie would whip your behind if she was here."

Elijah waved his hands to get them to quiet down. "I have news, and I ran here after the call. You remember I told you I had dinner with Stacy and her friends Ray and Rachel?"

"That name combination is still so weird to me," Zuri said absentmindedly. Elijah glared at her. "Sorry, continue."

"Anyway, guess who Rachel's father is?"

Reggie pursed his lips. "Can we not, and you just tell us?"

Elijah blew out an exasperated breath. "Whatever her dad is, Phillip Minor."

Zuri sat up at attention. "Brave One's Die Young, that Phillip Minor?"

One of the most prominent directors and screenwriters of their generation, Phillip Minor, had not made a film in two years. Everyone was waiting with bated breath for his next project. The rumor was that he wanted to work with a smaller studio, and many, including Ellis Films, had thrown their hat in the ring by reaching out.

"Yes, the Phillip Minor. He showed up to have dinner with us, and it floored me. When I told him I was an executive here, he became interested. Said we were on his shortlist of film companies he was thinking about working with."

"Holy shit, bro, Phillip Minor is like a millennial Spike Lee. If we work with him, that will solidify the studio," Reggie said.

"And it would help us get from under the dark cloud that Francis put us under." Zuri leaned forward. "Please tell me he said he's going to work with us?"

Elijah took out his phone and put it on speaker as a voice-mail message played. "Reginald, it was a pleasure speaking with you the other night. I've had time to discuss what we talked about with my associates, and I believe Ellis Films is where I would like to continue my work. Your family's passion for film dating back to your grandmother is impressive. I believe a black-owned studio would be perfect for the direction I would like to go in my career. Call me along with your family members when you can."

The three of them were silent for a moment as the message ended, then Zuri let out a cry of joy and wrapped Elijah in a hug. "Whatever you did, Eli, thank you."

Reggie got up and joined in with a hug of his own. "Yo, if this goes through, I promise I will stop flaming you about your receding hairline."

"Not even your slick-ass remarks can ruin this for me, Reggie. Now say it?" Eli said, standing back with his arms folded after they stopped hugging.

Zuri looked between them, confused. "What is happening right now?"

Elijah smiled. "Oh, he knows. Say it."

Reggie mumbled something under his breath as he sat back down.

"Nah, loud enough for us both to hear it," Elijah said, cupping his ear.

Reggie glared at his brother, but he raised his voice and said, "You're the best twin, and I bow down to your awesomeness." He gingerly got down from the chair and did a bow, prostrating himself on the floor.

Zuri laughed out loud. "You two still do this? Like seriously, are you 11?"

Reggie got up, and even though he looked annoyed, Zuri could see the amusement on his face. Despite their constant ribbing of each other, there was lots of love between them as well.

"So, I'm thinking of dinner tonight with our ladies to celebrate. What do you say?" Elijah asked, doing a little two-step.

"I'd love to, guys, but Gen is making dinner tonight. We've both been busy, and we need some alone time."

"I'll bet you do," Reggie said, wiggling his eyebrows.

Zuri threw a balled-up napkin at him. "Anyway, how about we do it this weekend? I can make a reservation at that place we like in Napa."

Elijah snapped his fingers. "Yes, that would be perfect. Then knucklehead over here can propose to Delilah."

Zuri did a little clap. "You're going to propose? Oh, that would be so sweet. She deserves all the good things for putting up with you."

Reggie gave her the middle finger, and Zuri laughed, mouthing *I love you too.*

"Eli helped me pick out the ring a few weeks ago; I just haven't found the right time to do it. But this would be a wonderful way to celebrate and surprise her," Reggie said.

Zuri watched her two cousins as they joked around and talked about how Reggie should propose. It was nice to be back in good spirits after the stress of the previous months. They had gotten through it, and she believed that their bond played a large part in that. She smiled as she thought about how proud her grandmother would be of the adults they had become.

* * *

Zuri pulled up to her house and turned off the car. In the past, this would be the time to decompress and get ready to face her home's silence. Now, Genesis was there more often than not.

As she sat there looking at the house all aglow, she heard the sounds of Alabama Shakes spilling outside. Gen loved to listen to music as loud as possible, and luckily for her, the nearest home was far enough away that she wasn't disturbing anyone. Zuri loved it because it reminded her of when they first met, and it made her heart skip a beat every time Genesis came into view when she first entered the house.

"Honey, I'm home," Zuri said, walking into the house.

Genesis couldn't hear her, but it entertained her to say it. Kuma came out from the living room to greet her, and she bent down to pet her.

"Hey girl, how was your day?" she said, rubbing her fur.

Until she got to be around a dog full time, she had no idea just how great their companionship would be. She liked to joke with Genesis that if they ever broke up, she would fight for partial custody of Kuma.

After hanging up her coat, she walked towards the kitchen but only found a pot boiling with pasta. Curious, she looked into the pan beside it and saw a sauce with some shrimp inside. Just as she picked up a fork , a hand grabbed hers and swatted her bottom.

"Are you sneaking food?" Genesis said, grabbing the fork out of her hand.

"Me? Of course not. I was just making sure everything was cooking well," Zuri said with a smirk.

"Good, because I wouldn't want to give you a spanking," Genesis said as she turned off the pasta.

Zuri leaned against the opposite counter. "Well, if that's the punishment, then maybe I need to change my answer."

Genesis emptied the pasta into a colander, then placed the pot back on the stove. She took off the oven mitts she was wearing and walked over to Zuri.

"Hi baby," she said, wrapping her arms around Zuri's waist.

"Hi," Zuri replied.

Their lips touched in a sweet kiss. Zuri's lips formed into a pout when Genesis pulled away.

"Hey, I wanted some more of that," Zuri said, reaching out for her.

Genesis ignored her and skipped into the living room. She came back with a stack of papers in her hand. Zuri looked at it as she handed it to her. One glance at the top and a smile spread across her face.

"You finished your business plan?"

"Yes, I did it, baby. I thought it was going to be another week, but I buckled down, and I got it done."

Zuri put the stack of papers down and pulled Genesis into a hug. The other woman squealed when she lifted her up from the floor.

"You have no idea how proud I am of you, Gen." Zuri put her down and picked up the papers again. "I'm excited to read it."

Genesis placed her hand on top of hers. "And I want you to, but not now. Now we eat. I just wanted you to show you I finished."

"Okay, I'll take it upstairs. Let me get cleaned up, and I'll be down in ten." Zuri tilted her chin towards her and kissed her again. "So proud of you."

Genesis blushed and shooed her away. Zuri strolled up the stairs as she read the first page. She could tell that Gen had listened to her advice on wording and getting into the meat of her company's goal.

When she got to the bedroom, she put the papers down on the nightstand. It felt good to help someone she loved reach such an important goal. Whatever the outcome, she planned on being there every step of the way.

After a quick shower and a change of clothes, Zuri headed back downstairs. Genesis had the table set and changed the music to something more mellow. Zuri kissed her forehead as she sat across from her, ready to dig into the meal.

"Before we eat, can I say something?" Genesis said, biting her lip.

"Of course, baby. What's up?"

Genesis cleared her throat. "I just want to say thank you for helping me as much as you have and for believing in me. It's taken me a while to have enough faith in myself to reach this point, and I am so happy to be with someone that not only makes me feel good but encourages me to reach my full potential."

"Well, you are amazing, and any help I can give you is my pleasure. You mean the world to me." Zuri got up and walked over to her side of the table. She made her stand up and hugged her close. "I'm never letting you go."

"Good, because I don't want you to." Genesis stepped back and looked into Zuri's eyes. "I love you."

Zuri looked into her golden-brown eyes and noticed Kuma out of the corner of her eye, resting in her dog bed. This was what she had wanted for so long, and now it was her reality. The thought made her tear up.

"Babe, are you okay?" Genesis said, her voice filled with concern.

"More than okay," Zuri said, pulling Genesis into her body again. "I love you too, Genesis, forever and a day."

Epilogue

One Year Later
Barbados

"Oh my God, how is it possible that this place is more beautiful than I remember?"

Genesis ran out to the pool area and admired the sun as it set over the ocean. She took a deep breath and exhaled. This was her first vacation since she started her accounting firm. After working with Reggie, word got around, and she started getting more clients. After six months, the work became more than she could handle, and she took on staff, including Lucy, who was more than happy to join her. Now they serviced some of Hollywood's elite, big and small.

She was also still heavy into her work at Beacon. While the role was part-time, she appreciated the balance it gave her. With a creative outlet and control over her career, she found herself the happiest she had ever been.

"I feel that way every time I get to wake up to your face," Zuri said, coming up behind her.

Genesis sighed as she peppered her neck with kisses. "That was cheesy, but sweet."

"Well, it's your fault; you've turned me into a big mushball. I swear I was much suaver before."

"Ok, keep telling yourself that," Genesis said, turning to wrap her arms around Zuri's neck. "This is nice, being back here."

"The few times I've come without you, it hasn't been the same. This used to be the place for me to get away from everyone, but now I can't be here without you."

"You say that now, but give it a few years. You'll be begging to come here alone."

Zuri caressed her face and tilted her chin towards her. "I doubt that."

Their lips connected, and Genesis sighed again. Every time felt like the first time, and she hoped that it would always be that way.

"I've got to talk to some staff. Go on and get settled in," Zuri said.

"I will. Don't take too long." Genesis placed another kiss on her lips.

As she walked away, Zuri smacked her bottom, eliciting a yelp.

Genesis walked over to the bar and grabbed a can of soda out of the small refrigerator. She chuckled to herself as she remembered sharing a drink with Tracy in that same spot and how the other woman had staked her claim on Zuri.

After finishing her drink, she picked up a few of their bags. Without thinking, she walked towards the guest house, then realized her error. She turned and walked in the opposite direction to what was now their suite.

Genesis put the bags down and went over to the glass doors, opening them. The ocean breeze washed over her, and she smiled. Leaving the doors open, she went to the bathroom.

She knelt beside the tub, her hand traveling over the porcelain. Memories from the night she hurt her foot and soaked inside came flooding back.

"What are you thinking about?" Zuri said, appearing in the doorway.

Genesis's eyes lit up. "Taking a bath in here, with you. Can we make that happen?"

Zuri's gaze turned dark as she licked her lips. "We can do it right now if you want."

Genesis smiled as she stood up and started removing her clothes. "Oh, I want, very much."

* * *

After watching a cut of Ellis Films' latest movie in the screening room, Genesis excused herself while Zuri went to make a drink. She didn't realize how much fun they would have returning to Barbados as a couple. The memories of their desire before they got together were fueling their current passion in the most delightful way. Zuri was already making plans for their next visit.

As Zuri sat at the bar, music came on over the house loudspeakers. It took her a minute, but then she recognized *Yeah, I Said It* by Rihanna. A smile appeared at the homage to the first time they met, but her smile slackened when she saw Genesis appear from their suite. She had changed into a black lace teddy that somehow was modest and suggestive at the same time.

As Genesis's body swayed to the music, Zuri realized that she was about to get a show and her insides burned with anticipation. She placed her glass down and watched as Genesis walked towards her. Once she reached the bar, she pulled Zuri from her chair and had her follow her to the couch. She pushed her down and rolled her hips as she slipped one leg between Zuri's. Biting her lip as she rubbed herself against Zuri's thigh, it took everything in her not to pull Genesis down on the couch and devour her.

Rather than give in, she sat with her hands at her side. Even though she hadn't been told she couldn't touch, Zuri knew that if she did, this would be over before it started. So she continued to watch and enjoy the sensations. Genesis winked at her as the song changed to *Touch Me* by Victoria Monet. She turned around and backed up, her barely covered ass against Zuri's center, mimicking the music's rhythm. As she pushed back harder, Genesis grabbed Zuri's hands and placed them on her breasts, holding her close. She bent back, and unable to resist any longer, Zuri kissed from her neck down to her shoulder blade.

"Please, baby," she whispered into Genesis's ear. She needed something, anything, to calm the fire she had stoked inside of her.

Genesis flipped around and straddled her leg again. The sundress Zuri wore had already risen so that only her underwear created a flimsy barrier between her and the heat of Genesis's body. They were soaked through, and a brush against her lips left her gasping. Her core ached for contact, and as if she could read her mind, Genesis lowered her hand and pushed her panties to the side. She stroked Zuri's clit before sliding one finger, then two, inside of her.

Zuri's head fell back against the couch as she rode Genesis's hand. Each stroke left her breathless and panting for more. Over the past year, Genesis had gotten much more comfortable being in control in the bedroom. Now, she had mastered it and showed no hesitation when they made love. All of her pent up passion was overwhelming in the best way possible.

"I love you," Genesis said as she leaned into her.

They kissed, and Genesis once again entered her. Pressure on her clit sent Zuri over the edge, her cries of pleasure almost drowning out the music. Even as she came down, Genesis was unrelenting. She dropped to her knees and pulled off Zuri's panties, tossing them to the floor. Her hands palmed Zuri's bottom as she brought her closer to the edge of the couch.

Zuri's body had gone limp, but the moment Genesis pressed her tongue against her, she was on fire again. Her hips angled up and into Genesis like they had a mind of their own. For a moment, she shut her eyes and disconnected from all the surrounding distractions. She reached out and latched onto Genesis's hair, gripping it as she rode out another orgasm.

Genesis kissed her thigh and laid her head on Zuri's leg, her hands hugging her. Once she caught her breath, Zuri pulled her up so that Genesis was straddling her leg again. Zuri then twisted so that she landed beneath her and used her body's weight to hold her in place.

Without hesitation, Zuri yanked down the top of Genesis's negligee, and her breasts spilled out. Her mouth watered at the sight, and she dipped her head down, taking one chocolate nipple into her mouth while massaging the other.

"I want you so bad," Zuri whispered. Her hand moved down and massaged Genesis, the buttons of the negligee brushing against her fingers. "Well, isn't that clever?" She brought her other hand down and yanked the material open. Genesis gasped, pressing against her hand.

She moved down her body, and they both groaned as she shoved Genesis's legs apart, and her tongue made contact. Her scent alone pushed Zuri's senses into overdrive, and she pulled

Genesis closer to her mouth. She dove into her heat, licking and sucking until Genesis's cries drowned out the music.

"God, you feel amazing," Genesis said, finally breaking her silence. Her hands massaged Zuri's locs, encouraging her to keep going. "Don't stop, baby."

Zuri had no desire to stop, not until Genesis had her release. So she persisted, sucking on her clit until she elicited the gasp that told her she was close. Then suddenly, her body shuddered, and she screamed out Zuri's name as her hips undulated and she rode out the orgasm.

"By the way, I love you too," Zuri said, kissing her hip.

"Oh, yeah?" Genesis said. "I would have never guessed if you hadn't said it."

Zuri nipped her thigh, and Genesis let out a yelp, then laughter. "Should we get cleaned up?" Zuri asked, laying her head back down on her stomach.

"Well, what's the point in that if we're just going to get dirty again?" Genesis said.

Zuri lifted her head and saw the naughty smile on Genesis's face. She gave her one of her own and dropped down again to give her exactly what she wanted.

* * *

Hours later, the ocean crashing on the beach was the only sound that punctuated the house's silence. When they finished having fun in the living room, they had retired to the bedroom to continue making love until they collapsed in a heap of delicious exhaustion.

Genesis was pleased with Zuri's response to her outfit and dance; it was something she had wanted to do for months.

"I wish it could always be like this," Genesis said, lifting her head off of Zuri's chest.

"It might not always be exactly like this, but I don't see why we can't maintain this level of happiness," Zuri said, stroking her back.

"Because you're naïve." Genesis dropped her head back down and snuggled in close. "It's sweet but unrealistic."

Zuri laughed. "I'm not sure if I should be offended by that."

"I don't mean it negatively; you weren't with anyone as long as I was. Circumstances change, people, change."

"Okay, but we can change together. This isn't an individual deal here," Zuri said, kissing her forehead. "I think if we're both willing to work at it, then we'll be fine."

"You think so? Genesis asked, raising an eyebrow.

"I know so."

Genesis untangled herself from Zuri and jumped out of bed.

"Where are you going?" Zuri said, laughing. "It's cold; get back here."

After disappearing into the closet, Genesis returned, kneeling on the floor beside Zuri. She grabbed her hand from under the covers and kissed the knuckles.

"My mom used to talk to Kenzie and me about agape often, which refers to the unconditional love that God has for humans and vice versa. I always thought of the ability to love as a gift that God gave to us, and sharing it with another person in and of itself has its own divinity." Genesis slipped a diamond ring on Zuri's finger. "You are the answer to a prayer I made so long ago, and I would be honored to have you as my wife."

Zuri stared down at her hand, then looked up at Genesis. "Are you serious?" she asked, her voice trembling.

"I love you, and I already know that I don't want to be with anyone else. We can have a long engagement. I don't care; I just need you to know that I'm in this for the long haul."

"You don't have to do this to prove that," Zuri said, caressing her face.

"I know, but I also know that you've been planning your wedding since you were a little girl. What's important to you is important to me."

"So things changing between us doesn't scare you?"

"No, I said I wish it could always be this way; I didn't say I wouldn't love you just the same if it weren't." Genesis wiped away the tears that slid down Zuri's face. "So, is that a yes?"

Zuri nodded her head. "I'm being proposed to by a beautiful naked woman spouting philosophical words about love. The answer is hell yes."

Genesis jumped back into the bed and wrapped herself around Zuri, kissing all over her face while she laughed. This was happiness, and she couldn't wait for them to spend the rest of their lives together.

THE END

Acknowledgments

I started this book in 2020 and all I can say is, I thank God for seeing a new year and being able to write. It provides me with a special kind of solace.

There are many people I adore, but the two who really made this possible are Israel and Pragueleen. You two mean the world to me and I can write about love the way I do because of you both.

You are loved, you are appreciated , thank you.

A special thank you to my readers. You inspire me to do better and make me feel that I have stories worth telling.

About the Author

Ava Freeman loves romance, the steamier the better. It was that love, and her penchant for storytelling, that inspired her to start writing.

When she's not crafting her next story, Ava can be found reading (of course) or watching horror movies (have to balance out those energies). That is when her daughter lets her get a quiet moment (usually when she's sleeping). She currently lives in New York with her partner and little rebel.

www.authoravafreeman.com